Hope Returns

Second Edition

A Novel

Dorey Whittaker

ISBN: 1518868940
ISBN 13: 9781518868948
Library of Congress Control Number: 2016900266
CreateSpace Independent Publishing Platform
North Charleston, South Carolina

This novel is dedicated to my loyal readers. Your love for the characters of *Wall of Silence* inspired me to continue this literary journey.

The books in this series:

Treasure in a Tin Box
Wall of Silence
Hope Returns

Prologue

THE GEORGIA OBSERVER

Serving the citizens of Jefferson, Georgia, for over 100 Years

LISA MILLER FOUND NOT GUILTY OF MURDER!

Thursday, July 18, 1985
Jefferson, Georgia

In a stunning turn of events on Wednesday, Lisa Miller was found not guilty of murdering her father, Charles Miller. The courthouse was shocked when Ms. Miller's attorney, Randall Duncan, called a surprise witness to the stand. Ms. Hope Winslow, a resident of Culver City, California, confessed that she was in Bascom's Bakery with her biological mother, Lisa Miller, the night Charles Miller burst into the bakery kitchen. Unaware of his connection to her at the time, Ms. Winslow told the court how this intruder displayed a handgun and announced his intention to kill them both.

Ms. Winslow testified that Lisa Miller threw a copper pot at the intruder, causing him to drop his gun. As he bent down to retrieve it, Ms. Winslow testified that she ran to escape through the back door, but the intruder caught her just as she exited into the back alley. She stated under oath that he slammed her against the alley wall, pinning her against the building with one hand on her throat and the other hand pressing his gun into her body.

She testified how Ms. Miller wedged her body between her and her attacker, forcing the intruder to release his grip on Ms. Winslow's throat as Ms. Miller and the intruder fought to gain control of the gun. Once free, Ms. Winslow swore under oath that she ran back into the bakery to find something to defend herself. She grabbed a wooden rolling pin, the first object she could find, and returned to the alley.

Her testimony was emotional as she described how her mother's face was turning blue as she struggled to get the gun away from the intruder. He had his forearm wedged against her mother's throat, and Ms. Winslow felt if her mother lost consciousness he would control the gun and they would both be killed. Fearing for her life, Ms. Winslow confessed she was the one who took the rolling pin and struck the fatal blow to the back of Charles Miller's head just as the gun went off.

Once the jury came back with a not guilty verdict, it was expected that Judge Kirkley would order Hope Winslow taken into custody at the close of court yesterday since, by her own testimony, Ms. Winslow left the scene of a murder – self-defense or not. As of today's deadline, no warrant has been issued.

THE GEORGIA OBSERVER

Serving the citizens of Jefferson, Georgia, for over 100 Years

LISA MILLER REFUSES ALL INTERVIEWS

Saturday, July 20, 1985
Jefferson, Georgia

Although thankful for her acquittal, Lisa Miller refused to comment on any possible legal problems that her daughter might be facing as a result of her leaving the scene of the crime. After finding Ms. Miller at the home of her longtime friend, Gladys Carter, and the person she credited for getting her off drugs eleven years ago, she was asked why she had covered up for her daughter since it was obviously self-defense. Ms. Miller merely responded, "I made a huge mistake. My daughter came forward on her own once she found out about the trial. I just pray that everyone involved will keep the promises that have been made to her."

Several attempts have been made to find out what these promises are and who authorized them. One unnamed source within the courthouse quietly warned, "Heads will roll, and that right soon."

Judge Kirkley also refused an interview, stating, "You need to allow the court time to confirm some questionable legal issues. This community has endured enough witch-hunts over the past five months."

THE GEORGIA OBSERVER

Serving the citizens of Jefferson, Georgia, for over 100 Years

PROSECUTOR GORDON TO BE CALLED BEFORE ETHICS BOARD

Monday, July 22, 1985
Jefferson, Georgia

This morning, Judge Kirkley officially filed a "Cause of Action" with the State Board of Review against Prosecutor Jeffery Gordon. Details of this action have not yet been made public. Within the hour District Attorney Samuel Crane placed Gordon on administrative leave in order to allow him time to answer these charges. A hearing has been scheduled for two weeks from today.

Gordon has been campaigning for the soon-to-be vacant position of District Attorney for Jefferson, Georgia. Some have speculated that this is the reason why Prosecutor Gordon worked extensively to bring Lisa Miller to trial so quickly.

THE GEORGIA OBSERVER

Serving the citizens of Jefferson, Georgia, for over 100 Years

GORDON WITHDRAWS FROM D.A. RACE

Thursday, July 25, 1985
Jefferson, Georgia

Soon after learning Judge Kirkley had filed a complaint against Prosecutor Gordon with the State Ethics Board, four of Gordon's most ardent supporters withdrew their financial support. These supporters swiftly moved to distance themselves from Gordon. Although no one is discussing the details, one unnamed source told this reporter that Gordon knew about Hope Winslow several weeks before she come forward.

Hope Winslow has refused all calls, referring everyone to her attorney, Randall Duncan, of Jefferson, Georgia. Mr. Duncan's only public statement is, "I will reserve all comments until these charges have been adjudicated before the State Board of Ethical Review."

THE GEORGIA OBSERVER

Serving the citizens of Jefferson, Georgia, for over 100 Years

ETHICS REVIEW BOARD MEETS BEHIND CLOSED DOORS

Tuesday, August 6, 1985
Atlanta, Georgia

Prosecutor Gordon's attorneys argued yesterday that all charges against their client remain confidential until the State Board has determined there is sufficient evidence to officially charge their client, Jeffery Gordon. The Board granted this request but warned that all depositions must be completed within one month. No names were divulged nor were the details of these charges.

After returning to Jefferson yesterday afternoon, this reporter questioned several citizens about the Board's actions today. The general consensus seemed to agree with Michael Buchannan, longtime resident of Jefferson, "I find it interesting that Mr. Gordon's right to privacy is honored, but when he was prosecuting Lisa Miller, dozens of stories appeared in the newspaper about her criminal past. By the time her trial began, everyone in town was convinced of her guilt. I guess you have to be one of 'them' to get a fair shake at justice in this town."

THE GEORGIA OBSERVER

Serving the citizens of Jefferson, Georgia, for over 100 Years

ONE MONTH AFTER NOT-GUILTY VERDICT

Monday, August 19, 1985
Jefferson, Georgia

While the citizens of Jefferson wait for news of criminal charges against Prosecutor Gordon, Lisa Miller has decided it is time to get back among the living. Having taken an additional month to recuperate from the strain of her murder trial, Bascom's Bakery, where Lisa Miller has been gainfully employed for the past eleven years, will again benefit from Ms. Miller's excellent pastry skills.

Although still refusing any interviews, we wish Ms. Miller all the best and publically apologize for having allowed certain parties to use this local paper for their own personal ambition. Although this newspaper never slandered Ms. Miller, we recognize the personal burden we placed upon her by dredging up her scandalous past without acknowledging her eleven years of recovery.

Hope Returns

A deluge of letters to the Editor showed this newspaper that our coverage of the Miller trial has caused our readers to feel misled. This newspaper promises our readership audience to be more careful and balanced in covering future stories. Integrity and trust must be the hallmark of a free and open press.

CHAPTER 1

I<small>T WAS</small> 3:00 a.m., and as usual, Lisa Miller could not sleep. The amber glow of her clock radio cast gloomy shadows in her bedroom. These shadows danced across the ceiling, changing shape whenever the clock updated the time. The reflection of the time and date being projected upon her ceiling had become an interesting metaphor of her life over the past five months. Watching the date blinking on the ceiling, Lisa pondered, "Has it really only been one month since I was found not guilty of murdering my father?"

Frustrated at not being able to sleep, Lisa made the mistake of looking over at the stack of newspapers setting on her dresser. Five months of articles exposed every ugly detail of her life. Having read every one of them dozens of times, she had no need to retrieve them because they were now emblazoned in her mind. Against everyone's advice, she had ordered copies of all the back issues that had been published while she was in jail. To these, she had added all of the current newspapers with articles about how the prosecutor in her case was now being taken before a peer review board for his unethical behavior during her murder trial.

These articles chronicled every foolish decision she had ever made in her life, and they beckoned her back into the shadowy world of what if? What if she had done this instead of that? What if the prison had warned her they were releasing her father as the courts had ordered? What if she had taken that weekend trip Gladys had talked about? What if her daughter, Hope, had not chosen that night to come looking for her birth mother? What if...?

Lisa turned away from the dresser, refusing to take the long journey down the path of what if again. Pleading with God to help her control her destructive thoughts, she prayed, "Lord, You know I spent years wishing I had never been born and blaming You for all of it. But now, at forty years of age, I would never change certain parts of my life—even if I could. Since I don't get to pick and choose which parts I would keep and which parts I would erase, I have to learn how to incorporate all of these segments of my life into one—now that it is safe to do so.

"God, I really am thankful my murder trial forced me to face it all. Ashamed of so much of my life, I felt the only way to survive was to lock away my secrets and just live in the present. I always looked at my life as three separate and distinct parts—my brutal childhood, my foolish and destructive youth, and finally my wonderful redemption. Even though I knew You had forgiven me, I was afraid to tell anyone about my baby girl. I had given her away and wanted to leave her in my past. I saw no reason to tell anyone about her since she was gone forever.

"I thought I was content to live the rest of my life with this one secret. After all, she was living that wonderful life I always wanted for her. I convinced myself that there was no reason to tell my sister or Gladys about my little girl after all these years, so I tucked her existence deep in my heart and grieved her loss alone.

"Lord, I don't know if I will ever have a chance to explain everything to my daughter, but I want to be honest with her and confess who I was and who I have become. I want her to understand that You are the reason I am now who I am. I never wanted her to be contaminated by me or my family. You know I was too much like my mother back then to be trusted with a child, so I gave her up for adoption twenty-two years ago to give her a better life than I had. But then that night everything changed in an instant. She came looking for me. I don't know how she found me, but she came walking into the bakery that night, wanting some answers from her birth mother. "

Suddenly, the memory of her adult daughter's face, standing at the bakery counter that night, trying to summon enough courage to admit why she was in the bakery, filled Lisa's heart with pride. Hope didn't have to say a word. One look at her and Lisa knew who she was and why she was there. "God, I was blindsided that night. Hope came walking into the bakery wanting answers. Even though You saved me almost twelve years earlier and I had not taken any drugs or sold my body since, I was not prepared to explain any of this to my daughter. But just as I started to tell her everything, my father burst into the bakery kitchen, determined to kill me. If it had not been for Hope, he would have succeeded this time."

A shudder ran down Lisa's back as she remembered the look of terror in her daughter's eyes. "God, I am thankful I did not die, but I wish Hope hadn't been the one to save me. The fact that she took a life—even though she had no choice—is a burden no one should have to carry.

"I really messed everything up, didn't I? I panicked and reverted back to my old life's method of dealing with stressful emergencies; I ran. Actually, I did something even more foolish, didn't I? I talked my daughter into running. In my panic, I didn't even think to ask for Your help, God. I just didn't want her life ruined. I wanted her to get out of the bakery, out of this town, and out of my life so she could be safe again. At the moment, my advice seemed so rational to me. But God, You and I both know that when it comes to my family, my rationale has never been very rational, has it?"

Overwhelmed with all this emotion, Lisa sat up in her bed and remembered Gladys' admonition earlier that evening, "Lisa, holding onto all these newspaper articles is like drinking a little poison every day. Every time you reread one of these articles, you allow them to drag you back into a black hole of despair. You need to toss them out. Holding onto them is holding onto the pain as well."

Lisa put on her robe and slippers, picked up the huge stack of news-papers, and headed for the trashcans at the curb. Resting the huge stack against her right hip, Lisa quietly lifted the lid with her left hand and allowed the stack of newspapers to slide out of her possession. A strange relief came over her as she stared down into the trash can. Gladys had warned her that reliving the ugly past makes focusing on the future im-possible. "Lord, is Hope ever going to give me a second chance? I foolishly talked her into leaving the scene of a murder. I thought I could take all of the blame and keep her out of it. But once Hope found out I was on trial for murder, she risked everything to come forward and testify at my trial. Even though it was a case of self-defense, it was my idea for her to run. As a result of my poor decisions, my daughter is all tangled up in Prosecutor Gordon's legal troubles because he found out about her halfway through my trial and threatened her if she dared come forward. God, I couldn't make a bigger mess of things if I tried. I thought my days of drama were over, but here I am again, asking You to fix me and to help my daughter."

Startled by a car's turning the corner, Lisa quickly replaced the trash-can lid and made her way back to her bedroom. Unable to sleep, she thought about jumping in the shower but noticed the clock was blinking 3:35 a.m. Reluctantly, she slipped back into bed. Just because sleep was eluding her, she had no right to disturb Gladys' sweet slumber. This was going to be a long night.

After two more hours of tossing and turning, the familiar click of her clock radio signaled it was finally 5:30 a.m., and her workday was about to begin. She quickly reached over to turn off the alarm before it had a chance to ring. Usually, before the alarm could begin to ring, she would be on her feet, heading for the shower, eager to start her day, but since that night in the bakery, her usual routine had been anything but usual. Studying the blinking clock, Lisa mused, "I have waited months for this day to arrive, but now that it is here, I'm not sure I am ready for it. Will I ever feel comfortable in my old routine again? For the past eleven years, my life has been Bascom's Bakery. For the past eight years, I have been responsible for opening up the bakery, firing up the ovens, and getting the pastry dough prepped and chilled for a long morning of doing what I do best—baking goodies for everyone in town at Ruth Bascom's bakery.

"I always looked forward to the three hours of solitude in my beloved kitchen before the bakery helpers started pouring in with chitchat and gossip. I seldom joined in the gossip fests with the young girls who worked with me in the kitchen. I was almost twice their age, and I knew what it felt like to be the brunt of gossip in a small, Southern town."

Lisa had again found herself the central topic of the town gossipers. She knew those who wanted a glimpse of the infamous town tramp were probably planning to make their way to the bakery today. "God, that really is what I am dreading today, isn't it? I know Ruth will try to protect me. But God, I hate the fact that she has to. Her bakery means the world to me, and I do not want to bring shame to it or to her. Twelve years ago, Ruth Bascom gave me a job when no one else would. She and Gladys believed in me when I didn't believe in myself. Gladys gave me a home, and Ruth gave me a job and taught me a skill that gave me a sense of pride for the first time in my life. I love being a pastry chef.

"Ruth was so strict with me. I had such a foul mouth and flash temper back then. At first, the girls would make nasty comments to each other about me. They were too afraid to go face to face with me because I would let go with words most of them had never heard. Ruth would pull me aside and remind me that those words were never allowed in her bakery, and she would make me apologize to my coworkers. Ruth knew how hard it was for me to apologize to those girls, but she made me do it anyway. Not all of the teasing was mean. Most of the time they were just trying to lighten my mood, but I didn't handle it well. I didn't know how to react to the girls without getting angry. Ruth would quickly step in whenever the teasing began to take on a mean spirit. Eventually, we would all chime in and repeat her warning, "Girls, I think we need to change the topic. If it isn't kind, then don't say it."

Remembering those early years both embarrassed Lisa and warmed her heart. Ruth Bascom and Gladys Carter were her angels from heaven, and she knew it. "God, they loved me because You loved me, and they taught me all about Your forgiveness. Several times Ruth had been forced to fire a worker because they could not, or would not, accept the fact that I had once been a drug-using prostitute. Although my past was not a daily topic of discussion, I never denied it or made excuses for it. I knew I had been forgiven, but I also knew that most people are not as forgiving. Gladys and Ruth were my anchors. Whenever I encountered such people, Ruth and Gladys would remind me that no matter how they behaved, I was to respond in love." Looking up at the ceiling, Lisa confessed, "I guess I have not fully learned that lesson yet, have I?"

Hearing the second click of the clock, the signal that the radio was about to come on, Lisa reached over to shut it off, but then remembered she had no reason to hurry this morning. This being her first day back to work since all of this started, she was not expected to show up at the bakery until eight-thirty. She leaned back against her pillow and listened to the morning weather report and was glad to hear that her walk to work would be bright and clear of any late summer showers. But that welcomed news was quickly followed by the hot topic of the newsroom.

It's a sunny day here in Jefferson, Georgia. On the local front, Prosecutor Gordon continues to defend his behavior in the recent murder trial of local woman, Lisa Miller. As we all know, Miller was found not guilty last month of the murder of her estranged father, Chuck Miller. Prosecutor Gordon has been given a leave of absence in order to defend his actions in this case, but unnamed sources close to the case have assured this reporter that Judge Kirkley is determined to make sure Gordon will never return to his former position.

Lisa climbed out of bed, turned off the radio and headed for the bathroom. "I sure hope this unnamed source knows what he is talking about. I just wish my name wasn't always dragged into every news report about

Gordon. Thirty-one days have passed since I was found not guilty of murdering my father. Thirty-one days since I have seen my daughter. Thirty-one days since Ben Jackson declared his intentions to seriously date me."

This last thought brought a smile to Lisa's face. "I can focus on Prosecutor Gordon, or I can focus on Ben Jackson. I can focus on my daughter, Hope, or I can focus on my first day back to work since this nightmare started. Although Hope is never out of my thoughts, I have to give her time to get over the horror of my murder trial. So today I intend to shower and get ready for my first day back to work. I've missed the bakery something awful."

Lisa noticed the time on her clock radio and hurried into the bathroom to take her morning shower.

CHAPTER 2

LISA STEPPED OUT of the shower and dried off just enough to slip into her bathrobe. Carefully wrapping her wet head in a towel, she caught her reflection in the bathroom mirror and stood frozen for a moment. Having just finished the novel, *A Tale of Two Cities*, she smiled at her own reflection and quoted her favorite line:

> *It was the best of times, it was the worst of times, it was the age of wisdom, it was the age of foolishness, it was the epoch of belief, it was the epoch of incredulity, it was the season of Light, it was the season of Darkness, it was the spring of hope, it was the winter of despair....*

"Yes, Mr. Dickens, that thought about sums up my life as well."

Lisa studied the face that had stared back at her for forty years, smiled, and then played back Ben Jackson's departing words to her the previous night. "Lisa, I am so proud of the woman you have become, and I always want to be a part of your life. I know it won't be easy, but would you at least consider taking our relationship to the next level?"

Lisa moaned, "How is it that the *best of times* always has a *worst of times* to take the thrill right out of it?" As always, the face in her mirror never seemed to have an acceptable answer to her deepest questions. Ben's words, "it won't be easy" reverberated in her ears until she almost screamed at the face in the mirror, "I know, I know. But it's never been easy, has it, Lisa? Ben Jackson is everything you ever wanted in a man and never thought you'd get—not you—not after everything you've done in your life." The face simply stared back at her. That face had heard this argument many times before, but this time, this time Lisa could finally smile with her heart. "Ben Jackson knows it all, and he still wants to have me in his life. He is the first man in my entire life who knows all of my secrets and still loves me, which makes this the *best of times*."

A flicker of embarrassment crossed Lisa's face as she remembered her first meeting almost sixteen years earlier with Officer Ben Jackson; she had been sitting in a jail cell on drug charges. "Ben Jackson was also there for *the worst of times*. How vile I was back then," she practically chuckled, "my *age of foolishness*. I can hardly believe that was actually me back then; it was, and I own it." The face just smiled back at her with that knowing look Lisa had come to admire. "I can own it because I have also come through *the epoch of belief*, and know that I have been forgiven and am no longer that person who once behaved that way."

In the distance, Lisa heard Gladys chatting with a neighbor as she picked up the morning paper. Then Gladys' cheerful voice called out "Good morning" as she reentered the house, signaling to Lisa that breakfast was almost ready; but she wasn't. Lisa hastily put on her uniform, pulled her hair up into a clip, slipped on her shoes and headed out to the kitchen. She had both dreaded and looked forward to this day for five months, and here it was: the day she was finally going back to work at Mrs. Bascom's bakery. Five months…had it actually only been five months? It felt like a lifetime ago—a lifetime that she never again wanted to relive.

The smell of hot coffee and Gladys' pecan rolls filled her senses as she walked into the kitchen and took her seat across from Gladys. Pouring Lisa's coffee, Gladys asked, "Are you ready for today? Everyone at the bakery is so excited to have you back. But Lisa, we all know how hard walking into that bakery for the first time will be for you. Are you sure you want to put in a whole day of work the first time back after your father's death?"

"Death? That's a polite way to phrase it." Lisa tried to make her response sound lighthearted, but it didn't come out that way. "I know everyone is concerned about how I will feel about being there, and I do appreciate it, Gladys. I know it will be hard, but I can't let the past rob me of my future. That bakery is more than that one night when my father came into it, intent on killing me." Then remembering *A Tale of Two Cities*, Lisa tried to lighten the conversation with, "talk about *an epoch of incredulity*."

Gladys quickly added, "And don't forget *a winter of despair.*"

A sad-faced smirk was Lisa's only response. She loved it when Gladys played along with her word games. They had spent every evening of the past month reading this novel out loud together, and Gladys knew how much this phrase had meant to her. She also appreciated the space Gladys had given her to pick the times when she was willing to talk. Most topics were out on the table now—all except for one. Lisa couldn't go there yet; it was just too painful. So bringing this conversation to an end, she quickly switched topics with, "Thanks to you and Mrs. Bascom, that bakery is so much more than just that one night. You two led me out of my *season of darkness*, my self-destructive, self-hating, drug-addled existence. You took me into your home and loved me when I could not love myself. Mrs. Bascom gave me a job and taught me the skill of baking. That was the season of my life where I learned self-respect and a good work ethic. I guess I'd call that my *age of wisdom, as well as* my *season of light*. During those twelve years, you and Mrs. Bascom poured wisdom into me and held up the Light of Truth until I could finally see it. I love you both, and I love that bakery."

Lisa had quoted that Dickens' phrase so many times, they both knew it by heart. Gladys observed the glaring absence of the phrase, *the spring of hope*. She knew this was no oversight on Lisa's part. The most important phrase in that whole quote was the only one Lisa had omitted. Sipping her coffee and letting Lisa lead the conversation, Gladys learned as much from the topics not discussed as those that were. Lisa's *spring of hope* was still in question and trying to push the conversation in that direction would only hurt her. Therefore, Gladys patiently waited until Lisa was ready to bring it up.

Quietly finishing her breakfast, Lisa wondered what it would feel like to walk into the bakery in just a few minutes. Five months and three days had passed since that terrible night. Turning her face away from Gladys, Lisa whispered, "If I take the back way, I'll have to walk through the security door off the alley."

Gladys remained quiet, knowing Lisa wasn't really talking to her. She was thinking out loud and simply needed to get it out. They both knew what had happened at that security door. "Gladys, I can't get the image of my father's bloodshot eyes out of my head when he had me by the throat. They were so hate-filled, but the most difficult image I still have to deal with is seeing her panic-stricken face as I looked over his shoulder." As if willing herself to face the memory, Lisa turned back toward Gladys and confessed, "Going through the front door of the bakery will be just as painful. The last person I saw walk through that door was my daughter, Hope."

Even though Gladys knew Hope was never far from Lisa's thoughts, this was the first time in two weeks that Lisa had spoken her name. None of the family knew Hope had existed before that trial. During the trial they learned that Lisa had given up her baby for adoption when she was just seventeen and never talked about her. They were halfway through the murder trial before anyone in the family learned that, not only did she exist, Hope had been in that bakery the night Chuck Miller had tried to kill his daughter. "Lisa, Hope will be okay. Only one month has passed since she had to testify at your trial. You need to be patient and give her the time she needs to absorb it all. Her parents…" Seeing the quick flash of pain in Lisa's eyes, she quickly corrected, "Her *adopted* parents said they are getting her into counseling to help her deal with the fact that she killed a man. That realization can't be easy for anyone, especially a young woman, to bear, regardless of the circumstances."

"I know that, Gladys. I just wish my heart could accept it. I never wanted my baby to be tainted by my family. That was exactly why I gave her up. Then she came looking for me—her biological mother. How could she have known she had picked the very night my father had decided to visit me at the bakery?"

"Lisa, Mr. and Mrs. Winslow seem like really nice people, and they love your baby girl." Gladys knew it was hard for Lisa to think of her daughter as a grown woman. Whenever Lisa did talk about Hope, she usually referred to her as "my baby girl."

"Do you really think she will ever come back here to Jefferson, Gladys? I have to hold onto the hope that Hope will return one day."

Brushing a strand of hair away from Lisa's face as she bent over to kiss her on the forehead, Gladys leaned back to look Lisa straight in the eyes and said with robust confidence, "Lisa, I do believe your *spring of hope* is coming. Love requires us to be patient. You have to give Hope time to resolve all of this. I know every day is an eternity to you; I know that." Then pulling Lisa to her feet in order to give her a big bear hug, Gladys whispered into her ear, "I love you, girl. I couldn't love you more if I had given birth to you. I know you are hurting and that you tend to bury your hurt in busywork. I want to help you walk through this, but not talking about Hope is not the way to do it. We need to be praying for her, and not just that she comes back here. You and I don't know everything this young woman is dealing with, but God does. So we will daily, if not hourly, place her in His hands and trust Him to protect her and heal her."

Returning Gladys' bear hug, Lisa suggested, "At the top of every hour, I am going to pray for Hope, and knowing that you are here at home doing so right along with me will bring me great comfort." Then feeling the necessity to confess her own need, Lisa added, "Gladys, would you also remember me while you're at it? I feel so vulnerable right now. I am so weak and torn. One minute I am up in the clouds in love with Ben, and the next I am in the blackest hole of despair over Hope. One day I feel like I can tackle anything, and the next day, I can hardly get myself out of bed. Why does life have to be so complicated? I love Ben. You know I do. But I also know just how hard life will be for him if we pursue this relationship. This is a small town in Georgia. Gladys, every preacher in every pulpit preaches repentance and forgiveness, but most people don't really believe it in real life—at least they don't when it comes to the type of crimes I committed. How can I ask Ben and his son to open up themselves to the kind of cruelty some people can dish out? Ben tells me to let him worry about that, but I don't think I can handle it. It is one thing when people treat me with cruelty; I deserve it. But Ben doesn't really know just how mean people can be and how hard it could be for his son."

"Lisa, you are not giving Ben enough credit. Ben knows people and he can handle it. Yes, lots of small-minded people live in this world. But we both know that just as many wonderful, good-hearted folks have accepted you without holding onto your past. Why not try to remember all of those people when you find yourself sliding into that black hole of despair? You can't do anything about rude, self-righteous, hateful people, except maybe pity them. Obviously, they have never come to know the forgiveness of God. When you encounter one of these people today, just say a little prayer for them and protect your heart from anger. As they judge you, you pray for them. I am not saying taking the high road is easy. It is one of the hardest things you will ever do. But Lisa, I know it works because God tells us to do it."

"I know you are right, Gladys. I simply don't know if I can do it yet. When I get those looks from people, and you know the looks I mean, I get filled with either shame or rage. The idea of praying for them right then seems beyond me. I am expected to show compassion to someone who is not showing compassion to me. It doesn't seem fair."

"It isn't fair, Lisa; that's the point. but your showing compassion is godly. When you get those stares today, and we both know you will, remember that God never looked at you that way. He offered you love and mercy, and He wants you to be His righteousness toward those who are still in darkness. Apart from your accepting that love and mercy, this is the best way of saying thank you to Him for all He has done for you. Loving the unlovely in His name is the godliest action any of us can do."

"Like you and Mrs. Bascom did for me, right? I was as unlovely a person as ever walked this earth, and you were God's arms offered to me."

Hearing the living room clock chime reminded them both that Lisa was now officially late for her first day back to work. "It's kind of good that I'm late today. I don't have time to worry about which door I'm going to take; I just need to get there and get busy. But Gladys, in thirty minutes, it will be the top of the hour so remember to pray for Hope—and for me." Lisa flew out of the door, turned down the driveway, and headed up the street as quickly as she could without actually running. She was determined that today was going to be one of those best-of-times kind of days.

CHAPTER 3

❧

Rounding the corner onto Sycamore Avenue, Lisa spotted Mrs. Bascom standing out in front of the bakery, chatting with the owner of the hardware store. For over twenty years, Pete Nuell and Ruth Bascom had shared a common wall and had built up their businesses to a comfortable level; yet they both still swept their front sidewalks every day. Ruth loved chatting with Pete about the different businesses on the block, finding out who was in trouble, who was talking about expanding, and how they could encourage more foot traffic—issues every small business owner needs to keep up on.

As Lisa approached, Ruth turned her gaze from Pete, who, in response, stepped aside for Lisa to pass. "Good morning, Lisa," Ruth offered with warm smile. Pete, on the other hand, simply nodded his acknowledgment of her presence and began sweeping his sidewalk again while the two ladies headed into the bakery to start their day.

"Missy and Brenda are really glad you are back. They have hated the early morning baking hours because it interferes with their late-night dating schedule. They had to get here at four in the morning to have all the pastries ready for the morning rush, which means early to bed. That schedule simply doesn't sit well with their young boyfriends, as I have heard repeatedly."

Pushing open the swinging door to the kitchen, Lisa called out the familiar phrase, "Coming through," as she entered her sanctuary—her kitchen. Oh, how she had missed this place! Both Missy and Brenda about knocked her over in their enthusiasm to greet her. "Thanks for the warm welcome, girls."

"We are so glad to have you back," Missy gushed in her thick Alabama twang. "Lisa, we've tried to keep things going, but we sure are happy to let you have your kitchen back!"

"I'm glad to be back; however, I have been told your excitement to see me is in no little way due to the fact that I will take back the four a.m. shift, starting tomorrow morning."

"Oh, that's not the reason we're happy you are back," chimed in Brenda. Then in response to Lisa's knowing smile back at her, "Well, it's *one* of the reasons—just not the only reason."

Hearing the timer signal something was ready to come out of the oven, Missy turned, grabbed an oversized mitten and slid a tray of Lisa's famous butter pecan rolls out of the oven and placed them on the cooling rack. Beaming with pride, Missy said, "See, Lisa, we followed your recipe to the letter."

"So you are not going to tell her about the five trays of pecan rolls we botched before we mastered it?" Brenda teased.

"Only five?" Lisa questioned. "I think I ruined at least six trays before I got Gladys's recipe down right, so you girls outdid me." Then wanting to end this meet-and-greet moment, Lisa asked, "So what is yet to be done today? Have you got the bread dough rising yet?"

"Yup," Missy said with pride. "And we have your pie crust made and chilling in the fridge for you. We knew you would want to get right into making your pies again, so we thought we would have everything cleared out and ready for you." Then winking at Brenda, Missy teased, "Your first pie was ordered way last week, Lisa. Officer Jackson wants to personally pick up one of your double chocolate meringue pies at noon today."

"Okay, that's about enough teasing from you two. Ben is a great guy, and we like each other; that is all. You two get busy on the bread trays while I get the pies started. Mrs. Bascom is going to handle the front counter for several more days so I can just keep a low profile here in the kitchen. Once things settle down and we get back to normal, we can decide who does what around here."

Brenda's knowing smile signaled to Lisa that she understood what Lisa was really saying, whereas Missy, a little less observant, simply took the instructions at face value and started in on the bread assignment. Waiting a few minutes for the right time, Brenda slid up close to Lisa and whispered, "Things have calmed down some already. Your taking that extra month was a good idea. People around here have short attention spans. At first, new customers kept coming in, thinking they might get a glimpse of you. When they didn't, they went on with life and forgot about you. Lisa, you know all our regulars still love you, right?"

"I sure hope so, Brenda. I don't want Mrs. Bascom to suffer on my account. I think it's best if I stay back here in the kitchen most of the time, at least for a while." Then giving Brenda a playful tug on her apron, Lisa's trademark replacement for a Southern hug, she concluded, "Brenda, I'm glad things have calmed down, but don't be mistaken. Lots of people in this town have very long memories. I will just have to deal with that when it comes. But right now, let's have some fun turning out the best stuff we can and wow them with our products!"

The women chatted and laughed as they scurried around the kitchen, attending to their individual tasks. Lisa caught up on the girls' love lives, as they tried to outdo each other with descriptions of just how wonderful their boyfriends were. Listening to the endless chatter of the girls kept Lisa's thoughts in check. She needed this distraction to keep her from dwelling on the fact that the swinging door to the front counter area remained closed today. For the past six years, once the ovens had been turned off and the kitchen had cooled down, they would prop open the swinging door so the luscious smells from the kitchen could fill the bakery and increase sales. Opening the doors also allowed their regulars to shout a word of greeting to Lisa, compliment one of her pies or pastries, or simply to carry on idle conversation as they noticed her at the big sink, scrubbing dozens of bakery pans or standing at the big work island, putting icing on some special order. The bakery had become a hub of gossip for many regulars who shared the news of who was getting engaged, married, or having a baby. Name what was going on, and the bakery was somehow involved. After all, Mrs. Bascom's bakery was the bakery for everyone in town. If something was going on, the bakery was where the details were discussed—the where, when, who, and how many.

Today, without saying a word as to why because they all understood why, Mrs. Bascom kept the swinging door closed. Lisa knew her employer was protecting her from curious eyes and even more—from unusually loud comments made by rude customers waiting at the counter. Every once in a while, Mrs. Bascom would swing open the door so a friend could shout a greeting to Lisa, but then the door would swing back closed. Lisa would remember Gladys' warning, "Protect your heart from anger." She was glad Mrs. Bascom had decided to keep the door closed for now because she wasn't so sure she could pray for "them" if she saw their faces, nor could she easily forget their rude remarks. "I guess they aren't the only ones with a long memory," Lisa chuckled to Brenda as they washed the last of the cookie sheets. "Ruth is trying to protect me from them, but really, I think God is protecting me from myself as well. I can carry a grudge as well as the next person, and right now I need to be very careful to forgive. You'd think that someone who has been forgiven so much in her life wouldn't have trouble forgiving others. I just wish it weren't such a hard lesson to learn."

Brenda said nothing; she simply reached over to give Lisa's apron a little tug. That gesture was enough. At noon the swinging door opened as Ben Jackson entered the kitchen. Blushing ever so slightly, Lisa pointed to his special order and chided, "Officer Jackson, it is customary for us to box up the special orders and have them setting behind the front counter for pick up."

"Well," smiled Ben, "I'm not here just to pick up my special order. I'm here to pick you up as well. Would you like to go down the street and grab a bite of lunch to celebrate your first day back to work?"

"I don't think that is a good idea, Ben. I'm not ready for any face-to-face confrontations just yet. Besides, I don't want the whole world to know about us either—at least not just yet."

Brenda and Missy tried to look busy and pretend not to be listening. Ben turned to Missy and pleaded, "I need some help here, girls. Can't you talk some sense into her?"

"I'm keeping out of this. Lisa knows what is best for her." Then giggling as she took this opportunity to head out front to fill the cookie display, with a twinkle in her eyes and sassiness to her voice, Missy added, "Or at least she *thinks* she does."

Lisa pushed the swinging door closed behind Missy and said, "Ben, the lunch counter is way too public right now. I'm having a really good first day back, and I don't want to risk messing it up. Do you understand?"

"I understand," Ben teased. "You are ashamed to be seen with me," then he quickly added, "I do understand, Lisa. I can be patient. You take all the time you need, but can Benny and I come over tonight and have dinner with you and Gladys?"

"Sure, I just need to call Gladys to let her know. She loves to cook, and she loves you and Benny."

"*She* loves me and Benny?" He emphasized *she*.

No one on the face of the earth could get away with teasing Lisa—no one except Ben. Poking him in the ribs as she pushed him out into the front of the bakery, Lisa whispered, "You know I do, but if I'm ever going to finish my work today so we can have that dinner together, you need to get out of here now."

With a huge smile on his face Ben ended their conversation by declaring, "Tell Gladys I'll be bringing dessert and, Lisa, don't you be late.

I know how you are when you get into a kitchen." He went to the front counter, paid for his special order and left the bakery a very happy man.

It was nearly 6:00 when Lisa finished with the last cookie sheets, checked the list of special orders for the next day, and then headed out to the front counter. "Ruth, everything is ready for tomorrow. I went through the pantry and confirmed we have enough supplies to get through at least three baking days, but we will need to start a shopping list if we want to bake anything on Thursday."

Flipping the closed sign on the front door, Mrs. Bascom slipped the bank bag into her leather tote, picked up a special order that needed to be dropped off down the street and said, "This was a really good day. It felt so good walking into my kitchen and hearing you three girls laughing again."

Lisa smiled at the thought of being called "one of the girls." It had been years since she felt like a girl. "Ruth, none of us opened the alley door today, but you still might want to check and make sure the security alarm is still set." Lisa knew she didn't have to explain why she hadn't done it herself before coming up front. It was just too soon to touch that door—the doorway where her father had died.

"That's okay, Lisa; I plan to leave the back way after everything is secure out here. Would you mind dropping off this special order since it is on your way home? It's for Myers Law Firm up the street around the corner. They are having a late-night session and want some pastries in their conference room. All you have to do is drop this box at the receptionist's desk. They will plate everything themselves."

"Sure, Ruth, I'll be happy to." Taking the pastry box as Ruth opened the front door, Lisa returned Ruth's confident smile, even though she felt anything but confident. She had hoped to get through this whole day without coming face to face with any customers. "Are you sure the receptionist will still be there at 6:00?"

"If not, just set it on her desk and leave. Someone at the firm will find them." Then shooing her out the front door, Mrs. Bascom added, "Tell Gladys I will be joining you all for dessert tonight. She wants to make this a little party to celebrate your first day back."

Walking past the adjoining storefronts had never bothered Lisa. Mr. Nuell's hardware store was usually the only other store still open this time of night. Painter's Beauty Parlor always closed at four now that Mrs. Painter was well into her sixties and could not put in the long hours anymore. Beyond the beauty parlor was Hodges' Five & Dime. Years earlier, when Woolworths wanted to pull out of Jefferson, old Mr. Hodges thought he could still make a go of it and bought it, "lock, stock and barrel," as he always said. Walking into Hodges was like stepping back in time. The old hardwood floors creaked underfoot as you walked beside the old-fashioned counters that displayed everything from thimbles and thread to model airplane kits. Hodges had even kept the old popcorn machine for which the five and dime ad been famous. Many a customer entered his doors just to enjoy the smell of popcorn. Hodges was no fool, and he was a great salesman. Very few customers ever left his store without a complimentary bag of popcorn as well as something they could not live without. No one knew how he kept his doors open these days, but they were all glad to have him on the block.

Turning the corner at the Five & Dime, Lisa could see the lights on at Myers Law Firm. As she climbed the six steps to the large oak doors, she could see the receptionist's empty desk through the ornate glass inserts in the doors. She quickly opened the door and headed for the desk. Intent on getting out of the office without being seen, she set the pastry box where it would be easily spotted. Lisa could hear voices echoing down the hall and hurried toward the front door. She recognized one of these voices all too well, and she had no intention of coming face to face with Mr. Gordon tonight. Gordon had been the prosecutor who had tried to get her convicted of killing her father, simply to use her trial as a stepping stone to the position of district attorney. He had also threatened her daughter when she offered to step forward and explain what had really happened that night in the alley.

Running down the front steps, Lisa heaved a huge sigh of relief, knowing she had made it out without being seen. Looking back at the lighted windows of the conference room, she wondered why Gordon would be at

Myers Law Firm at this time of night. For the last month, the local paper had been full of editorials about what a snake Gordon was, a very Southern description that fit him to a tee. It was also common knowledge that Judge Kirkley was determined to bring up Gordon on charges and was trying to have him disbarred. *So why is he here at Myers Law Firm?*

For months, as Lisa sat in jail waiting for her trial to start, the local paper had run story after story about her colorful past. By the time the trial was scheduled to start, almost everyone in Jefferson was convinced that she had killed her father. So when the truth finally came out, everyone felt lied to, which really hurt the editor's reputation and the paper's credibility. Small-town people don't like it when people they should be able to trust betray them. Realizing he had been used by Gordon to accomplish his own selfish goals, the editor was now on a personal campaign to expose Gordon and ensure he never again held office in this town. The troublesome part of this whole ordeal was that Lisa's story came up every time the editors wrote about Gordon.

Lisa again found herself the victim of someone else's drama. She had lived her first thirty years in such a stew of anger, it had almost destroyed her. Remembering Gladys' warning this morning, "Protect your heart from anger," Lisa questioned, "That doesn't mean Gordon? He deserves everything he is getting. He needs to be stopped." But having had this conversation with Gladys many times over the past month, she knew what Gladys would say. "Lisa, anger is an emotion that only destroys the user. People know what he did, and they are going after him. You need to let them handle it and release Gordon to face his own consequences. He will not get away with anything."

Seeing the house just two doors up the street, Lisa knew Gladys was right. She knew that anger simply keeps you connected to the very person from whom you need to walk away. Anger is a tether that binds you to that person. Leaning against the gate, Lisa confessed, "God, You know I'm not as strong as Gladys. I know she is right, but I've never been good at this. Not toward others and not myself. This morning I thought I would have to forgive some customer for a rude remark. That would have been so much easier than this. Why Gordon? Why did I have to hear his voice and deal with all of this drama? Why did I have to start with such a hard person? I know if I hold onto these feelings, they will just destroy me and poison any chance Ben and I might have for happiness. I don't want to hold onto this anger, but I need Your help." Then remembering Gladys' famous saying, "Confession is the first step toward healing," Lisa reached for the gate lock and headed for the front door, confident that, as hard as it was, she had indeed protected her heart from anger today. She had owned it. She had confessed it. And she had asked for help. Reaching for the door knob, she smiled and said, "Tether disconnected—at least for now."

CHAPTER 4

B<small>EN WAS ALREADY</small> at the house when Lisa walked in. He had tucked one of Gladys' dishtowels into his belt, which made Lisa chuckle as he greeted her at the door. "I washed the lettuce and got water all down the front of me so Gladys insisted it was either one of her aprons or this dishtowel."

Lisa slipped her arm around Ben's extended arm as he directed her toward the kitchen. "I think it looks good on you, Ben. Besides, Benny would throw a fit if he walked in here and saw his father in an apron."

Lifting the lid on the huge pot on the stove, Lisa asked, "What can I do, Gladys?"

Turning Lisa toward the hallway, Gladys gave her a gentle push as she ordered, "Nothing. You go get changed out of that uniform into something comfortable. Ben and I have everything in order. Benny should be here as soon as football practice is over, and then we can eat."

As Lisa changed her clothes, she could hear Ben's deep masculine voice telling Gladys one of his famous jokes. Ben could hardly finish them without breaking into a belly laugh himself. The listener never knew if he was laughing at the joke or simply because hearing Ben laugh made him want to laugh. Humor had never been part of her past, but Ben seemed to make it easy to see the humor in almost anything. This gentle giant of a man reminded her of a teddy bear. She loved it when he put his arms around her, told her something funny, making them both laugh. Ben's body would start to quiver, and a deep resounding chuckle would erupt from him until Lisa was in tears and had to beg him to stop. There was absolutely nothing about this man she didn't love. Sometimes that fact scared her.

She and Ben were not officially dating. Officer Benjamin Jackson had been assigned the duty of escorting her from her jail cell to the conference room during the three months her attorney was preparing for trial. As the trial got underway, he escorted her back and forth from the jail to the courthouse and stood at attention just a few feet from her throughout the trial. Very little about Lisa's life was left unexposed to Ben Jackson, a fact that both comforted and mortified her. During the long, lonely afternoons in that jail cell, Ben would usually find some excuse to stop by for a chat.

Knowing any discussion regarding her trial was not permitted, Ben would always plan some safe topic to start their conversations—the opening of the new Winn Dixie out on the highway, the Methodist fundraiser that was rained out, and her favorite, the time the Moose Lodge had a chili contest during the Fourth of July celebration and how almost everyone in town came down with the runs. Ben could get so animated in his storytelling she could actually envision the dignified ladies of town making a run for the port-a-potties. "Pun intended," he had added.

Ben was fun to listen to, and she had begun expecting and looking forward to his daily visits. He always treated her as a real person, so the days he was unable to stop by became very long days. On the days when Ben could stay a little longer than usual, the conversation would slowly drift to more personal topics—but never in great detail. Ben didn't believe in dwelling on the past, but Lisa never got the impression he was trying to hide anything. She knew he was a widower and had a teenage son. He attended church regularly, as did most people in this small Southern town. He seldom talked about his wife, except to say she had endured a long battle with cancer—one she eventually lost. Lisa knew that Ben and his son, Benny, had been alone now for seven years and that Ben had never dated.

Recalling the afternoon the conversation about dating came up, Lisa remembered how uncomfortable Ben had been as he explained, "I've been on dates, just nothing serious. You can't be a widower in this town without everyone's trying to set you up with some friend of theirs. It's not that I want to live the rest of my life alone, but right now I need to focus on my son. Watching his mother waste away was really hard on him. I didn't think it would be good for him to have me drag women in and out of his life, so I would not be lonely. He is going to be a senior this year and then off to college. I've waited this long; another year won't kill me."

Opening the bedroom door, Lisa thought about Ben's determination to "wait until his son went off to college," and how he'd said, "another year won't kill me." Lisa knew she and Ben needed to have a long talk and soon. More than a week had passed since that conversation took place, and neither of them had liked its conclusion. Even though they were not officially dating, the gossipers in town were frantically flapping their tongues. As a result, several of the guys on Benny's football team had taken it upon themselves to keep him informed of everything being said about the newest couple in town.

One night after dinner, Ben opened their conversation with, "It's sometimes hard to live in a small town. I know these boys like Benny, but that isn't stopping them from being cruel to him. Actually, I think the real reason they are being so cruel is because they really are jealous. The three boys who are giving Benny the most trouble have absentee fathers. One is a doctor who is never home. Another has gone through two wives and is currently pursuing his third target, while the third one has had two DUIs and couldn't care less what happens to his son.

"Throughout high school, Benny had been the guy they all liked and admired. When these three guys were busy complaining about how stupid or selfish their fathers were; Benny would stay quiet. I tried never to miss a game. After a game, if their dads were not able to make it, Benny and I would invite these boys out for burgers. But now, these same boys are the ones making life unbearable for Benny."

"It's because of me, isn't it?" Lisa asked as calmly as possible. "Ben, remember when you told me you didn't want to drag women in and out of Benny's life? You said waiting another year wouldn't kill you, remember?"

"Well, that was before I fell in love with you. Now it would kill me to wait another year, believe me on that one."

"Ben, we have to think of Benny right now. This is his senior year and then he will be off to college, and then we can start our life. I don't like this situation anymore than you do, but we can't make our happiness Benny's burden, can we?"

"But Lisa, our putting off getting married won't make this unhappiness go away. I am not willing to stop seeing you, not talk to you, and pretend we don't care for each other for a whole year because of three selfish boys who don't know any better."

"Ben, we have been talking about getting married at Christmas, right? That way my sister and the whole family would be together. We are only talking about six more months. We can be patient, can't we?"

"Lisa, being patient is not the issue. I can wait another six months. I'm not a foolish teenager who lives only for today. We are talking about what it will cost us to make the gossip die down. That is what I am unwilling to do."

Lisa was almost afraid to ask her next question. "Well then, Ben, what is Benny willing to endure? How does he feel about all of this?"

Hanging his head, his shoulders heaving as he took a deep breath, "Benny wants us to cut it off." Turning toward Lisa, he clarified. "Benny likes you, Lisa. He really does. He is a seventeen-year-old who can't see past tomorrow, and tomorrow seems unbearable to him."

With more calmness than she was feeling, Lisa responded, "Well, I guess we either make ourselves happy and Benny miserable, Benny happy and us miserable, or we find a way to help Benny come to terms with the fact that not everyone in this world is going to play fair. We need to find a way to help him deal with these people in a way that we can all live with."

"It's not fair, Lisa. You and I have both been waiting for years to fall in love. No one has the right to determine our future."

Taking hold of his hand, Lisa almost whispered, "We won't have a future if we don't handle this right. Benny is hurting, and we need to help him deal with this so we don't have to look back someday and know that we were selfish. We can give Benny some time and the help he needs so he doesn't have to ever look back and regret how he handled this as well. Benny knows how much you have sacrificed for him, and he knows how much you love me. If we simply cut it off because he wanted you to, he will always know it was because that was the easy way out for him. That truth will never sit well with him—once he grows up and is out on his own."

"When did you get so smart about teenage boys?"

"I'm not so smart," quipped Lisa. "You notice I didn't tell you how we'd help Benny. I don't know how we will go about this, but I know where we might start."

Ben responded, "Prayer, right? But I seldom do that in front of anyone. Years of church services, community service projects, hauling Benny's youth group friends to every social on the calendar was easy. This is such a private act, and I always feel so clumsy with words."

"Ben, first of all, I'm not just anyone. I'm the woman you want to spend the rest of your life with, remember? We need to start getting comfortable praying in front of each other. Besides, Ben, God doesn't care about the words we use. He cares that we talk to Him.

"Ben, it took me two long years of listening to Gladys talk to God about me before I was willing to do it myself. I loved to hear her pray for me—even when I protested its value. I know it does work, especially when you don't have a clue about what to do next."

Taking Lisa's hand in his big mitt, Ben reticently said, "Well, that about sums up our situation because I don't have a clue what to do next." Lifting Lisa up off the sofa, Ben timidly suggested, "So before we talk to Benny, let's talk to God together."

CHAPTER 5

The first thing Lisa noticed upon entering Gladys' kitchen that morning was the absence of the morning paper. For the past eight years, she and Gladys had always read the paper while having breakfast. Ever since she had come home from jail, the paper was often missing during breakfast. Lisa waited until Gladys was finished filling their coffee cups before asking, "So Gladys, what is in today's paper that you are trying to shield from me?"

"You don't need to start your day with all this poison," Gladys cautioned. "You know the editor is out to get Gordon, and he is using your trial and history to keep everyone in attack mode. What he doesn't realize, or more to the point, what he doesn't care about, is just how hard this is on you."

"Gladys, we can't stop any of this. Gordon was hated by many people in this town well before my trial. None of these people care about the backwash to my life, let alone to the lives of those around me. They have a single-minded purpose—to drive Prosecutor Gordon out of office, out of politics, and out of our town. I am simply the tool they can use right now."

"Well, we don't have to let it spoil our breakfast, do we?" Gladys gently suggested.

"No, but everyone I care about is reading these stories. I cannot pretend that they don't exist. Every day, after one of these planted stories, Ben's son gets teased at school. He has been shoved into a locker, had his lunch tray flipped, called all kinds of names, and just yesterday, he was suspended from school for three days because he punched someone in the face when the guy called his dad a name that Ben would not tell me." Buttering her toast so hard that it crumbled in her hand, Lisa added, "Benny is the one feeling the brunt of all of this negative publicity. He has lost most of his friends, he and his dad are not getting along, and now he can't even play in this weekend's football game because of the suspension."

Pouring them both a second cup of coffee, Gladys confessed, "I thought when we walked out of that courtroom with a not-guilty verdict that everything was finally behind us, but I guess I was being naïve. Happenings like this don't just go away." Then replacing the coffee pot on the counter, Gladys paused, "I'm worried about you, Lisa. It's hard enough to take all this when it is only directed at you, but when it starts hurting those you care about, it goes to a whole new level of emotion."

"Gladys, Ben doesn't know what to do. Benny is angry about everything. He is questioning everything he has ever been taught. Ben told me the other night that Benny locked himself in his bedroom, tore up all his friends' photos, and smashed all three of the model airplanes the two of them had spent all last winter putting together before Ben got the door opened and stopped Benny's tirade." Looking toward Gladys with pleading eyes, Lisa declared, "And it is all because of me! None of this mess would have touched Ben or Benny if I had simply followed my own counsel. I knew it was a bad idea to let Ben into my life; I knew it. I warned him about this possibility. I should not have allowed Ben to get involved with me. He was happy; I was happy. Why couldn't we have just kept things the way they were?"

"Because neither one of you was truly happy until you found each other. If I had been given the privilege of designing the perfect man for you,

I could not have done a better job than Ben. And regardless of what you think right now, you are perfect for him."

The phone began ringing, so Lisa stood up to answer it and said, "I doubt that Ben is feeling that way right now. Seeing Benny so angry is killing him." On the other end of the phone, she heard, "Lisa, Benny took off last night, and I don't know where he went. He wouldn't go to any of his friends' homes because right now he has no friends."

"Ben, we will find him. Did he take his truck? Do you dare issue a BOLO on the truck without having to tell everyone you work with why you need one?"

"Right now I don't care who knows what. I just want to get my boy back home safe and sound." Then remembering the boathouse at the lake, Ben suggested, "I think I might know where he went. I'm going to call in a personal day and drive up to Lake Charles. Benny spent two weeks there this summer and talked about how quiet it was up there. Maybe that is where he went. I'll give you a call when I get back," and without waiting for a response from Lisa, the line went dead.

She just stood there for a moment staring at the receiver before hanging it back on the cradle. "Gladys, Benny has run off, and Ben is out looking for him." Returning to the breakfast table, Lisa dropped into her chair with a profound thud. "One week ago last night, Ben and I started asking God for wisdom. But right now, I don't feel very wise."

"Lisa, wisdom isn't a gift that comes to us all at once. When you came to live with me, I was terrified of your drug habit and criminal history. Boy, did I need wisdom. Every day was something new with you, and I didn't know what you needed from me. But Lisa, I did know the One who did know, and that knowledge gave me comfort. I had never been around someone addicted to drugs. Lisa, your addiction really scared me, and I felt totally unqualified. But because I wanted God to use me to help you, I kept asking Him to tell me what to do. God was telling me to keep loving you and when I needed wisdom, it would come."

Lisa slid closer, placed her head on Gladys' shoulder, and began to cry, "Gladys, I've never been as strong as you. I can't do this. I am so afraid of all these feelings I'm having. I just wish I'd never fallen in love with Ben. Love hurts. Caring hurts. And being responsible for hurting others is the worst kind of hurt."

Brushing away the tears from Lisa's cheek, Gladys said, "Lisa, you and Ben have asked for wisdom. How do you think that wisdom is going to come if there is no issue that needs greater wisdom than you have right now? When Ben finds Benny, and I am confident he will, he needs to have a truthful conversation with his son. He needs to listen to Benny, and he needs to be honest about all of these adult issues. So today, you and I will add Ben and Benny to our top of the hour prayer request list, right?"

"Right," Lisa responded without much enthusiasm.

Gladys continued, "Wisdom is a precious commodity that few people acquire because it is costly. Wisdom is not acquired by simply reading books and gaining knowledge. It is never acquired when we choose the safest and easiest path in life. Opening up yourself to loving another person is costly. Anything worth having is going to expose you to hurt. Don't be so afraid of getting hurt that you close up your heart and walk away from love. Ask God to give you enough wisdom to handle what comes today. Don't worry about anything else—only today. Ask for just enough wisdom for today for you, ask it for Ben, and ask it for Benny."

While at work, Lisa replayed Gladys' words from that morning over and over in her head. "Love exposes you to hurts. Love is costly. Accepting love into your life is choosing not to take the easy path." With every pie placed on the cooling rack that day, Lisa had a conversation with God. "You know I'm a coward. You know I am weak. You know I don't want to get hurt again, and I don't ever want to hurt anyone else. But God, I so want to grow into the person You want me to become. I don't want to remain a coward all of my life. I do want to become strong, like Gladys, full of faith and wisdom. I do want it, God. Please give me the strength not to run from this. Please pour Your wisdom into me."

Hours had passed since Lisa had heard from Ben. 3:00, After her top of the hour prayer, Lisa decided to call Ben's home phone to see if he would answer. The wait was agony. The phone kept ringing, and Lisa did not want to leave a message so she quickly hung up before it went to the answering machine. It was almost ten-thirty before Ben's call came. Lisa grabbed the phone, "Did you find Benny?"

"Yes, he was at the boathouse. Benny and I sat on the dock for six hours today, just talking. We talked about everything. He talked a lot about his mother and how much he missed her, and my boy and me did a lot of crying. At first, I wanted to just shake him for scaring me that way, but as soon as I saw his face, I knew this situation wasn't about me and my feelings. It was about my hurting boy, and I needed to get him talking. So I simply walked up to where he was and sat right next to him on the dock and waited. I didn't ask any questions. I didn't lecture him. I just quietly sat beside him, asking God for wisdom while I waited. I had no idea what Benny was really struggling over. I thought it was all the teasing and his suspension and being out of the football game this week. I thought he didn't want me to date you because he couldn't get over your past and that he had bought into the town gossip that the shame of your past would become his. I thought...I thought. Lisa, I was all wrong. I wasn't even close to having a clue what Benny's real issue is."

Almost afraid to ask, Lisa ventured, "So do you know now?"

"Yup, I sure do. Did you know that wisdom comes when we shut our mouths and open our ears? Sitting on that dock praying my heart out, I kept getting this feeling like I needed to just shut up and listen, so that is what I did. At first, Benny talked all around the moon, but I just listened. He talked about how it felt being the brunt of everyone's jokes and the laughingstock of the whole school. But even as he was talking about that, somehow I knew it wasn't the real issue. Oh, yeah, it is an issue, but not the real one.

"He is so confused. The truth is Benny is afraid of loving you. It has nothing to do with your past. He really doesn't have an issue with that. He said, 'If God can forgive Lisa, who am I to hold her past against her?' I can't tell you how hearing my boy say that made me feel. I started crying like a baby. Then Benny started crying, and we sat there and hugged for a long time. It felt so good to hold my boy."

"So Ben, why is Benny afraid to love me?"

"He feels like he is being disloyal to his mother by liking you so much. He said seeing me so happy with you makes him glad and sad at the same time. He said when he punched that kid in the face, he was more mad at himself than the stupid kid. Wanting to defend your honor against anyone and everyone proved to him that he really does care about you, and he didn't quite know what to do with those feelings, so he punched the kid's lights out and got into trouble for it.

To lighten the conversation, Ben laughed one of his deep, resounding laughs and added, "We both laughed over that one, but I told Benny he couldn't do that ever again. Hitting people is never the answer to a problem. But then again, I doubt that any kids at school will risk teasing him anymore!"

"Is Benny feeling better now that you two have talked?"

"Yes, but he and I decided that we both could use some counseling. We need some help sorting out feelings—something guys are especially bad at. Benny needs to come to terms with his mother's loss and learn how not to feel guilty having feelings for someone else, namely you, Lisa."

Remembering all of the petitions and requests for wisdom she had offered that day for Ben, Lisa summed up the day. "Ben, if wisdom is learning what you didn't know, gaining understanding about something you didn't understand, and not being too stubborn to ask others for help, I believe you and I gained a little bit of wisdom today, don't you?"

"Isn't that what we have been asking for, Lisa? Even Benny and I prayed together out on the dock today. I was really uncomfortable at first. He knew that I prayed, just never in front of him. But today we've started afresh, and we will keep praying together about all of this. All three of us are going to get through this together."

CHAPTER 6

❧

THE ARTICLES IN the paper continued. About once a day, someone would come into the bakery trying to get a close-up view of Lisa. Ben and Benny were talking about important things, and life was moving forward. Lisa finally agreed to one lunch date a week at Hodges' Lunch Counter. Being as big as he was, it was always hard for Ben to be inconspicuous, let alone when he would start one of his jokes. But Ben was also hard to dislike, so Lisa felt somewhat assured of everyone's behavior while she was with him.

As they were finishing up their lunch, Mr. Hodges walked up behind them, slapped Ben on the back and said, "Haven't seen you in here for months, boy. I remember a time when your feet couldn't even touch the floor while sitting on one of my stools. You always liked the grilled cheese basket lunch, Ben. Is that what you ordered today?"

"Yes, sir, Mr. Hodges. No point in messing with a good thing." Ben joked back with him.

"Don't you forget to stop by and pick up a complimentary bag of popcorn as you leave. And Ben, I have a few model airplane kits you might want to take a look at on your way out. A boy is never too old for model planes! Right, Ben?" Hodges was always the inveterate salesman.

"I'll be sure to do that, Mr. Hodges. It's nice seeing you again."

As Mr. Hodges started to head toward his front counter, he remembered why he had made his way to them in the first place. He turned to Lisa and said, "Lisa, bet you can't wait to see that girl of yours next week?"

The shock of his question made Lisa's head begin to swirl, and she had trouble breathing. She simply nodded a polite acknowledgment of his comment, and Mr. Hodges continued on his way, unaware of the impact his casual comment had made. Leaning in closely, Ben asked, "What is he talking about, Lisa?"

"I don't know, Ben, but I intend to find out."

Ben quickly paid their bill, picked up the bag of popcorn, waving it in the air toward Mr. Hodges, and headed back to the bakery. Entering the bakery, Lisa turned to Ben, "I need to call my lawyer, Mr. Duncan. He is representing Hope and her father. He will know if Hope really is coming back here next week, and why. Ben, I guess I need to read the paper after all. The fact that old Mr. Hodges knows more about my daughter than I do is rather upsetting. The only thing that would bring her back here, apart from visiting me, and we both know that wouldn't be the reason for this visit, is because someone is digging into Prosecutor Gordon's behavior, and they need something from Hope."

"Lisa, I have to get back to the courthouse, but you call me as soon as you know anything."

Lisa wasted no time getting in Mr. Duncan on the phone. He had been her lawyer during her murder trial, and she both loved and respected him for all he had done to help her. "So is it true, Mr. Duncan? Is Hope returning? Is she actually coming back to Jefferson next week?"

"Lisa, I had intended to call you today, but things kept getting in the way. Yes, Hope and her father are coming next week. I tried to get them to do her deposition in California so she wouldn't have to come back here so soon after your trial. But since Gordon hired Myers Law Firm to represent him in this case, they refused to sign off and want both Hope and her father back here for their depositions."

Remembering the night she dropped off the pastries, Lisa said, "So that was why Gordon was at Myers Law Firm that night. I thought he was there getting hired, not becoming a client."

"Hired? Lisa, right now Gordon couldn't get hired as dog catcher. Last week he was asked to step down as city prosecutor, and yesterday he officially removed his name from the ballot for district attorney. He knows he is finished here. His only fight right now is to save his license to practice law, and that is a fight he won't surrender to easily."

"Will he be questioning Hope?" Lisa asked with fear in her voice.

"No, Lisa, he won't. His lawyer will, but he will be present." Then redirecting the conversation, Duncan asked, "Have you talked with Hope since the trial?"

"No. I got a sweet letter from her about a week after she left. She said how sorry she was for everything. She apologized for waiting so long to come forward—even though we all know that her running away was my idea. Mr. Duncan, you are sure Hope cannot get into trouble for leaving the scene of a murder, right?"

"Lisa," Duncan tried using his most grandfatherly voice, "I know you are still worried, but I have it in writing from the district attorney that no charges will ever be filed against Hope."

"I know, Mr. Duncan, but it is so hard to trust anyone after what Prosecutor Gordon did. I know it was just as much my fault, but I don't want Hope to pay for my foolishness. She has enough to deal with having taken a life—even one taken in self-defense. Hope hasn't offered me any encouragement about more communication—calling, writing, visiting, anything. Gladys and I decided we needed to give her some space for now, and then I find out about this."

"Lisa, I've spoken to both Hope and her father several times. I will be representing their interests in this matter, even though they have both been assured that no charges will be issued against either of them. I intend to make sure everyone keeps his promises. Lisa, Hope and her father will be arriving next Wednesday afternoon and will be staying out at the West End Hotel. They will be here until Sunday afternoon. If you would like, I can tell Hope that you would like to visit with her during her stay. Would you like me to?"

"Yes, but please tell her I'd understand if she is not ready. I don't want her upset any more than necessary right now. Would you tell her that for me?"

"Rest assured that I will, Lisa. Is there anything else I can do for you right now?"

"Yes, actually there is, Mr. Duncan. Do you think it would be easier for Hope if my sister, Susan, came down from Atlanta for this meeting? That is, if there is going to be a meeting."

"I think that would be a great idea, Lisa. Susan is your greatest advocate; other than Gladys and Ruth Bascom. Her presence might make it less uncomfortable for both of you. You call Susan and see when she might be able to drive down here to Jefferson, and I'll get back to you about the time."

"Thank you, Mr. Duncan. I know you are a busy man, so I will let you go and wait for your call. But Mr. Duncan, don't you worry about me if Hope says no. I won't fall apart on you," and she hung up the phone.

She filled in Gladys on everything as soon as she got home and then called her sister, Susan. Four months had now passed since the trial, and she missed her kid sister. They chatted on the phone every week, with Ben's being the most constant topic of discussion. Of course, Hope was never out of their thoughts. "Answer the phone, Susan. Don't you know I need to talk to my sister right now?" Instead, she heard the familiar click, signaling the answering machine was about to record her message. Lisa thought about hanging up. *How can I leave such an important message on a machine?* Then she heard a loud click, and her brother-in-law Scott said, "Don't hang up! We are here." He was out of breath because of running to answer the phone.

"Hi, Scott, it's me, Lisa. Is Susan there?"

"Sure, Lisa, she just needs to get in the house. We had driven into the driveway, and I heard the phone ringing. I made a mad dash for it, leaving Susan to get the kids out of the car by herself. He knew something was up because Lisa usually had lots to say to him, even when she really wanted to chat with Susan. Signaling for her to hurry up, he stretched out the phone so Susan could take it while he lifted Matthew out of her arms. "Hi, Lisa, how are you?" Susan said as she dropped onto the sofa. "So how is Ben?"

"Ben is fine, Susan. I'm not calling about Ben. Susan, Hope is coming back to Jefferson next Wednesday and will be here until Sunday."

Sitting up straight, Susan asked, "When was that decided? I thought you hadn't heard from her, except for that one letter."

"I haven't. She was subpoenaed to appear, so the prosecutors can get a deposition from her regarding the Gordon case. Hope and her father are coming here. Mr. Duncan said he will talk with her and try to set up a meeting for me. If she is willing, would you be willing to come down and visit her with me?"

"Of course, I will. Let me clear my calendar and get Mom to take care of the kids so I can be there." Lisa knew, without Susan having to clarify it, that "Mom" meant Scott's mom—not theirs. No one in their right mind would ever leave their kids with Marjorie Miller, nor would she offer or accept the job.

"I'm really nervous, Susan. I don't know what I'll say to her. I'm sure her parents have told her everything they learned while sitting in the courtroom. I have so much I need to tell her, but I'm not sure she really wants to know any of it. Gladys said to let Hope take the lead and only answer the questions she asks."

"I would agree with Gladys, except…" Susan paused for a second, not sure if she should broach the subject.

"Except what, Susan?"

"Except…what if Hope fears she might upset you by asking certain questions she needs answers to?"

"Susan, you mean about her biological father, right? You think she might hold back for fear of making me feel uncomfortable with the question? She has to wonder. Once she heard about my past, she might be fearful that I don't even know who it might be. You are right. If I get the chance to meet with her, I need to make it really easy for her to ask me who her father was."

"Lisa, I'm not asking you to tell me who it is. The day we all found out about Hope, you said you wouldn't tell anyone who it was until you were able to tell Hope. But if you tell her, and I'm saying that you should tell her, are you worried about her seeking him out after all these years?"

"No, Susan, I'm not. When I tell Hope you will understand why I'm not worried."

"Wow!" Susan mused, "Hope is returning to Jefferson next week."

"Yes, she is," responded Lisa. "It certainly isn't going to be as hard as last time and definitely not harder than the time before. Maybe this time Hope can just get the answers she has waited for her whole life—and only that this time."

All week long Lisa practiced just how she would say it. She imagined sitting and looking at Hope, telling her everything. She didn't want to sound evasive, making Hope think there was anything more to hide. She also did not want to use so many words that the beauty of the truth would get lost. By the time Wednesday arrived, Lisa felt as ready as she possibly could, under the circumstances. Duncan called as soon as he had picked up Hope and her father from the airport and had them safely tucked away in their hotel rooms. "Lisa, even though Hope is in town, I do not want you to call her or meet with her until after both depositions. Hope's deposition is tomorrow morning, and her dad's deposition will be Friday morning. I want her as calm as possible for her deposition. But she has agreed to meet with you and Susan at 2:00 Friday afternoon. If I give you the name of the hotel, can I trust you to be patient and wait until then?"

"Yes, Mr. Duncan, you know you can trust me. Does she want us to come up to her hotel room?"

"Lisa, Hope seems a little frazzled, but I think she is looking forward to spending some time with you. Just be in the lobby by 2:00, and she will call the front desk when she is ready. You take care and don't worry about a thing."

CHAPTER 7

L̲ᴵˢᴬ'ˢ ᴬɴˣɪᴇᴛʏ ᴡᴀꜱ palpable as she waited in the lobby of the West End Hotel on Friday afternoon. Hope had set the meeting for 2:00; therefore, she and Susan made sure they were sitting in the lobby by a quarter to the hour. The clicking of the huge clock above the fireplace began to wear on Lisa's nerves, as if, with every click, it was saying, "Almost time." Looking over at her kid sister, she simply smiled and nodded her acknowledgment. Susan knew how important her presence was right now, but she also knew that they had talked enough and that she wanted to just sit there quietly. Nothing anyone could say would make this wait more tolerable.

The ringing of the lobby phone startled them. The receptionist at the front desk had told them she would forward the room call to the phone in the lobby when their guest was ready to receive them. Seeing that Lisa could not move, Susan reached for the phone and said, "Hello? Yes, we are sitting here in the lobby. We will be right up."

Turning her gaze toward her big sister, Susan saw the tears welling up in Lisa's eyes. "Take a deep breath, Lisa. I'm sure Hope is just as nervous. You and I need to make this as easy for her as we can. Lisa, you have practiced and practiced what you are going to say to her. You have asked for the right words. You simply have to trust that God will direct this conversation and that He will show you what Hope needs to hear today. You and I are not walking into that room alone; you keep that in mind, and let things unfold the way they should."

Hope was standing in the doorway of her room as the two sisters stepped off the elevator. Her father gave her a quick hug, acknowledged her guests with a smile and nod, and then retreated to his room across the hall. Hope stepped back from the doorway, signaling both women to enter without any intention of offering, or accepting, a hug of greeting. She directed them to the two club chairs across from the sofa and asked, "Would you like something to drink? The hotel just brought up a large pitcher of sweet tea."

"That would be much appreciated, Hope," Lisa responded, sounding more calm than Susan knew her to be. "Did you have pleasant flight from California?"

Pouring the tea as she spoke, Hope tried to carry on small talk about the trip, avoiding any mention of why she was here. "The flight was fine. We had a three-hour layover in Chicago, but there wasn't enough time to do anything but grab a bite to eat. I don't really like flying very much. The air gets so stale, I usually get a headache."

Accepting the glass of sweet tea, Lisa simply smiled her response. She hated chitchat—especially when something important needed to be addressed. As Hope turned toward Susan and offered her a glass, Lisa signaled to Susan that she needed help. Taking the glass, Susan offered, "I don't get headaches, but I do get leg cramps on long flights. Have you done much traveling, Hope?"

"Not a lot. I flew back and forth to college, but those were just two-hour flights. I was supposed to fly to Europe after graduation, but I wasn't able to do it. My parents gave me the trip as a graduation present, but Michael didn't want me to go without him, so I didn't."

Keeping the conversation light, Susan asked, "Michael? Is he your fiancé?"

Beaming with pride, Hope responded, "Yes, his name is Michael Guthrey Gundersol. He and his family are very important people in California. He is the third generation of Gundersols expected to hold office there. His father was a state senator for twelve years, as was his grandfather. My father and his father went to college together, and both of my parents have been involved with his campaigns forever. They are all working to set up Michael to run for office this next term."

"So he has never been to Europe?" Susan asked without thinking.

"Oh, yes. He actually spent his freshman year of college in Europe." Seeing Susan's knit brow at her answer, Hope felt compelled to explain, "He just didn't want me to go there without him. He wanted to be the one to show me Europe. He is really thoughtful in that way. He wants me to see it through his eyes, so to speak."

Quickly trying to change the subject, Lisa asked, "Hope, what did you major in at college? What is it you want to do with your life?"

"I was an English Lit major, but Michael doesn't want me to have a job. He says I will have my hands full being his wife when he gets into office."

Tossing a quick glance toward Lisa, Susan said, "Well, it sounds like this Michael has your life pretty much mapped out for you. He sounds like a man who knows who he is and where he is going."

"Yes," Hope declared with pride, "He is wonderful. He is so much more experienced than I am. He has been exposed to the political world his whole life and believes he can do some great things for the people of California."

Her gaze drifted away for a second as Hope confessed, "I just hope I have not hurt him by getting into all this mess back here. He is very concerned about what this incident might do to his campaign if people find out his fiancée was involved in a murder."

"Hope, it wasn't a murder. It was self-defense," Lisa pleaded. "No one could ever blame you for what happened that night."

"You don't understand," Hope said defensively. "Both Michael and his mother told me not to come here. Mrs. Gundersol did not think it was wise to look you up, let alone come back here to meet you. Michael told me that she already had a problem with my being adopted—unknown blood-lines and all."

Susan caught Lisa's eye and gave her a stern warning to be careful. She wanted to change the direction of this conversation before Lisa said some-thing she would regret. "Hope, you can never fully understand how very sorry we are about how it turned out for you. You did not deserve that. But as Lisa's younger sister, I will forever love you and thank God that you were there that night. If you had not been there, I would not have my sister today. That fact is without question."

Picking up on Susan's redirection, Lisa suggested, "Hope, from your last letter I understand that your parents filled you in on our miserable life story." Lisa then waited until Hope responded with an acknowledging nod before continuing. "So you know what our parents were like, you know the lifestyle I lived for fifteen years, and you know that I am no longer that person, right?"

"Yes, Lisa, my parents told me everything. They said I should be really proud of you, and I am, really. I am so sorry you went through all of that. It must have been terrible."

"It was terrible, Hope, but I am not using it as an excuse for why I became what I became. No excuses will be offered here today, just some explanations for why it happened, and to give you the missing piece of your family puzzle."

Relief flashed across Hope's face as she said, "You're talking about my biological father, aren't you? So you know who he is?"

"Yes, Hope, I know who he is," Lisa reassured her.

With excitement in her voice she could not cover up, Hope asked, "Does he know about me? Did he ever try to find me, ever?"

Lisa had prepared for this talk for four long months and here it was—her time to tell it all. "Hope, once I tell you the whole story, you will have all your questions answered. Some of it you might think is simply rehash-ing what was said at my trial, but if you allow me to tell it in a way that puts it all into context, you will finally understand everything regarding your birth."

Without waiting for a response, Lisa started in. "As you know, Susan and I grew up in a terrible household. For most of our lives, our father beat us regularly and brutally. Our mother was no better, so Susan and I were all we had. Many a day started with the question, 'Will this be our last day?' Since I was eight years older than Susan, I always felt responsible to protect her. I was seldom successful at it, but I really did try.

"We lived under stringent rules. Our father's rules were absolute and intractable. If he even perceived that we had violated one of them, let alone out and out disobey one, his beating were nearly unendurable."

Seeing the look in Hope's eyes, Lisa ended this description. "Well, Hope, you saw how he was that night. Just imagine a little kid's facing that temper on a regular basis and you have a glimpse of Susan's and my childhood."

"Moving forward," Lisa said with a forced lightness in her voice. "As fearful as that kind of life is, a person can only endure so much of it before he just don't care anymore. How can you care when you can do nothing to stop it? I held on for as long as I could because of Susan. I knew what life would be like for her if I was gone, so I stayed until I had no other choice."

Smiling over at Susan, Lisa continued, "We were told never to talk to the neighbors. We were ordered to get home from school and get into the house, period. But when I turned fifteen, I decided to start breaking his rules. At first I would defiantly sit out on the front lawn, as if to show him he no longer controlled me. However, I did make sure I kept my eye on the far corner so I could see when his car made the turn, and I could make a run for the house before he spotted me. I would drive Susan crazy with fear. I remember her begging me to come into the house, but there I sat.

Within a week or two of doing this, the neighbor boy, Steve Reiner, started sitting out on the lawn with me. He and his mother were well aware of what was going on in our house, and Steve was so nice. For months we'd find different ways of communicating with each other. Lots of times, when my parents were home, I would walk out of the kitchen door and sit on the trash can lids that were stored beside the fence that separated his house from ours. I would pretend to be reading some homework assignment, but Steve was on the other side of the fence, quietly talking to me. I could tell him anything, and he would understand.

He had seen my father in so many tirades; he knew exactly what my father was capable of, so he was very careful not to put me in harm's way. He was my best friend. Actually, he was my only friend other than Susan. But I couldn't talk to Susan. She was just a little kid, but Steve understood what I was going through, and he cared about me."

Sliding her fingers along the chain that hung around her neck, Lisa displayed a locket as she said, "On my sixteenth birthday, Steve gave me this. He had taken my picture a few weeks earlier and cropped it, along with one of himself, and put them in this locket. Except for the times in jail, this locket has never been off of my neck."

Reaching for the clasp and releasing the chain, Lisa handed it to Hope as she said, "Open it Hope, but be careful. A lock of your hair is also inside it, along with a picture of your father, Steven Reiner, and myself."

While Hope stared at the picture, Susan's brain was frantically searching her memory bank for mental images of Steve and Lisa back then. Image after image of their sitting out under the tree in Mrs. Reiner's front yard, laughing together, flashed before her. She sorted through her memory bank and remembered all the times Lisa sat on those trash cans while she would climb up into her favorite tree. She thought her sister was only reading out loud, when all the time, she was talking with Steve.

"Hope, what Steve and I did was wrong, but I loved him so much and longed for someone to touch me with gentleness, if only once. I began slipping out of our bedroom window late at night, and he would meet me at the end of the driveway and, at first, we would just walk the quiet neighborhood, dreaming of the day when we could run away together. Of course, I knew that day would never come because his mother was a sweet widow, and he knew it would kill her if he ran away. But still we dreamed. One night we let things go a little too far. Steve was so ashamed. He took full responsibility, but I knew it was just as much my fault, and I also knew that was not going to be the last time we did it either.

"I was so hungry for his affection, I didn't care about the consequences. I didn't think about what it would mean to both of us if I got pregnant. I was a stupid sixteen-year-old kid living for the moment, and I made it very hard for Steve to say no to me. He wanted to and he tried to, but I always won.

"I had missed my second period before it dawned on me that I might be pregnant, and then I panicked. Suddenly, all the horrible consequences of our actions became crystal clear to me, and the daydreams ended."

Watching Hope's face as she said, "Horrible consequences," made Lisa stop to explain. "Hope, you were never one of the horrible consequences—never. That night I realized I could never again allow my father to beat me, not for my sake, but because of you. I could not risk his hurting you. I also knew that Steve was in real danger."

Susan's head nodded vehemently, knowing full well exactly what their father would have done to Steve.

"I had to do something, and quickly. I knew I could not tell Steve about you. He would never have let me go if he knew. I knew I could not stay there. Beatings were such a regular part of our lives that, even if I could keep you a secret for a couple of months, enduring any one of his beatings meant I could have lost you.

"I had three people I felt responsible for…and none of them were me. First of all, I needed to protect my baby. Secondly, I needed to protect Steve. And finally, I was sick with fear for Susan, but I was only sixteen and had no power to do anything but run."

Hope had held her breath for several seconds before she exhaled, and asked, "So you ran away to save us both? Did you ever contact him later on to tell him why you left?"

"Sadly, Hope, I did not. I had made my way out to California, found an adoption agency that would help me during my pregnancy, and found you a good home. For several years I thought about writing to him, but I was afraid. How could I tell him I'd given our baby away? So I simply tried to forget everything—Steve, you, and Susan. I tried to numb myself of anything that had ever mattered to me. Consequently, I just fell apart, and you know the life I fell into.

"It wasn't until Susan and Gladys got me off the drugs and off the streets that I started to care again. One day I went to the library while I was in Atlanta visiting with Susan. Years had passed since I had stepped foot in Atlanta, and I was afraid to go by the old house to see if Steve or his mother still lived next door. I went through old newspaper issues, trying to find some mention of Steve."

Susan sat reeling from all this new information and tried hard to let Lisa and Hope have their own personal time together without her interrupting. As Lisa kept talking, she remembered that July day in 1974—just days before her wedding, when she and Scott had called on Mrs. Reiner. Susan had wanted to have someone from her past attend on her special day, so they had driven to her old neighborhood in order to personally invite her sweet elderly neighbor.

While listening to Lisa tell Hope how hard she had searched for information, Susan sat there knowing exactly where Steve had been all these years but wanted to wait and see if Lisa had found out the truth for herself.

Lisa then said, "Hope, I was shocked when my lawyer, Mr. Duncan, told me that Mrs. Reiner was going to testify at my trial. He didn't know about you at the time, and he would not agree to let me meet with her, or any of the witnesses, because he did not want their testimony questioned. By the time Duncan knew about you, he still did not know how you connected with Mrs. Reiner. It's probably a good thing too. It was hard enough for me to sit there listening to her testimony, knowing what I had cheated her of. She sat in the courtroom the day you testified, never knowing she was looking at her own granddaughter."

With a broken and fragile voice, Hope responded, "I never looked around. I wasn't allowed in the courtroom during anyone else's testimony. I should have looked around. I should have paid more attention."

Susan decided that now would be a good time to offer some encouragement. Leaning forward to take hold of Hope's hand, she said, "Hope, you did exactly what Mr. Duncan asked of you. You stepped forward, told the truth, and saved your mother's life. I'm actually glad none of us knew all of this during the trial. It was hard enough staying on point; I can't imagine what it would have been like to have all these other facts swirling around in that courtroom." Looking over at Lisa for approval, Susan said, "Lisa, I think I have some information that both of you need to know. I've had this information for eleven years, but I did not know it would be important to you."

Responding with great curiosity and with full trust in anything Susan might say, Lisa asked, "Well, what is this information you've had for eleven years?"

Not wanting to simply blurt out her news, Susan started by explaining how she had come across this information. "Hope, I got married in 1974. Wanting someone from my past at my wedding, I went to see Mrs. Reiner just days before my wedding. As Scott and I visited, I noticed there were no recent photographs of her son. I remember picking up a photo of Steve in his uniform and was kind of afraid to ask about him."

Both Hope and Lisa stiffened, their minds running ahead of her, preparing for the worst.

"Mrs. Reiner told me that Steve seemed to fall apart during his senior year of high school. He had dropped out of sports, stopped caring about college, and basically seemed lost." Turning to Lisa, she added, "At least now we know why he fell apart. Anyway, she said he barely made it through graduation and spent that summer driving his motorcycle like a madman. She finally convinced him to join the Marines. 'He needed something to get him out of his funk,' she said."

Taking a deep breath, Susan plunged ahead, knowing what she was about to say was going to profoundly hurt both of these women. "Steve was almost through boot camp when he and a buddy decided to take their liberty by hopping onto Steve's motorcycle and heading for the nearest big city. Mrs. Reiner said Steve lost control of the motorcycle on a turn and went right into the path of an oncoming semi. He was killed instantly."

Susan sat quietly, allowing this information to sink in. Lisa fell back against her chair and cried softly. The love of her life had been dead for all these years, and she didn't even know.

Hope sat there staring at the photo of her father in the locket while tears streamed down her face. "I didn't even get to meet him. I found him and lost him all at the same time."

Seeing her mother in so much pain, Hope extended the locket toward Lisa, "Here, he gave this to you. It's yours."

Lisa did not take the offered locket, but instead clasped both of her hands around her daughter's hand and, closing Hope's fingers around the locket, and said, "Hope, I held onto that locket for years, hoping someday to give it to you. I always wanted you to know that you were conceived in love. You were given up because you were loved. This necklace is now yours."

Lisa's heart so wanted to take her daughter into her arms and hug her, but she sat frozen with doubt. Would Hope accept affection from her? She envisioned Hope's making a dash for the door, running to the only father she had ever known—the one sitting in the room right across the hallway. Watching her daughter struggling to absorb all of this new information, Lisa thought about something Ben had said the night before. "Lisa, you have asked for wisdom. Let that wisdom guide you tomorrow. Listen to it and don't get paralyzed by fear."

Lisa gave Susan a confident smile, released her hands from around Hope's hand, and gently raised her daughter from the sofa and took her into her arms. This was not a time to what-if things. Her daughter was right in front of her, and she was hurting. As Lisa's arms drew Hope to her, Hope surrendered to her embrace, and her full weight rested against her mother.

For the next several hours, Hope listened while Lisa and Susan told her all about her father, Steve. Their stories were filled with laughter. This young man Hope was getting to know through these two women was someone she had yearned to meet. However, knowing her biological father would only happen through their remembrances.

In the hallway, Daniel Winslow put his ear to Hope's door, trying to hear what was going on in his daughter's room. He was surprised to hear laughter. He wasn't really sure what he had expected to hear, but he knew he did not expect to hear people laughing. Checking his watch, he realized that their dinner date was going to be delayed. Closing his door, Daniel mused, "Well, at least things seem to be going well for Hope. Guess I'll give her another hour before ordering room service."

Back in Hope's room, the laughter continued. "Hope, your dad had a great sense of humor, and he got that attribute from his father. I remember way back, I must have been twelve, and Susan was about four. The Reiners had a huge veggie garden in their backyard, and I would hide in our garage, peeking through the cracks in the siding, watching his family work in the garden. Once, Mr. Reiner picked some veggies and yelled, 'Veggie fight,' and tomatoes started flying. Steve was laughing so hard, he couldn't get a tomato off before his dad would get him with another really gushy one. Mrs. Reiner just ran for cover.

"Mr. Reiner was always doing something crazy. Another time he was painting their house, and he filled a paint bucket with water, pretending it was paint. When Steve came out to bring him a glass of water, he stepped under the ladder his dad was on so he could hand it up. Mr. Reiner pretended to lose control of the paint and dumped the whole bucket on Steve. It took Steve a few seconds to realize it was just water, and Mr. Reiner actually had to climb down off the ladder because they were laughing so hard.

With a faraway look, Susan added, "They were always laughing over there. Hope, I remember once when I must have been about six years old. Lisa and I climbed up in my fig tree just to watch the Reiner family working out in their yard. This time Steve got the better of his dad. I guess Steve must have set up his joke earlier in the day. When his dad had finished weeding the veggie garden, he asked Steve to turn on the hose so he could give everything a good drink of water. We watched Steve signal his mother to move out of the way, and then he turned the hose on full force.

I'm not sure just what he did to that hose, but his dad got soaking wet and started yelling at Steve to shut off the water.

"At first, Lisa and I were scared, thinking Steve was in real trouble, but his dad started laughing. We didn't really understand them very well, but we both knew we'd rather be living in the Reiner house than ours."

Lisa and Susan took turns telling one story after another, laughing at whatever funny thing Steve or his dad had done. By the end of the afternoon, Hope had a very clear imagine of her father, and was laughing along with Susan and Lisa. Susan noticed that both Lisa and Hope seemed much more relaxed, and every once in a while, Hope would grab Lisa's arm, begging her to stop a story so she could catch her breath. Susan also noticed the look in Lisa's eyes every time Hope reached out and touched her with a casual freedom as well as with laughter in her voice. Today could not have turned out any better.

Susan knew Lisa did not want this day to end, but it had to. There would be other days, of that they were now sure. Checking her watch, Susan suggested, "Hope, do you think your dad is waiting dinner for you? I can't believe it is almost 6:00."

Trying not to sound pushy, Lisa offered, "Hope, would you and your dad like to get out of this hotel for the evening? Gladys can put a dinner on the table faster than anyone I know, and she would love to have some time with you."

"That offer sounds so tempting, but this has been a really long day, and I'm exhausted from all the tears and laughter. I promised to call Michael, and I'm sure my parents are worried about how today went." Then turning a beaming smile toward Lisa, Hope said, "I can't wait to tell them all about my wonderful birth father and that I have an amazing mother."

Putting her arms around Lisa, Hope suggested, "Can I have a rain check? Are you busy tomorrow?"

Lisa's knees almost buckled beneath her out of pure ecstasy. "Tomorrow will be great. How about nine-thirty? I am sure Gladys will go all out with one of her famous Southern breakfasts. Be sure to tell your dad he is more than welcome to come too."

Pondering this invitation for just a moment, Hope decided, "No, I think I want to come alone tomorrow. My dad will understand. We've talked a lot about how hard it is going to be to let you into my life, without feeling disloyal to my parents. They understand it better than I do. If my dad is there, I will be worrying about how he is feeling instead of how you and I are feeling. He's had my love for twenty-two years, and he knows that will never be taken away from him. You and I only have tomorrow and then I have to fly back to California, and I'm not sure when I'll be able to come back. I don't want to share you right now. I want to learn as much as I can about you and Aunt Susan," flashing a big smile Susan's way, "and even my new sort-of grandmother, Gladys."

Hope kissed her mother on the cheek, then lifted the locket up and asked, "Mother, would you please put this locket around my neck before you leave?"

The Miller sisters were quiet as they pulled out of the hotel parking lot. Neither one wanted to break the spell they were under. This afternoon had been more than either of them could have asked for.

Seeing Lisa walk in the kitchen door answered all of Ben's and Gladys's questions. The smile on her face said it all. Flying into Ben's waiting arms, Lisa burst into joyful tears. Ben did not say a word; he simply cradled her in his arms, feeling very thankful. During supper Lisa and Susan filled them both in on the visit. As Lisa repeated everything she had said to Hope, Susan watched Ben's expressions carefully as he heard about Steve for the first time. As Lisa told them all of her secrets, Ben kept patting her arm to comfort her. Susan glanced over at Gladys, who had also been watching Ben, and gave her a knowing smile. He was fine with all of her revelations.

CHAPTER 8

—⚜—

Everyone was up early Saturday morning. Hope was coming around 9:00, and Gladys had her pecan rolls in the oven by seven so the kitchen would be cool before Hope arrived. Gladys was always the rock when everyone else was rattled, but not this morning. Lisa had never seen her so flustered. She tried to offer help, but Gladys wanted the kitchen to herself and shooed both Lisa and Susan out to set the dining table.

"I've never seen her this way before," Lisa giggled. "She is finally going to really meet her *granddaughter*. Yes, Susan," looking over at her sister, "Gladys considers Hope her granddaughter, just as she considers me her daughter."

"That is not news to anyone in this family, Lisa," Susan teased. "The two of you are closer than most mothers and daughters. I am glad Ben suggested that he not be here today. He is right. Hope only found out about her birth father yesterday and is just getting comfortable and free with you. There will be plenty of time to introduce Ben into her life later on. Today, it's just the four of us women."

Gladys, finally comfortable she had everything under control, joined the girls in the living room. "Gladys, Susan and I were just talking about something that bothered both of us yesterday. Maybe it's nothing. Maybe Hope simply doesn't realize how her words make Michael sound, but warning bells went off every time she talked about him."

Gladys cautioned, "It is still too early to draw any conclusions. You don't have enough facts, and you don't really know Hope all that well. Let's just see how things go today. Let's not grill her about this young man, but if she volunteers information about him, we all need to be very careful not to react in a way that makes her feel defensive. Maybe Hope was only very nervous yesterday and misspoke."

Hope arrived and quickly warmed up to Gladys, just as everyone did. Lisa and Susan decided to sit back and watch Gladys guide the morning's conversation, watching her make her guest feel welcomed and relaxed. Before they knew it, she had Hope meandering through her youth, telling them stories that gave them a vivid picture of a very happy childhood. Gladys could ask questions few others could get away with. Her absolute sweet nature made it obvious to the questioned party that there was no guile whatsoever in her heart.

They were almost finished with breakfast when a gentle knock and a "Hello there," at the kitchen door signaled someone was coming in. Gladys quickly said, "Oh, Lisa, Mrs. Bascom said she wanted to stop by just to say hello to Hope. I didn't think you would mind sharing her for just a few moments."

Hope was a little taken aback as a tall, slender, well-dressed black lady came into the dining room. Mrs. Bascom was dressed in a lemon-yellow box suit with a beautiful pale-yellow silk blouse. Hope watched as this woman, obviously at ease in this house, made her way around the table, giving both Lisa and Susan a quick peck on the cheek as she greeted them before turning to the one she had come to see. Extending her hand, she said, "Hello, Hope. I am Ruth Bascom, Lisa's employer. I can't tell you how grateful I am for all you did for our Lisa."

Smiling shyly as she took Ruth's hand, Hope said, "I understand I, too, have lots to say thank you for. Lisa…my mother, told me how much you and Gladys did to help her. I think my debt is much greater than yours. Mrs. Bascom, even though I don't get into the religious things myself, I can see it really means something to all of you, and I respect that."

Gracious as always, Mrs. Bascom gave Hope a big smile and replied, "Lisa was worth every single moment of the struggle. Showing your mother that no one can ever be so bad or so lost that the love of God cannot save him or her, gave Lisa the hope she needed. I'm just going to keep praying that Lisa's little Hope can one day come to understand it too. Gladys and I sometimes argue over whose daughter Lisa really is, so we both claim her. Therefore, if you don't mind, Hope, I will just talk to God about you, instead of talking to you about God."

"I would appreciate that, Mrs. Bascom. I sure could use someone praying for me."

"Sweetie," Mrs. Bascom almost giggled, "everyone in this room has been praying for you, and we will continue to—just you rest assured of that." Then graciously switching gears to take the pressure of the conversation away from Hope, Ruth said, "Lisa, when I got to the bakery at 5:00 this morning, I was surprised to see that you had already been there and had made several trays of pastries for me. I'm not complaining, mind you. Your work made my morning rather easy. But when I gave you a two-day vacation so you could spend time with your daughter, I did not expect you to beat me into my own kitchen and do all the hard work."

"I just could not sleep after yesterday," Lisa responded. "Baking always calms me down and helps me think straight. Besides, Gladys wouldn't let Susan or me do a single thing in her kitchen this morning."

Not wanting to intrude any longer, Mrs. Bascom explained, "I have a bakery order I need to deliver, so I need to run. Hope, I am so happy to have finally met you." Ruth slipped out the kitchen door so the four women could continue their visit.

Gladys suggested, "You three go into the living room while I do these dishes."

"Not on your life, Gladys! Susan and I can clear the table for you. Hope, how would you like to dry the dishes for Gladys?"

"Sure, I'd love to," Hope responded. "I still have lots of questions for you, Gladys. Maybe you can answer them while we do the dishes?"

After the dishes were washed and put away, Gladys quickly prepared a dinner in the crock-pot, and they all settled down in the living room for an afternoon of good ol' Southern visiting. For fear of missing out on even a few moments of this precious time with her daughter, Lisa did not even want to excuse herself for a quick trip to the restroom. Gladys focused her stories on all the things she felt Hope needed to know about her mother. No one could champion the achievements of Lisa Miller as well as Gladys Carter could—even if they embarrassed the one being addressed. After one or two of these stories, Lisa said, "All right, that will be enough!" Gladys would lovingly retort, "You just never mind, Lisa. I am allowed to brag on you. And who better to brag to than your own daughter?"

Throughout the afternoon the four women shared stories, laughing at the silliest things. At one point, Susan pulled out her camera and began taking photos of Hope and Lisa sitting on the sofa laughing together. She wanted to record these moments for Lisa.

Hope shared all about her high school and college years with such a sense of pleasure, but when she would speak of more recent times including Michael, Gladys noticed a slight strain in her voice. More than once, Hope out and out apologized for having embarrassed him by her naïve behavior.

Lisa and Susan watched as Gladys masterfully wove her questions about Michael in and out of other more mundane questions. Hope was so relaxed and unguarded that she began sharing how he sometimes made her feel stupid. "I know how important it is to be careful," she started. "My mother is a very close friend of Mrs. Gundersol, and sometimes after a dinner at her home, my mother will get a phone call; then I get a lecture." With a deep sigh, Hope confessed, "Maybe I'm not cut out for public life. After all I am only twenty-two years old. Even though my mother thinks this is a chance of a lifetime, I'm not so sure. Don't get me wrong; I love him. He is wonderful. It's just that he expects so much of me, and I hate disappointing him all of the time."

Gently, as if just pondering out loud, Gladys offered, "Hope, have you considered putting off the wedding for a little while? If you feel you are too young to handle all of this pressure, maybe a year of working a job will give you some time to grow up a little more."

"Michael would not stand for that suggestion," countered Hope. "Neither would his mother; therefore, neither would mine. Plans have been made, calendars have been inked in—as Mrs. Gundersol says. I wouldn't dare go against her again."

"Again?" asked Susan.

Embarrassed at her faux pas, Hope struggled to turn her comment around. "Yes, well, kind of…. You see, Mrs. Gundersol had very strong opinions about my looking for you, Lisa. She has very strong opinions on everything, but especially about adoptions. She and my mother have had some rather strained conversations regarding my origin over the years. I think I am the only topic my mother has ever taken a stand with her. My mother really values her friendship with Mrs. Gundersol, and Mother will drop everything whenever she calls. She loves all the teas she is invited to, all the grand political dinners she and my dad are allowed to partake in. My dad is the one who knew the Gundersols first. He went to college with both of them. Dad isn't as dazzled by all the power and glitz as is my mother. Sometimes I think my mother would be even more upset than Michael, if I ever found the strength to stand up to all three of them." Then almost as an after-thought, Hope ventured, "But I think my dad would secretly enjoy it."

The timer began ringing in the kitchen, indicating dinner was ready. Knowing it wasn't wise to press Hope any further right now, Gladys stood to leave and simply replied, "Well, I'm sure you will make the right decision, Hope. Just don't let anyone push you into a lifelong commitment that you are not ready for."

Dinner was almost over when the telephone rang, and Gladys went to answer it. Coming back to the dinner table, she announced, "The call is for you, Hope. You can take it back in the hallway if you would like some privacy."

A puzzled look crossed Hope's face as she said, "Is it my dad? He is the only one who knows I am here."

"Sweetie, I'm sorry, I didn't think to ask who it was. Would you like me to?" Gladys asked.

"No, that's okay, Gladys. You said there is a phone in the hallway? I'll just be a minute," she said as she excused herself.

Lisa, Susan, and Gladys sat quietly, trying not to listen, but finding it hard not to. They wanted to discuss what Hope had shared about Michael and his mother, but they were afraid she might hear them talking. Instead, they sat still and strained to listen to Hope's one-sided conversation.

"Hello, this is Hope Winslow."

"Oh, it's you. How did you get this number?"

"Oh, right; my dad, of course."

"I tried calling you last night, but you were not home. I did not want to leave a message with your mother."

"I know I promised you."

"Please don't get that way."

"Michael, that is not fair. I tried to keep my promise, and I did not simply choose to come here. I was subpoenaed, remember? But now that I'm here, I am certainly glad I came. Michael, I have learned a lot about my birth parents on this trip."

"But…but…but it is important to *me*."

"No, I didn't. I guess I should have kept trying, but Dad wanted to go to dinner.…

"Michael, was I supposed to sit in my room without dinner because you were not at home awaiting my phone call? Why is this my fault? Why didn't you stay home and wait for my call?"

By now the three listeners knew a long pause meant Hope was getting a very long lecture, and Gladys gave Lisa a warning sign—first with a single finger up to her lips and then simply placing her hands flat together. Without a word, both women knew exactly what Gladys was instructing.

"I do see your point, but Michael, couldn't I just have this weekend without your trying to control my every move? I'm not a child—no matter what you and your mother think. I've been back here doing important legal business. I have also accomplished some wonderful personal business. I find it sad that you have not even asked me about that. Don't you even care about the things that I care about?"

Lisa shot a hand signal indicating, "Okay, Hope," as they heard Hope ask this question. Then just as quickly their hopes were dashed as they heard her reply, "I know you have a lot on your plate. I know you are a very busy man with lots of important engagements to attend. I'm sorry I wasn't more understanding; I really am. I am grateful you let me come back here when it wasn't the best time for you. I really am grateful, and I apologize for sounding so disrespectful just now. I will see you tomorrow night. Goodnight, Michael, I love you."

Sick with concern for her daughter, Lisa knew she could not say a word right now. Hope returned to the dinner table, offering a lame excuse for why Michael had called. All three women observed that the young woman who returned to the table was no longer open and available. Her words were now guarded, her gaze downcast. It was obvious to all that Hope had lost that conversation, and she did not want to discuss it. No one spoke of the call the rest of the evening. With a promise to try to come back sometime during the holidays, Hope departed. The three women walked back into the house and sat quietly together around the dining table. No one spoke for several minutes. Gladys played with a fork, turning it over and over, as if by doing so, it might change into something else.

Susan finally broke the silence, "Lisa, you and I grew up in a home with two tyrants. Our father displayed tyrannical physical outbursts, and our mother tyrannically betrayed us in order to protect herself. What Michael is doing to Hope is exactly how tyranny in the home starts. Oh, he is much more polished than our father, but he is headed in the same direction. First he demeans her, making her question herself constantly. He controls her every move and expects her to put his wishes and interests, not only above hers, but she isn't even allowed to have any interest that isn't centered on him. You and I both know when he gets tired of this game, the game will switch; he will get physical. We cannot let another generation of our family endure that kind of life. Our mother felt like she had nowhere to turn when Dad invaded her life. Her parents were no support, and she wasn't strong enough to stand up to him on her own."

A quick flash of anger came across Lisa face, "Susan, don't you dare compare my daughter to our mother. Hope is nothing like her."

"I'm sorry, Lisa. I didn't mean to compare them except to say that, unlike our mother, Hope has you, me, Gladys, and her father. All of us care about her, so I was simply making that comparison, which should give you some comfort."

. "I know, Susan, and it does. But how do we help Hope see what he is before it is too late? I don't even know where to start. She has three very strong people pushing her, and I am afraid she won't listen to me. Two of them treat her like dirt, and the other seems to turn a blind eye because her eyes are so filled with the power and prestige the other two represent. I'm really frightened for my little girl."

"Then we need to pray," declared Gladys. "She needs wisdom and strength, and we need wisdom and strength. When we can't talk to the ones we love about what they need, it is best to talk to the One who loves them the most and ask Him to give them everything they need. Jeremiah 29:11 is a verse I am going to claim for Hope. I am going to quote it as a prayer every day—until I know Hope can claim it for herself." Smiling at Lisa, Gladys added, "Actually this is the same verse I prayed over you, Lisa, so it is kind of a family verse. *'For I know the plans I have for you,'* declares the Lord, *'plans to prosper you and not to harm you, plans to give you a future and a hope..'* "

CHAPTER 9

THE NEXT MONTH was uneventful. Hope had returned to California, calling only occasionally. Ben and Benny were deep in counseling, finally coming to terms with the loss of Beverly. The local newspaper was still full of stories about ex-prosecutor Gordon. Many months would pass before Gordon would actually go on trial, but the editor was determined to redeem his reader's trust by exposing every dirty little trick Gordon had done under his cover of authority.

The first big holiday for the bakery was fast approaching, and Lisa had more than enough distractions to keep her busy. Their Thanksgiving special orders made for very long workdays. During one of Hope's weekly phone calls, she shared, "Mom does not want me to go back there for Thanksgiving. Michael has two very important fundraiser dinners that week, and he wants me on his arm. Besides, Mrs. Gundersol has invited all of us to their Thanksgiving dinner, and my mother would not even consider missing that event."

"I understand, Hope. Hers is not an unreasonable request," all the while dying inside at the idea of Hope on that man's arm.

"But I told him I do want to come back there for part of the Christmas holiday. I want to spend more time with you, and I would like to meet Mrs. Reiner. Do you think you could arrange that?"

"I'm sure that can be arranged, Hope." Lisa said with a voice that revealed her great pleasure at her request. "Is Michael okay with this plan?"

"He isn't okay with lots of things right now, Mom. This is only one of them. As soon as I returned home, I decided to apply for a job—even though he and his mother had forbidden it. Two companies in town were looking for proofreaders. With my degree in English Lit, I was sure I could get one of them, so I applied for both."

As Hope continued, Lisa's mind kept focused on Hope's use of the word *forbidden*. "How dare he *forbid* her," Lisa's heart demanded.

"The one I really wanted and thought was a sure thing was withdrawn at the last minute. Later, I found out that Mrs. Gundersol had made a call to the owner, who happens to be a close friend of the family, and suddenly they no longer needed a proofreader. But that didn't stop me. My mother gave me a really hard time about pursuing a job when the Gundersols were so dead-set against it, but I decided I needed to develop some adult skills before being manhandled by the Gundersol family and never being allowed to do anything on my own ever again."

"So did you get a job?" Lisa asked.

"Yes, I did. Actually I missed two phone calls from this company." Hope paused, obviously trying to decide just how much she should say. "My mother 'forgot' to give the messages to me. Once I found out about the calls, I went down to the company, and I was hired on the spot. I started last Monday, and I love my new job."

"What wonderful news, Hope! But with a new job, do you really think you can take time off to come back here during the holidays?"

"Yes, I can. This company closes down for the last two weeks of the year. The HR director told me they never get much business accomplished during that time anyway, so several years ago the owner decided it was best to close down and avoid all of the distractions."

Lisa was almost afraid to ask, "How is he handling this decision of yours?"

"Neither Michael nor his mother are happy about it. Mrs. Gundersol is not accustomed to having her wishes ignored. I cannot tell you how many times I have heard that phrase over the past month. But every time I hear it, it stings a little less, and right now I really don't care about her wishes."

Lisa said a silent, "Praise the Lord," upon hearing such a determined statement coming from her daughter.

"He is making a lot of schedule demands on me. I think he is only trying to show me how inconvenient my little job is to his important schedule. He is not accustomed to hearing "No." But Mother, I am starting to like the sound of no coming out of my mouth. I've even been using it to my mother. Please don't get me wrong; I love my mother, I really do, and she loves me. She simply doesn't see Michael and his mother the way I am starting to see them."

Lisa mused silently, "Asking for wisdom really does work, Lord," before asking, "Hope, so you must be really busy, holding down a new job while attending all those fundraiser dinners in the evenings."

"I am really busy, but I love it. I finally feel useful and appreciated. It is such a good feeling to hand over my work and be praised for it. I haven't had that since college and didn't realize how much I was beginning to doubt my abilities."

Then remembering the real reason for her call, Hope said, "Mother, with all of your long hours at the bakery, my busy life now that I'm working, not to mention the three-hour time difference between us, I decided to have a private phone line installed in my bedroom. I bought my own answering machine too. This way I will never miss one of your phone calls, and you won't have to leave a message with my mother."

Lisa thought, "...another little step of independence," before replying, "That was a good idea, Hope. It is hard finding a time when we are both free to chat, but let's still make time at least once a week to talk together. I love our chats."

"As do I, Mother, but this upcoming weekend Michael has two huge fundraisers scheduled, and then we move into the Thanksgiving week. Only having a three-day work week will mean I have to get five days of work done in three days, as well as two additional evenings tied up with Michael's dinner schedules. I don't think I will have any time to myself until Thanksgiving evening. Even if it is really late for you, would you mind if I called you after I get back home from the Gundersol event?"

"Hope, you can call me any time; I will be here at the house. You remember I told you that Gladys and I decided not to drive to Atlanta for Thanksgiving once we knew you were not coming?" Pondering if now was as good time as any to bring up the subject of Ben, Lisa made a decision. "Hope, I've been meaning to tell you something, but I could never find the right time. At first, I wanted to keep our relationship uncluttered so you could focus on getting to know who your dad was. I wanted to wait for the right time to tell you that I finally have another man in my life. I want you to know because I don't want to keep secrets from you. Neither do I want Ben to feel like a second-class citizen in my life because he isn't."

"I am so happy you have someone, Mom." Hope's response to this news was so open and unguarded, it thrilled Lisa's heart. Hope added with a giggle, "Having met Gladys and Mrs. Bascom, I am sure this Ben of yours has passed muster with them, right?"

"Completely, Hope, with a resounding 'Amen' from both of them." Lisa's voice was so filled with excitement Hope could not help but laugh with happiness for her. "I can't wait to introduce Ben to you, and though you do not know it, he has already met you. You see, he was the police officer who was guarding me during my trial. He watched you on the witness stand, and he can't wait to give you one of his famous bear hugs for coming to my defense."

"Well, I can't wait to meet this Officer Ben. If Gladys and Mrs. Bascom think he is worthy of you, I am sure I will also. Can I meet him during my Christmas visit?"

"I'm sure that can be arranged. Ben has been a widower for many years. He and his son, Benny, have been invited to Atlanta to share the

Christmas holiday with the Thomas family. Bill Thomas is Gladys's younger brother. He is also Susan's father-in-law. You see, it was through Susan that Gladys came into my life. You are going to love all of them, Hope. So this Christmas you will meet the whole family, and we will arrange to take a day and go meet Mrs. Reiner. What a wonderful Christmas present you will be to her! You will be like giving her a piece of her son back this Christmas." With this image, they ended their conversation and returned to the work at hand.

Thanksgiving week was crazy. To keep up with all of the pie orders, Lisa decided to start baking at 3:00 a.m. instead of 4:00. By Wednesday afternoon the bakery counters were filled with dozens of pie boxes, tagged and ready for pick up. The customers had been warned that their orders needed to be picked up by 6:00 that evening. All four of the women were in the front, behind the counter, keeping the customer's orders flowing out the door as smoothly as possible.

Ben stopped by to pick up his order right at 6:00 so he could be there when Mrs. Bascom closed the bakery. He knew the cash register would be full today and wanted to make sure his presence was clearly visible, standing by the front door in his uniform. As the last customer left the shop, Ben locked the door and flipped the sign to indicate the bakery was now closed. While Mrs. Bascom took the cash drawer back into the kitchen to count the money, Ben stood sentry, only opening the door to let Brenda and Missy leave.

Lisa had already made sure the kitchen was clean and ready for Friday morning, so she and Ben chatted while Mrs. Bascom filled out her deposit slip, placed the money in her bank bag, put the bank bag into her large leather tote and then returned to the front counter. Handing the leather tote to Ben, Mrs. Bascom placed the cash drawer back into the register, being sure to leave it open so anyone looking in the front window was sure to see the drawer was now empty.

They quickly set the alarm as they stepped out front, locked the door and walked the three doors down to the bank's night deposit slot. Ben opened the leather tote, all the while keeping his eye out for anyone who might be watching. Ruth pulled out her bank bag and entered her pin number on the keypad, which opened the night deposit door. She slid the bag safely down the chute and secured the deposit door before thanking Ben. "It sure does help to have your very own police protection on a night like this. Thank you, Ben. I really do appreciate you. Now you and Lisa go have a wonderful Thanksgiving."

Other than a family phone call to Atlanta, Thanksgiving was all about Gladys, Lisa, Ben, and Benny this year. Hope would not be calling until well after midnight, so Lisa focused on making sure the four of them had a great day together. Benny was feeling better about his dad's relationship with Lisa and was starting to handle the teasing with more appropriate responses. He had discovered the counselor was right when he had said, "Teens get bored with things pretty quickly. Once all this news becomes old hat to them, they will move on to other topics. You just focus on what is important for you, Benjamin. You can control your temper by understanding what was making you so angry. Guilt is a hard taskmaster. Now that you realize you are not being disloyal to your mother, the guilt reflex can go away; you can move forward."

After dinner Ben ordered, "Gladys, you and Lisa go sit in the living room while Benny and I do the dishes. You worked so hard making this lovely meal; it is the least we can do to say thank you."

Lisa had just gotten comfortable when the phone started ringing. "Gladys, I'll get it. It is probably Susan anyway. You stay seated." Lisa checked her watch as she ran for the phone and saw that it was only 3:00 as she answered, "Hello, Happy Thanksgiving!"

Through the sobs she heard, Lisa could barely make out Hope's voice on the other end of the line. "What's the matter, Hope? I didn't expect your call until midnight."

"I wasn't going to call you at all, Mother, but the last two days have been so terrible I just needed to talk with you." Hope tried to gather her emotions so she could get out a sentence. "After all of his demands of me, Tuesday afternoon Michael up and announced that he was not going to be home for Thanksgiving. He decided he was going to Mammoth on a ski trip with some of his buddies."

Lisa measured her response, "Well, that is an interesting turn of events."

"Oh, this is so typical of him," Hope offered. "He wants what he wants and doesn't care that he left me high and dry, sitting here when I could have been there with you. I think he did this on purpose just to punish me."

"So how comfortable was it at the Gundersols without Michael?" Lisa probed.

"Oh, Mother, that is really the worst part of this. Actually, to be very honest, I wasn't even that upset when he told me he was leaving. Sad, isn't it? I should have been, but he is so very difficult to be around, I rather like it when he goes away."

Pulling the telephone into her bedroom, Lisa sat on the bed as she asked, "So why are you so upset?"

"Because when he announced he wasn't going to be there for Thanksgiving, Mrs. Gundersol cancelled. Now my mother is really upset with me. Lisa, she said it is all my fault that Michael pulled this stunt. According to my mother, if I hadn't been such a brat in trying to show Michael how independent I am, he never would have done this. I've never seen her this angry."

"Hope, I suspect that Mrs. Gundersol is putting pressure on your mother so she will put pressure on you," suggested Lisa.

"That is usually how it goes," Hope's frustration was obviously bubbling to the surface. "I actually told my mother this morning that I am seriously considering calling off the wedding. That announcement surely did not sit well."

Guarding the thrill of hearing this declaration, Lisa calmly asked, "Hope, are you seriously considering calling off your wedding?" What she actually wanted to say was "Run, Hope! Run! Run as fast as you can! Run here—run to me." Instead she continued, "Hope, you have taken some bold steps recently. You found a job, decided not to allow them to keep you away from us, and you are demanding some respect. If Michael can't handle that independence, maybe you should call it off. At least put it off until he grows up a little."

"I did learn one very important lesson this morning," Hope snickered. "I will never ever quote you to my mother again. I know my mother feels threatened by you or at least my feelings for you. She has to sit there, day after day, listening to Mrs. Gundersol's opinion of *wretched women*, and those are *her* words—not mine. She does not believe anyone can change, and she demands that anyone who is to be her friend must believe as she does. Then my mother comes home and tries to convince me that I, too, need to fall in line. When I don't and then dare to quote some wisdom from you, well, you can guess the response I get from her."

"I think you are right, Hope. It is best you not quote me. I see no reason to pour fuel onto the fire. Your mother needs reassurance from you that your love for her has nothing to do with our relationship. Even more importantly, it has nothing to do with the Gundersols. Until your mother realizes that her friend is using her, I think she will continue to be a pawn in Mrs. Gundersol's quest for control."

"You are right, Mom. I think my mother fears losing everything—and everything to her is me and the Gundersols. One day she will have to decide which one of us is more important to her.

CHAPTER 10

$\maltese$

Lᴀᴀ's ᴇᴍᴏᴛɪᴏɴᴀʟ ᴄʀᴇsᴛ, knowing Hope was beginning to see Michael for who he was, did not last very long. The following Tuesday, as Lisa changed out of her uniform, she clicked the button on her answering machine and heard a very different sounding Hope.

"Hi, Mom, this is Hope. I know you are still at the bakery, but I wanted to let you know that things have changed out here. You won't believe how sorry Michael is for having pulled that stunt on Thanksgiving. Mom, he really is sorry, and he promised me he would never do that again."

As she listened to this message from Hope, Lisa just dropped onto the bed in utter disbelief. "Hope, please don't tell me you bought that line?"

"Mom, he said he just didn't realize that I would get so upset, but because I was upset, he feels I have proved to him how much I do love him."

"Oh, brother," Lisa bellowed at the answering machine. "Hope, don't you see Michael is so vain, he interpreted your being upset as missing him—not that you were upset at his behavior? Hope, you cannot be this blind, can you?"

"Mom, he made me promise not to talk about cancelling the wedding. He asked me to give him another chance to prove that he does respect me and my feelings. He is trying, and I need to be a little more understanding. Mom, I'll try to call you Saturday. Have a great week. Love you, Mom."

Lisa sat on the bed, replaying this message over and over. Every time she pushed the button, she was hoping the message would change, but of course, it didn't.

Gladys sat quietly on the living room sofa, hearing this message over and over, knowing her girl's heart was breaking with every replay. Lisa came out a few minutes later, took her usual seat across from Gladys, and offered, "I suppose you heard all of that. Can she really be that gullible?"

"I don't think Hope is really gullible, Lisa. I think she is trying to find a way to keep loving Michael, but in order to do so, she has to ignore lots of warning signs. We need to be very wise right now. If we go on the attack, she will feel obligated to run to his defense."

"Gladys, I am so thankful that was the answering machine and not Hope on the phone. I don't think I would have been able to shut my mouth."

"Lisa, if he is the kind of man we all believe him to be, Hope will see it."

"But when, Gladys? After she marries him? After it is too late? She has so many people working on her, lying to her, pressuring her."

With great assurance, Gladys answered, "Hope has just as many people here who care about her and are asking God to open her eyes. We might not be able to tell Hope what we believe is best for her, but we can ask the One who knows what is best for her to help her."

Knowing that Gladys was always right, Lisa pondered out loud, "*It was the best of times; it was the worst of times*, right, Gladys? Hope gives in to Michael's pressure—*worst of times*, but she also said, 'I love you, Mom'—*best of times*." Pausing for a moment, Lisa determinedly stated, "Christmas is coming—*best of times*. Hope will be joining us for Christmas—*best of times*. I have a sneaking suspicion that Ben is planning to officially propose to me on Christmas Day—*best of times*. But Hope is still in danger—*worst of times*." Turning a weary glance toward Gladys, Lisa asked, "How do parents get through things like this without God? I know God loves me. I know God loves Hope. I couldn't survive this without that knowledge."

"Well, not to be corny or anything," Gladys replied. "To quote our favorite movie line from *Fiddler on the Roof*, 'Then we must leave it in God's hands.' "

Throughout the week Lisa could be heard whispering, "I must leave it in Your hands," as she went about her daily routines. As soon as she got home each day, she would check her answering machine and find no message. "I must leave it in Your hands." For six long days, there were no messages and no phone calls—just silence. Then late Wednesday night, the phone call came, and Lisa was almost too afraid to answer it. "Good evening."

"Hi, Mom, how are you tonight?" Hope's voice sounded strained, but controlled.

With Gladys's warning swirling around in her head, "Don't attack—no matter what Hope says. Let God handle this," Lisa simply replied, "It has been crazy busy here, Hope. How about you?"

"I'm okay." Hope responded, although she did not sound okay. "I guess you are looking forward to Christmas in Atlanta, right?"

"Yes?" Lisa answered with a question instead of a declaration. "We leave here after church next Sunday." Then almost afraid to ask, "Hope, you are still flying in next Monday to join us, aren't you?"

"I want too, Mom; I'm just not sure I should. Michael is really upset. Ever since Thanksgiving, he has been absolutely wonderful. He even told his mother to back off—something he never does. He listened, as I told all about my work days, even giving me compliments without a 'but' at the end of his sentences."

Dreading the answer, Lisa asked, "So what happened?"

With anger in her voice, Hope said, "He knew I had already purchased my airline ticket. He knew that well before Thanksgiving."

"Right…and so?" Lisa prodded.

"Last night everything blew up. After a wonderful dinner together and a relaxing stroll through the mall, we stopped at his favorite coffeehouse and, out of the blue, he said, 'Hope, I've accepted an invitation to attend an awesome Christmas Eve party. Absolutely everyone who is anyone in this town will be there. I'd like you to wear that hot pink suit that I like so much.' "

Astonished at this man's audacity, but careful with her words, Lisa asked, "Christmas Eve? But Hope, you will be here on Christmas Eve."

"That is what I told him, but he flew into a tirade right there in the coffee shop. He said he merely assumed that since we were getting along so well, I would not think of abandoning him during his Christmas. Then when I reminded him that I had already purchased my tickets, and the family was expecting me, he exploded, saying, 'After everything I have done for you this past week, you dare to do this to me? I do not deserve to be treated like this, and I will not tolerate this kind of disrespect from my future wife. You will cancel your trip, and you will accompany me to this party. Do you understand me?' "

Dying inside, pleading silently for the right answer, Lisa asked, "So Hope, what are you going to do?"

"I've just decided. I am coming. If he thinks that a few days of pouring on the charm is all it takes to blind me to his faults, he is sadly mistaken. Before I board that plane, I have one week—one week of listening to my mother's badgering, his threats, and Mrs. Gundersol's relentless posturing about all of her son's wonderful qualities! But I am coming."

"Good, Hope! I am so happy you made that decision." Feeling the need to offer only one warning, Lisa added, "I sure wish this coming week was already over. But Hope, if Michael is this upset with you, maybe you should make sure you are not alone with him this week."

"Oh, Mom, he would never hurt me. He is simply spoiled and wants his own way."

"Enough said, don't make her defend him," Lisa thought. "Hope, I guess I'll see you in one week. Take care, sweetheart. I love you." Then as she hung up the phone, Lisa repeated, *"Then we must leave it in God's hands."*

For the next several evenings, Lisa and Ben went Christmas shopping together, meeting Benny for dinner at their favorite Italian restaurant and then shooing him home to get his homework done while they continued shopping. Lisa tried to stay in the moment, enjoying her time with her two guys. Benny was always trying to get his dad laughing, which did not take much effort. On the last Friday night before Christmas week, Benny made a request of Lisa that proved the worst was now over for him. Dinner was over, and they were sitting together chatting when Benny asked, "Lisa, Sunday, after church, we are all heading to Atlanta for the holidays, but before we leave town," Benny hesitated for a second, "before we leave town, can we stop by the cemetery and wish my mom a Merry Christmas, together, as a family?"

Soft-hearted Ben's eyes immediately filled with thankful tears as Lisa took Benny's hand. "I think that would be a wonderful start to Christmas, Benny. I wish I could have known Beverly. She must have been a wonderful mom because she had you, Benny."

"She would have loved you, Lisa." Benny hesitated and then added, "I know it because I love you."

Two days later, while Gladys sat in the car guarding all of the presents packed for Atlanta, Ben, Lisa, and Benny walked into the cemetery with a bouquet of flowers. They were gone for only a few minutes, but those were very important minutes. As they returned to the car, Gladys noticed that Ben was on one side of Lisa, and Benny was on the other. Both men had their arms around Lisa, and all three of them were smiling.

CHAPTER 11

—⚜—

Ben pulled into Bill and Caroline Thomas' driveway right at 5:00. The house was ablaze with Christmas lights, and before he had time to turn off the engine, everyone inside of the house began pouring out to greet them. Scott Thomas, Lisa's brother-in-law, opened the back door to help his aunt out of the car. Little Matthew, his youngest child, pushed his way past his daddy in order to get the first kiss from Auntie Gladys. Lisa Anne, much too grown up for pushing past her younger brother, stood quietly waiting for her Auntie Lisa to acknowledge her. "Auntie Lisa, can I help you with those packages?"

Lisa smiled at her namesake, lifted the packages off her lap, setting them down on the now empty driver's seat and pulled Lisa Anne onto her lap. "Merry Christmas, sweetie pie. Do you know how much I have missed you?" Hugging her niece closely, Lisa whispered in her ear, "And in case you think I had forgotten, I did bring my bag of knitting supplies. You and I are going to make something very special for your mommy. I've been working on it for days, but I left the most important part for you, sweetie. We have three days to finish it and get it under the tree."

Beaming with excitement, Lisa Anne gave her favorite aunt a kiss, then leaned down to get a good look at the huge man who had climbed out of Auntie Gladys's car. Giggling, as only a young girl can, Lisa Anne whispered, "Auntie Lisa, my mommy told me you have a boyfriend."

"Yes I do, sweetie," Lisa confessed, "and that is his son, Benjamin, but he likes to be called Benny."

Scott made his way around the car, spun Ben around and gave him a huge bear hug. "Welcome, Ben. It sure is nice to see you out of uniform—finally." Then checking to see if Lisa was listening, Scott leaned forward, ever so slightly and said, "Everything is set for tomorrow."

Ben just winked and then quickly changed the subject. "Wow! What a beautiful home! Hey, Benny, this is how the other half lives."

Benny simply smiled as he hurried to get all of the luggage out of the trunk, when Bill Thomas, Gladys' younger brother, stepped up and suggested, "Benny, just take out Gladys' and Lisa's luggage. You and your dad are going to bunk at Scott and Susan's place, while Gladys, Lisa, and Hope will be staying here."

"Yes, sir, Mr. Thomas," Benny agreed. "My dad told me we are staying at your son's home, but I have to get all of this luggage out of the trunk in order to get the presents that are packed way in the back."

"Well, let me help you with those. My wife has supper ready to serve, and believe me, no one in this family wants to be late for one of my wife's holiday suppers," Bill said with a wink.

Placing the last present under the Christmas tree, Benny hesitantly followed his dad into the dining room. "Benny," Mrs. Thomas suggested, "you take that seat next to your dad. Lisa you take the seat on the other side of Ben." Benny was thrilled to see that he had not been relegated to the children's table in the kitchen. Even though carrying on a conversation with adults made him feel awkward, having to entertain a bunch of little kids was beyond his comfort zone.

Benny watched with pride how his father seemed to easily join into the adult conversation. He could tell that Scott really liked his dad, which made him more relaxed and able to enjoy the meal. As seconds were going around the table, Benny turned to his dad with a smile and said, "This is our first really fancy holiday supper since Mom died. I guess not everyone has frozen casseroles for Christmas. A guy could get used to this!"

Ben reached around his son and slapped him on the back, "Boy, men were not created to live alone. Without women, we'd all be living on casseroles, hot dogs, and Chinese takeout. At least these two boys would."

Mrs. Thomas smiled hugely at Benny as she handed him her famous corn pudding casserole and said, "Benny, this meal has never been frozen. You can eat to your heart's content. I know seventeen-year-old boys have a bottomless pit."

As the conversation drifted into planning the next two days, Scott asked Lisa, "What time does Hope's plane arrive?"

"Scott, she is supposed to arrive at 4:40 tomorrow afternoon. I just hope she got on that plane."

"She will be here, Lisa," Scott offered with all of the gentleness he could muster. "You and Susan are meeting Hope at the airport, right?"

"That is the plan. We should have her back here by 6:00 at the latest "if" her plane is on time." Everyone at the table understood that her "if" was intended for more than the plane's arrival.

To lighten the mood, Scott suggested, "Since Ben and Benny will be staying at our house, I thought we'd give you girls some free shopping time tomorrow. I offered to show the guys around Atlanta, but we will make sure we are back here by 6:00 to meet Hope."

Mrs. Thomas chimed in, "Carol Anne and Harry should be back in town late tomorrow afternoon. His mother isn't doing well and cannot handle the grandkids in her house for more than a few days. At least they were able to make this one last trip while she is still able to enjoy the children. I'm glad they made the effort, and I know Carol Anne wants to be here when Hope arrives."

Benny turned to Lisa and asked, "Who are Carol Anne and Harry?"

"Carol Anne is Scott's younger sister, Bill and Caroline's daughter. She is my sister's very best friend." Giving Benny a huge smile, she added, "You are going to like Carol Anne, Benny, but you are going to love Harry. He coaches the wrestling team at his school, as well as track and field. You were on your wrestling team last year, weren't you?"

"Yes," Benny said with an embarrassed shrug, "but I wasn't very good. I don't have my dad's size, and the coach said I didn't have a killer instinct."

"I wouldn't say that, Benny," Lisa teased. "I've seen you run guys down and tackle them, and they were guys much bigger than you. You never let your size stop you on the football field."

Benny sat back and smiled at her words of praise.

After Scott and Susan took their houseguests home, Mrs. Thomas, Gladys, and Lisa headed upstairs to get settled in. Pulling out extra pillows, Mrs. Thomas said, "I'm putting you two in Scott's old room because it has twin beds. I'm saving Carol Anne's old room for Hope. I think she will be more comfortable in a room by herself. Besides, that room has its own bathroom. I hope you don't mind."

"That is perfect, Caroline. Hope is going to be overwhelmed after meeting so many family members for the first time; she will need a quiet place of retreat after one of our holiday gatherings," Lisa joked. "And by the way, I want to thank you for also extending an invitation to Hope's parents. That was really sweet of you. I'm sorry they turned down your invitation, but maybe after things settle down and they get used to my being in Hope's life, they might join us one of these years."

As Gladys took the pillows from Caroline, she offered, "I'm kind of glad they turned it down this year. This is Hope's first holiday with the family and will be the first time she meets her other grandmother. I think having her parents here might have been too much for her."

"I think you are right, Gladys," agreed Caroline. "But I felt I needed to at least extend the invitation to them. I didn't want them to think we were shutting them out. Mrs. Winslow was very gracious and said Hope was really looking forward to her time here."

Lisa decided to keep her own counsel and not mention the pressure Mrs. Winslow had been putting on Hope since before Thanksgiving. She simply said, "I'm sure this has been hard on all of them. I can't imagine how Mrs. Winslow must have felt sitting in that courtroom hearing her girl testify about taking a man's life and seeing Hope so upset."

Climbing into bed, Gladys looked over at Lisa, who was again checking the time on her watch. "Lisa, Hope will get on that airplane tomorrow. We have prayed for her safety all week long. You have to trust that she has taken your advice. She promised she would make sure she would never be alone with Michael this week. We know she doesn't agree that he could become physical with her, but she did promise to be careful. That is all you can do right now."

Reaching up to turn off the light, Lisa simply smiled and repeated, *then we must leave it in God's hands*, right? Goodnight, Gladys."

After breakfast, Scott gathered up the kids and had them all in the van before Susan was even out the door. "Mom and Gladys will watch the kids while you and Lisa have a day of shopping together. You are going out to the new mall on the west end, right?"

"Yes." Susan studied Scott's face, wondering why he cared where they were going today. "I want to take Lisa to that new tearoom on the highway. The West End Mall is right there, why?"

"No reason," Scott said teasingly, "except Ben and Benny want to buy Lisa her Christmas present today, and I'm sure they don't want to run into her without it wrapped, that's all. So you girls go to the West End, and I will take the guys to the downtown mall." Closing the car door behind Susan, Scott blew the kids a kiss and waved goodbye as they drove off.

Running back into the house, Scott bellowed, "All right boys, 'Project Get a Ring' has commenced."

Only half-joking, Ben patted his pocket, "Wallet, checkbook, and credit cards, I am ready." Clapping his son's back, he added, "Okay, Benny, let's get our lady a beautiful ring today!" The three headed in the opposite direction.

All day long Susan did her best to keep Lisa busy so she didn't just think of Hope. They bought all kinds of last-minute items, had a wonderful lunch at the tearoom, and then Susan surprised her sister with a trip to her favorite salon for a pedicure. They were served scones with orange glaze and their choice of specialty drinks. Susan laughed as Lisa struggled to keep still while they scrubbed the bottom of her feet. She was so ticklish, it was almost more painful than enjoyable.

They talked all about Ben and all about the special things he had done to show how much he loved her. Lisa filled her sister in on what Benny had done the day before and what that gesture really meant to all of them. "Susan, sometimes I think none of this is real. In my wildest imagination, I could never have dreamed of someone like Ben loving me." Lisa knew the girl working on her feet was listening to every word she said. She hesitated for a moment before deciding to say what was on her mind anyway. "Susan, I said that to Gladys about a week ago, and she said that is exactly how it is when we realize exactly how much God loves us. We are not worthy of His love, but oh, how wonderful it is to see all the ways He shows us just how much He loves us!"

Lisa winked at Susan when the girl quickly excused herself, saying she needed more towels. "I'm so happy, Susan. Who would have thought that those two little girls in that bedroom back on Elm Street would someday be sitting here talking about having two such wonderful men in their lives?"

"And Lisa," Susan responded, "the same will be true for Hope one day. If God could bring you and me this far, you know there is hope for Hope too, right?"

Lisa reached over to squeeze her sister's hand. She dared not speak for fear of falling into tears of thankfulness. She knew God was protecting her little girl because Hope was in God's hands.

On the other side of town, Ben and Benny were on a mission to find the perfect ring for Lisa. Ben had known Lisa back in the day when her life had been a real mess. She had been in and out of the jail where he worked for years. He had seldom spoken to her back then because her responses were always full of foul insults and filthy offers. The less time he had spent around her jail cell the better.

As he and Benny examined the trays of rings before them, Ben thought about how profoundly Lisa had changed into the woman he was now willing to ask to join him in marriage. For years, Lisa had been a regular guest at the jail, then without any warning, she had disappeared. He had forgotten about her and had gone about his business.

Eleven years had gone by without any contact or thought of where she was or what she was doing; after all, she had simply been one of those lost souls bent on self-destruction. Then Ben looked over at Scott Thomas and smiled, remembering the morning he and Susan came into the jail demanding to see Lisa. Studying Scott today, with his arm around Benny, laughing as they held up pretty rings, Ben remembered that morning, only nine months earlier, when Lisa was back in his jail, accused of murder, but definitely a different Lisa than he had known before.

The change had been so profound, he was intrigued. This could not be the same woman. Ben remembered how curious he had been, watching this woman interact with the sweet old lady, who turned out to be Gladys, as she had visited Lisa in jail. He began making a point of stopping by her jail cell with any excuse he could muster, just to chat with her because he had felt desperate to know what could have caused this change in her.

Ben smiled as he remembered all the late afternoon chats with Lisa and how much he had looked forward to them. She and Gladys would allow him to join in their visits whenever he could arrange to be on duty in her area. He loved to listen to them talk about trusting God in this terrible situation. During these chats, he learned how Gladys had taken in Lisa and had nursed her back to health after one of Lisa's many drug overdoses. He learned how Gladys had shared the love of God with a soul so desperate to know that she still had worth—both to God and to Gladys.

By the time Lisa's trial began, Ben was convinced of her innocence, fearful of her future, but assured of her salvation, and he knew he had strong feelings for her. Her past was her past. Having known her back then and seeing what she had become made his feelings even stronger. What courage it must have taken to fight so hard to come back from where she was! He knew only a loving God could have done this, but Lisa had accepted that help and had now become someone he truly admired.

After her acquittal, he had stopped by often to see how Lisa was doing; at least, that is what he had told himself. But very soon both he and Lisa knew they were in love. Within a month he was talking marriage, but Lisa feared the effect this proposal would have on his son, so they had waited. Benny's feelings needed to be taken into account, and Ben loved her even more for that.

Two weeks had passed since he and Benny had made the decision to ask Lisa to join their family. Ben was certain that Lisa would say yes because they had talked about a future together, but only after the plan was acceptable with Benny. As soon as that last hurdle had been removed, he had gone to Gladys for advice about when to ask Lisa to marry him. She had suggested, "Ben, I think when everyone who loves Lisa is present would be a good time. If you can hold on for a few weeks, we will all be together for Christmas. Then the whole family can celebrate with the two of you."

Tucking the ring they had purchased into his pocket, Ben said, "Benny, even though I want to ask Lisa to marry me right now, I need to be patient—not because I fear her response but because I want to be sensitive to all of the emotional upheaval in her life right now."

"But Dad," Benny questioned, "wouldn't asking Lisa to marry you be good?"

"I sure would like to think so, Benny," Ben laughed. "But in life, wisdom is more than just knowing the right thing to do; it is knowing when to do it. We need to respect the fact that Hope, if she comes, will just be getting to know us."

"If she comes?" Benny probed.

"Son, Hope is under a lot of pressure from her fiancé. Lisa said he resents Hope's coming here to spend time with her, and she is not sure Hope will have the will to withstand all of his pressure."

"Wow! I didn't know that was going on, Dad," Benny said with great compassion. "She must really be upset that her daughter is going through all of this. So what you are saying is that you are not worried that she would not accept your proposal; you don't want to ask while she is under so much pressure, right?"

"That's right, son. Loving someone means you also pay attention to what that person is going through instead of just thinking about what you want at the moment. Remember, even if Hope does come, Lisa still has the Thursday meeting with Mrs. Reiner. Lisa has a lot on her plate right now."

"Dad," Benny questioned, "aren't those good reasons to do something positive for Lisa?"

"Benny, I'm not saying I won't pop the question tonight. I am saying that I need to pay attention to more than my wants tonight. If Lisa needs to keep her focus on Hope for the next few days, I need to respect that and be patient. We will have to wait and see, but it will happen. I'm happy you love her almost as much as I do."

Later that afternoon, Lisa and Susan were at the terminal gate early, waiting for the passengers to disembark. The plane sat on the tarmac for several minutes before the ground crew rolled the ladder up to the plane's door. Lisa watched as these men seemed to take forever securing the blocks under the wheels. Then they climbed the ladder and knocked on the door, signaling to the stewardess that it was okay to open the door. One by one the passengers deplaned, their arms filled with wrapped Christmas presents. The travelers seemed to take their time—as if deliberately intending to cause Lisa agony. Then Lisa caught a glimpse of Hope's standing behind a fairly large man, but it was definitely Hope. Lisa grabbed hold of Susan and spun her around as she declared, "Hope is here! Now Christmas can officially start."

CHAPTER 12

DRIVING HOME FROM the airport, Lisa tried to keep the conversation light. She asked no direct questions about the past week. "Hope, how did that rewrite go that was causing you so much trouble?"

"I'm still working on that, Mom. I only have two days once I get back home to turn it in, and I want it to be perfect. This is the first really big task my boss has assigned to me, and I don't want it to have any mistakes," Hope replied. "I wanted to bring it along and work on it on the plane, but because this is a hush-hush project, my boss said he didn't want anything removed from the office."

"So you love your job then?" Lisa questioned.

"Yes, I do," Hope responded with great confidence. "I never realized how rewarding it would feel to have others review my work and be pleased with it."

Susan remained quiet as she drove them home, listening to her sister ask impartial questions that kept the conversation safe and hearing Hope begin to bubble with excitement as she answered the questions. As Susan pulled into the Thomas' driveway, Hope said, "Mom, it feels good to be respected. I am actually beginning to feel like an adult, but enough about me. Am I going to meet this wonderful man you keep telling me about? Is your Ben coming for the holiday? "

Beaming with pride, Lisa answered, "Yes, Hope, Ben is here, and I can't wait for you to meet him." Helping Hope with her luggage, Lisa quietly reviewed their hour-long conversation in the car. "Not one word of Michael. I wonder if that is good or bad." She studied Hope's demeanor closely, wishing she knew her daughter better. "Is this a facade of happiness Hope is putting on?" Lisa was bothered that she did not know the subtle little signals to pick up on when you know someone really well. But she knew that would come in time.

Scott, Ben, Benny, and Harry came out of the house as soon as they heard the car turn into the driveway. "Let me get that suitcase, Hope," Scott offered, while Ben made his way around the car to introduce himself to Hope. "Welcome to Atlanta, Hope. I'm Ben. Did you have a nice flight?"

Hope studied this gentle giant of a man smiling at her with his hand extended. "It's nice to finally put a face to all of my mom's stories about you, Ben. I guess you already know my mom is crazy in love with you, right?" Hope teased.

Ben's face turned bright red as he pushed Benny forward, "This is my son, Benny."

Stepping forward, Benny offered, "Let me take that garment bag for you, Hope. I'll make sure it gets into your bedroom. By the way, Hope, I was just helping Mrs. Thomas set the dinner table, and she placed you and me together. I guess they realize we are too old for the kids' table and too young for the real adult conversations." Then embarrassed at saying she was not an adult, he added, "Well, at least I'm not old enough. I'm only seventeen, but I am closer in age to you than you are to any of the adults at the table. I will try not to bore you."

"I doubt that you could bore me, Benny. I would be honored to have you as my table companion." Then with a wink, Hope added, "Besides, then you can fill me in on the romance between our parents."

"So you don't mind that my dad loves your mom?" Benny probed cautiously.

"Not at all! I think it's great. Lisa deserves someone special in her life after all she has gone through." Leaning closer, Hope probed, "Your dad is great, right, Benny?"

"He sure is," smiled Benny, as Hope placed her arm around his shoulder and teased, "Looks like you and I might become related one of these days."

Holding the front door open for her, he whispered, "Maybe sooner than you think, Hope."

Benny carried the garment bag and suitcase upstairs and placed them in the bedroom reserved for Hope. He couldn't wait to tell his dad about their conversation. Benny rushed back downstairs, made his way over to his dad and waited patiently for an opportunity to whisper his news in his dad's ear. "Dad, I don't think Hope has a problem with you and Lisa. She teased me that she and I might end up brother and sister one of these days."

Putting his arm around his son, Ben cautioned, "That's great, son. At least that is one less issue to worry about, but I still need to decide if Lisa can handle that kind of distraction right now. You just keep your eyes and ears open. Between the two of us, we will know when the time is right."

After everyone was introduced, Hope laughingly suggested, "I think I need everyone to wear name tags for the first twenty-four hours. Not only can't I remember all your names, but keeping track of who belongs to who is going to be a real problem."

Harry chimed in, "Hope, if you see anyone with red hair, they belong to me."

"Got it, Harry," Hope teased right back, "red hair goes with Harry and Carol Anne, right?"

"Right," Scott interjected, "and all the other kids without red hair belong to Susan and me. That makes it real easy."

Benny walked up next to Hope and offered, "Actually, Hope, it will take longer than twenty-four hours to get everyone's name and relationship down." Teasingly, Benny added, "Just do what I do, address all the adults as 'sir' or 'ma'am' and then start talking. They won't realize you don't know who they are; they will just think you are a well-bred, good ol' Southern child."

Hope giggled, "That might work for you, Benny. You are a good ol' Southern child. I'm from southern California, remember?"

Holiday dinners around the Thomas table were always lively, but this year was proving to be exceptionally so. Harry, the hilarious, as he had been dubbed, now found himself the perfect cohort for his humor. As soon as Harry realized Ben's susceptibility, he made it his mission to drive Ben into uproarious laughter, which, in turn, had the whole table unable to breathe. Once or twice, Ben excused himself in order to gain self-control. Once he was reseated, Harry needed only to cast a questioning look in Ben's direction, and Ben would again dissolve into crippling laughter.

Mrs. Thomas allowed this horseplay to go on for quite a while, until finally tapping her knife against her glass of water, "I think that is quite enough, Harry. You are going to make Ben sick if you keep this up."

Taking a submissive pose, Harry agreed to dial it down and asked, "So Benny, I understand you were on your school's wrestling team last year. Maybe you and I can spend an hour or so tomorrow over at my gym so I can see some of your moves. What do you think about that?"

Feeling uncomfortable, Benny said, "I'm not very good at it, Coach. I didn't even make the team this year."

"That's okay, Benny," Harry said, noticing his discomfort. "We can just have some fun. You won't be trying out for a position on my team so there is no pressure here."

As the conversation turned to adult topics, Hope observed the demeanor of everyone at the table. Although Harry seemed to take the lead, no one dominated the discussion. Everyone seemed at ease to join in and share his or her opinion without being insulted or instructed as to why they were absolutely incorrect in their thinking.

The conversation slid from topic to topic with ease. Hope noticed that, unlike Michael's dinner table, there were no prolonged diatribes of political significance. No one was demanding unquestioned allegiance from those being forced to endure it—not simply a quiet reservation, but demanding an assertive compliance to it.

As Hope watched this family having a pleasant mealtime discussion, she could not help but compare this with all the hundreds of dinner discussions she had endured around the Gundersol table. She thought of the endless reviewing of the Gundersol family history, their recounting, ad nauseam, every political victory ever achieved by a Gundersol. As tiresome as she found these diatribes to be, they were nothing compared to the hand-pounding tirades of Mr. Gundersol when he would begin his admonishments toward his son. "Failure is not acceptable, Michael," he would shout. "A Gundersol must never lose to lesser men. With all of my money to back you, with the Gundersol name, the education you have been afforded, any failure will sit squarely on your shoulders." Then Hope recalled the line Mr. Gundersol always ended with, "You are a Gundersol, son, and don't you ever forget it. Don't you ever let anyone else forget it either!"

Sitting here, listening to the light-hearted tête-à-tête from everyone, Hope dreaded the idea of ever sitting through one more dinner meal at the Gundersol table—let alone a lifetime of them.

As dessert was being served, Mr. Thomas tapped his glass for attention. "Hope, Ben, and Benny, we have a tradition in this house. Tomorrow evening is Christmas Eve. Caroline, my beautiful wife, will have Christmas Eve dinner ready to serve at 4:30, after which we would all love to invite you three to join us at our Christmas Eve service at church. Then we come back here for dessert and an evening of watching all of our old home movies. We have done this for the past fifty years in our family and would love to have you join us."

"We'd love to, Bill," responded Ben with enthusiasm.

Hope chimed in behind him. "So would I, Mr. Thomas. That sounds like a sweet tradition, and I'm looking forward to it."

Ben squeezed Lisa's hand under the tablecloth because he knew Hope's response was exactly the one Lisa wanted. All evening, Lisa had kept her eyes on Hope, watching her banter back and forth with different members of the family. She observed her daughter's ease as topics went from the profoundly silly to the profoundly serious. The only topics Hope did not join in were those touching the topic of faith. She did not appear to be offended, but rather uninformed and, therefore, ill at ease.

Often, Lisa would return her gaze to Ben, smile hugely at him, and whisper, "I am so very happy. You are on my right, and my daughter is on my left."

Just as Bill started to rise, signaling the dinner gathering was now over, Ben cleared his voice and asked, "Mr. Thomas, might I have everyone's attention for just a moment?" Sliding his chair back a little so he could stand, Ben took Lisa's hand in his. "As all of you well know, I love this woman with all my heart. So before everyone who cherishes her as much as I do, I would like to ask…'Lisa Jane Miller, would you accept this ring as my eternal pledge to love you, protect you, honor you, and cherish you for the rest of our lives? Lisa, will you please marry me?' "

No one at the table even waited for Lisa's response because they all knew it was going to be yes. The cheers drowned out her "yes," but Ben heard it, and that was enough. As Lisa stood in front of everyone wrapped in Ben's arms, Susan and Gladys exchanged a glance and cried happy tears for her. Hope quickly offered her congratulations, then turned to Benny and said, "See, I told you we would soon be related, Benny."

CHRISTMAS EVE DAY was filled with activities. Knowing Hope would be exhausted from traveling, and from their late-night gab session, Lisa suggested Hope sleep in while she got up early in order to go over to Susan's in time for breakfast. By the time she arrived, Harry and Carol Anne were already helping with breakfast and setting the table. "Good morning, everyone," Lisa said as she walked in the front door. "I intended to get here extra early so I could make some cinnamon buns, but I just could not drag myself out of bed this morning."

Seeing the smile on her sister's face, Susan questioned, "Did you and Hope have a chance to chat last night after we all left?"

"Yes," Lisa replied as she walked up and slid into Ben's open arms. "We sat on her bed and talked until almost three in the morning. I guess our family dynamic, even with our Harry the hilarious over here, really impressed Hope."

Giving Lisa a boyish grin, Harry offered, "I do my best, Lisa."

"Oh, Harry, she thinks you are great," Lisa clarified. "Hope kept comparing you to her fiancé and wished he was a little less serious all the time." Then patting Ben's chest, Lisa announced, "Hope is so impressed with my Ben. She said anyone who can laugh like he does must make life interesting and fun for everyone around him." Turning around, Lisa asked, "Where is Benny? I wanted to tell him she always wanted a little brother and thinks he is awesome."

"Benny just got up and is in the shower," Ben offered. "Not exactly sure why, since all of us guys are headed over to the high school gym after breakfast. Harry was able to open the school gym for a few hours, so Scott, Benny, and I are going to get in one of Harry's famous workouts. We can then eat all the holiday goodies we know you and Aunt Gladys brought with you." Turning to Scott, Ben warned, "Scott, I helped them load the tins of cookies, boxes of fudge and Christmas candies—not to mention the two cakes and three pies. We will need more than a three-hour workout with all those goodies laid out before us."

"It is the same every Christmas around here, Ben," Scott moaned, patting his belly. "Get used to it. Between Aunt Gladys, my mom, and Lisa, the house looks like a pastry shop."

"I've never heard you complain, Scott," Lisa teased. "As a matter of fact, you are always the first to ask for seconds, true?"

"Very true, Lisa," Scott admitted, "but now that I am in my early forties, I need to slow up on the sweets." He hesitated for just a second before adding, "Well, maybe I'll slow down next year."

Turning to Susan as she brought in the breakfast casserole, Scott asked, "So what are you gals doing today?"

"As soon as you guys leave, Lisa and I are packing up the kids and going back to Mom's house. I want to spend some quiet time with Aunt Gladys and Hope. Lisa has some secret project she and Lisa Anne are doing. Besides, I want to help Mom with dinner—if she will let me."

Drawing the discussion back to Hope, Susan asked hopefully, "Lisa, you said Hope is comparing our family with Michael's family? Do you suppose she is having second thoughts about him?"

"I certainly hope so, Susan," Lisa answered back. "But just as she says something critical of him, she follows up with some statement like, 'but he will get better once we are married,' or 'when we have our own place and he is no longer under his father's thumb…' I did my best to keep quiet and just let her make her own comparisons. Hope told me every dinner at the Gundersol mansion is a war-game strategy session. But then she said, 'but when Michael is elected, that should go away.' "

Looking around the table, Lisa paused and then said, "You guys are all great. I can't tell you how many times last night Hope recounted to me something one of you said or did that impressed her. She is watching how you men are treating us women, and she is struggling because, even with all her excuses, he never treats her very well." Tearing up with thankfulness, Lisa said, "Thank you guys for showing Hope what she should be able to expect from someone with whom she intends to spend the rest of her life. She has to see it because right now she will not hear it."

Ben waited until he was sure Lisa was finished talking about Hope before he asked, "Susan, would you mind driving over to the Thomas' house without Lisa? She and I have had no time alone together since I asked her to marry me." Turning to Lisa with a huge grin, Ben asked, "You don't mind giving me about two hours of your day today, do you?"

Once in the car Ben filled her in on his little secret. "Lisa, you and I are not kids anymore. Neither of us is interested in a big fancy wedding. We just want to get married, right?"

"Right, Ben. So what's up? You aren't kidnapping me and running off to elope, are you?" Lisa questioned, only half kidding.

"No, but I do have another proposal for you. The city hall will close at noon today. I think we should go there and get our marriage license. I know you want everyone who loves you at your wedding. Hope is here, and we sure don't want to have our wedding the next time she has to come back for Gordon's trial, so why not now? I talked with Scott last night, and he said he could call their pastor to see if he would be willing to come to the Thomas' house on Saturday afternoon at 2:00 to marry us in front of all our family before we have to get Hope back to the airport for her 6:00 flight."

Ben sat quietly looking at Lisa as she tried to absorb all of this new information, when she leaped into his arms and shouted, "Let's do it, Ben!"

"And by the way, Lisa, we can have Sunday, Monday, and Tuesday for our honeymoon. Just in case you said 'yes' to all this, Scott went ahead and booked us the honeymoon suite at the Old Plantation where he and Susan were married. He said that is their wedding present to us, and they will keep Benny busy while we are away."

"I love that place, Ben. Susan took me out there a few years back. It is perfect. But can we keep this a secret for now? Just until after we meet with Mrs. Reiner. Hope has enough to think about right now. On Friday morning we will tell the family, and on Saturday we will get married."

"Just one thing, Lisa, we do need to tell Mr. and Mrs. Thomas they are going to have a wedding in their living room on Saturday. That is something you just can't spring on people."

Lisa smiled in agreement, "You are right. Besides, Mrs. Thomas would not forgive me if I denied her the opportunity of decorating the cake for us. I don't know how she is going to do it and keep it a secret." Then remembering they would tell everyone Friday morning, she added, "She won't have to keep it a secret after Friday morning, so we are good to go." The couple left for city hall.

All afternoon family was in and out of the Thomas house. All of the grandkids were busy with their secret little Christmas projects in the basement, coming up only to tell everyone they could not come downstairs. Grandpa had set out different things for each child to make for Mommy or Daddy, and Grandma was always ready with beautiful wrapping paper as each child completed his or her special gift. Finally, when every child had his or her gift wrapped and labeled, they all marched up the stairs together and placed their presents under the Christmas tree, assured that their present was the very best one under the tree.

By 2:00, all of the grandkids were down for naps. They were promised they could stay up extra late that night and share in the holiday festivities if they took a nap. So by 2:30 the house was finally quiet. Caroline and

Gladys made quick work of preparing the dinner before coming into the living room to join Carol Anne, Susan, Lisa, and Hope for some quiet conversation.

Their discussion was casual, unscripted and gracious. No one invaded Hope's personal space, avoiding any probing questions about Michael or her faith. Hope knew these were very religious people, so she had fully anticipated being questioned at some point. Instead, Caroline told them about her latest project—a cake decorating class. Carol Anne talked about some of the silly things she and Susan had done as kids and Gladys, being the most proper of Southern ladies, shared about her latest victory—growing a beautiful African violet that earned an honorable mention at the fall festival that year.

By the time dinner was over and everyone was collecting a coat to leave, Hope found herself actually looking forward to their Christmas Eve service. When she was a young child, her family had attended church, but around the age of ten, something had happened. Since her mother no longer wished to go, they didn't. She never asked, nor was she told why. They simply stopped going, and life went on. Then in high school, she learned that no reputable scientists believe there is a God, and in college she learned that only weak-minded people have to lean on a crutch called religion.

Climbing into the car next to Lisa, Hope silently pondered what she had been taught. "But these people are not weak-minded people. They aren't shoving their religion down my throat every chance they get; neither are they apologizing for their faith. I'm not sure if religion is really a crutch, but it sure made a difference in my birth mother, that is for sure. How else could anyone explain such a profound change in a person? Maybe, at least for some people, religion really does work."

Walking out of the Christmas Eve service, Hope whispered to Lisa, "Does your church in Jefferson have a service like this one?"

"Yes, although not nearly as grand as this, but Gladys and I love it," Lisa said with fondness. "Did you enjoy the service?"

"Honestly, Mom, I really did. I didn't expect to…" Hope confessed, "I'm not exactly sure what I expected, but certainly nothing as nice as that was."

"I'm glad you enjoyed it, Hope. I know you don't go to church, and I want to respect your right to hold a different view than I have." Stepping aside to let the others go on out to the cars, Lisa decided this was the time to share her personal feelings about her faith with her daughter. "But Hope, I did want to show you my world, and that must include what you heard tonight in that service. I would not be honest with you if I denied what God did for me when He saved me eleven years ago. Just as the pastor said tonight, 'God sent His Son, Jesus, into this world not to condemn people but to offer them the gift of salvation.' First, He changed my relationship with Him by forgiving me and then He started the process of changing my life. My life did not change overnight. It has been a day-by-day journey. It is not religion, simply following strict rules and behaving in a certain way. I could never have done that. God began to change me from the inside out. He still has a lot more work to do in my life, but I know He loves me because I see what He has already done in my life."

"I can see your faith is very important to you, Mom. No one could ever deny that something very powerful took place in your life and for that I am very grateful." Hope turned toward her mom, looked deep into her eyes, as she said, "I'm just not sure it is something that I need right now. Can you accept that and love me anyway?"

"I will always love you—no matter what," Lisa responded, while sliding her arm around her daughter as they headed out to join the others. "I will never try to force my faith on you, but I also cannot pretend that I am not a person of faith when I am around you. I have to be true to who I have become because I know what I once was. I was rescued from the absolute pit of hell, and I know who I now am because of what

God has done in my life. I can no more deny that truth than I can deny my love for you." As they reached the car, Lisa offered, "So Hope, you be the real and truthful you, and I promise that I will be the real and truthful me. We will both respect each other and love each other as we are, okay?"

Before stepping into the car, Hope leaned over and kissed her mom on the check. "Okay, Mom, honesty and truth between us."

Arriving back at the Thomas house, all of the grandkids raced upstairs to get out of their church clothes and into their new Christmas jammies. Every year Grandpa and Grandma Thomas bought all the grandkids new jammies for Christmas Eve, and every year the grandkids looked forward to getting into them right after church. With great anticipation, they also looked forward to sitting on the family room floor, eating Christmas cookies and drinking hot cocoa while watching Grandpa's home movies until they finally fell asleep. All of the children knew that when they awoke, it would be Christmas morning.

After everyone had piled their plates with goodies and were comfortably seated, adults on sofas and armchairs, the kids on the floor, Hope and Benny decided to sit down on the floor with the little kids. Benny leaned against his dad's knees, and Hope, right beside him, leaned against her mother's knees. When everyone was settled, Grandpa Thomas announced that movie night had officially started.

As they did every year, they started with slides of photos of family long gone before Bill Thomas ever received his first Bell & Howell 8mm camera when he was in high school. As each photo came up on the screen, someone would yell out the name of the relative, something special about the person, or how they were related. Benny and Hope had a crash course of the family history. They saw pictures of grandparents, great-grandparents, aunts and uncles who were just names and faces to them. They saw Gladys and Bill as little kids, and Hope said, "Gladys, it is hard to imagine you ever being that little kid."

"Did you think she arrived fully grown, Hope?" teased Benny.

"You know what I mean, Benny," Hope laughingly retorted.

As the next photo came up on the screen, Hope was able to recognize a teenage Gladys but did not recognize the young man in the photo, and innocently asked, "Who is that in the photo with you, Gladys?"

Lisa quickly reached down and placed her hand on Hope's shoulder and whispered, "I'll tell you all about him later, Hope."

Immediately embarrassed at possibly asking an inappropriate question, Hope whispered over her shoulder, "Sorry."

Noticing Hope's discomfort, Gladys sweetly offered, "That's okay, Hope, we have no secrets here. That is Bill's and my older brother, Charlie."

Hope saw the gleam in Gladys' eyes as she said his name but dared not ask any questions.

"Charlie was our family's golden boy, our parent's firstborn son, heir apparent, and Bill's and my hero," Gladys quickly cast a loving smile at her younger brother, Bill, and continued, "Charlie was a senior in college when I was a senior in high school, and Bill was in eighth grade. Bill and I were convinced that there was nothing our big brother could not do. He was kind, smart, athletic, and he loved us both, didn't he, Bill?"

"He sure did, Gladys." Bill said with a smile.

"That picture was taken at Bill's thirteenth birthday—just a few months before we lost Charlie." Gladys looked around the room at all the young children sitting and listening to every word and knew this was not the time nor the place to give any more details, so she said, "I'll tell you all about him when the kids are not here, Hope."

Hope quickly gave a nod of acceptance, and Grandpa Thomas continued on to other pictures. Once they had completed the still photos, they moved on to the home movies and eventually made their way to the ones that interested Hope and Benny—the ones including Lisa. At first, they saw a frail woman who refused to smile at the camera. In this movie Lisa sat very close to Gladys, obviously uncomfortable in her own skin. Hope reached up and took hold of her mother's hand that was still resting on her shoulder. No words were needed.

The next few Christmas movies were like watching a time-lapsed study of Lisa. Benny and Hope watched as, year after year, before their eyes, Lisa blossomed into a healthy, happy, smiling, person, who was no longer frail and no longer apologetic for being present. She had become a woman who was obviously loved and accepted in this family. Leaning over to Hope, Benny said, "That is so cool, Hope. It is like watching your mother get better right before our eyes."

Squeezing her mother's hand, Hope said, "Benny, you and I just saw what that preacher was talking about tonight at church. God is in the business of changing broken lives, and Lisa is a perfect example of it. No one could deny the change in her. No one."

Ben quietly leaned over and wiped the happy tears from Lisa's face as he kissed her. He knew her heart was full and blessed, hearing her daughter give God credit for her change.

CHAPTER 14

LEAVING ALL THE grandkids sleeping right where they were was half the fun on Christmas morning. Bill and Caroline quickly laid out their special gifts, always wrapped in Sunday's funnies newspaper print, so the little ones knew exactly which presents they could open as soon as they woke up. No other presents were to be touched until after Christmas morning breakfast.

Late that night, as Scott and Susan were taking Ben and Benny back to their house, Benny questioned, "So what is the story about Charlie? Obviously Gladys did not want to talk about it in front of all the little kids."

Scott smiled at Benny in the rearview mirror and said, "Benny, I think Gladys should be the one to tell that story. I imagine Hope is also curious, so I suspect that once the kids go down for their afternoon naps tomorrow, Gladys will tell you the story of my Uncle Charlie."

Curious, but respectful, Benny said, "Okay, Scott."

By the time Scott and Susan had their house guests back at the Thomas's house the next morning, there was barely controlled bedlam in the house. Caroline and Gladys had already fed the grandkids and were trying to keep them entertained with cartoons in the basement until all of the adults were finished with breakfast and ready for opening presents.

Benny did his best to keep the little boys under control but quickly felt outnumbered. Smiling toward his dad, he said, "Man, our Christmas mornings were sure boring. We were done after two presents each and a drive to Denny's on the highway for a turkey dinner and pumpkin pie."

"Benny, can you open this for me?" little Matthew asked as he climbed up onto his lap. "I need help," Matthew pleaded. Though only two years old, Matthew wanted to be included with the big boys and was never far from Benny's side.

"Bring it here, Matthew. Mommy can help you," Susan offered.

"No, my Benny do it," Matthew insisted.

Benny added, "That's all right, Mrs. Thomas. I don't mind. It's kind of fun."

By the time all of the presents had been opened and the wrapping paper and ribbons had been collected, the smell of Caroline's roasting turkey began to fill the house with a wonderful aroma. The plan was to have Christmas dinner around 1:00 and the grandkids down by three for a much-needed nap—both for them and for the adults.

After dinner the men gathered up the kids for a long walk around the block while the women made quick work of putting away all of the food and washing the dishes. Everyone was ready for some quiet adult conversation, so as soon as the guys returned, the kids were all marched upstairs for two-hour naps. Even those who protested their need for a nap were fast asleep within a few minutes. Caroline made a fresh pot of coffee as they all made their way back into the family room. As they were enjoying the peace and quiet that only comes when all the children are fast asleep, the conversation found its way back to Charlie. "I know you must be curious about why I didn't want to talk about our brother, Charlie, last night," Gladys began.

"It is okay if you don't wish to share it with us, Gladys," Hope offered. "I gathered it was something painful enough that you didn't feel the kids should hear about it."

"Yes, you are right, Hope," Gladys agreed. "Little children don't need to hear about adult issues. Things go on in this world that cause people great pain, and no one is immune. At some point in everyone's life, someone or something, will rock that person's world, shattering everything he holds dear. How you deal with that hurt is what matters."

"You're talking about what happened to your brother, Charlie, aren't you, Gladys?" Benny probed.

"Yes, Benny, I am." Gladys admitted. "You see, the tragedy of Charlie's death was the single most difficult thing I have ever had to endure. It wasn't just that Charlie died; it was how he died and how I responded to it. But this is Christmas Day, and this is not a story that should be told on such a day as this. There will be other days—days more suited to the telling of stories. I promise then to sit down with both of you and tell you Charlie's story and mine.

"I agree, Gladys," Hope replied, "let's focus on pleasant things today, but someday I do want to hear your story."

Changing the subject, Lisa asked, "Hope, did you make that photo album we talked about? The one you were planning to give to Mrs. Reiner tomorrow?"

"Yes," replied Hope. "I have it in my purse. Actually, you have already seen it. It is just like the one I gave to you for Christmas."

"I didn't get to look at it," Susan chimed in. "Pull it out and let's see what Hope looked like as a child."

For several hours the family listened to stories behind the photos in Hope's album. Eventually, the conversation drifted to how they were going to break the news to Mrs. Reiner. They imagined how she was going to receive the news that Hope Winslow was her only grandchild. They listened to Lisa's ideas of how she would start the conversation, making suggestions about how they would do it, but in the end, everyone knew, no matter how it was said, Mrs. Reiner was going to have a wonderful surprise tomorrow.

To keep the afternoon light, Bill Thomas challenged Ben to a game of pool in the basement, while Gladys spent several hours showing Hope all kinds of knitting tricks. Harry, Scott, and Benny made their way out front to show Benny some great wrestling moves. Susan, Carol Anne, and Lisa chatted about wedding plans, while Caroline relaxed and enjoyed the last hours of another Christmas with her family.

The afternoon slowly faded into evening and, one-by-one, families gathered up presents, loaded their cars and said their goodbyes. Everyone knew that Lisa, Hope, and Susan had a full day ahead of them and did not want to have them exhausted for their big day. Lisa walked Ben out to the car, knowing she would not see him the next day. "This was a great Christmas, wasn't it, Ben?"

"It sure was. I loved it because I really like this family, but most of all, because I got to share it with you. I can't imagine going through another Christmas like the ones Benny and I have endured these past few years, but thankfully, we won't have to anymore." Kissing Lisa goodnight, Ben held her extra-tight and said, "I will be thinking about you all day tomorrow. I know it will turn out great. I know Hope is a little nervous, but she will do great."

The house was eerily quiet as Lisa walked back inside after waving goodbye. An exhausted Gladys, Bill, and Caroline had headed to bed as soon as Scott and Susan walked out the door, and Hope was upstairs taking a shower. Lisa walked into the family room and stood in the dimly lit room, thinking about what she had said to Hope at church the night before. She played back every word, measuring their impact on this young woman who did not believe in God. "God," Lisa prayed, "You know I am not good at expressing myself. I don't have Gladys' gift for words or Ruth's Bible knowledge. I feel like the blind man who Jesus healed. All I can say is, once I was blind, but now I can see. God, I can be ashamed of what I once was, but I can never deny it because if I deny that, I can't tell people who You have made me into. I only want Hope to understand that it was You who did it—not me."

Picking up her stack of Christmas presents, Lisa headed for the stairs. A glimmer of light shimmered across the album from Hope, and Lisa said, "God, I gave her up as a baby to save her life. Now You have brought her back to me, so I can share Your truth with her. You have graciously given me another chance to be part of saving her life, but this time, it is to save it for all eternity. God, please give me Your wisdom."

Susan was at the house before anyone was up. She had slipped in the kitchen door and started a pot of coffee before she spotted the cinnamon rolls left to rise on her mother-in-law's pastry shelf. "She must be up," Susan surmised, "no one beats Mom to the breakfast fixins!" Susan chuckled. Sure enough, just then Caroline came up from the basement with a clean load of towels to fold, "Good morning, Susan. You are up early today. Would you mind popping those rolls in the oven for me? I hear the shower going upstairs, so folks are beginning to stir."

The towels were all folded and ready to take upstairs when Caroline asked, "Did you notice that Hope never called home yesterday? You don't think she was afraid we would mind her making a long-distance call, do you, Susan?"

"No, Mom," Susan responded, "I'm sure that is not the reason Hope didn't call home. You also noticed there were no calls coming in for her either, right?"

"Yes I did. You'd think that fiancé of hers would at least call her on Christmas Day," Caroline stated. "Rather a curious situation, don't you think?"

"Mom, Lisa and Gladys don't like this guy at all. Hope is under a lot of pressure to marry him, but Lisa thinks she is having second thoughts." Then Susan added, "Lisa is dying to know what has gone on with them since Thanksgiving. Hope told them lots of things Michael does that bother her, and Lisa tried to judiciously warn her to take her time with him. Hope did not respond to that advice very well, and now Lisa is afraid to push for information, for fear of offending her again."

"Well, right now is not the time to focus on him anyway," Caroline wisely interjected. "Today is a big day for Hope, and it will be an emotional day for all four of you. Let's just keep our minds on today. Everything else can wait for another day."

"You are right, Mom. I know Lisa is focusing on how Hope is going to feel meeting Mrs. Reiner today and how Mrs. Reiner is going to feel meeting Hope. Mom, Lisa isn't thinking about how hard it will be standing on Mrs. Reiner's front porch—like I did eleven years ago. She has not been back on that street since she was seventeen years old. I doubt she has thought about just how many horrid memories are going to flood her mind when she looks over at our old house and remembers all the terrible events that happened to her there."

"Susan, all we can do is pray for her today. Memories only have control of us when we have not dealt with them. For years, Gladys has tried to get Lisa to deal with all that happened in that house years ago. Lisa has come so far and grown so much, and we are all very proud of her. But this one area has always been off-limits to Gladys. Lisa is convinced that she has handled what she needs to handle and wants only to move on."

Susan smiled, "I know, Mom. I was the same way, remember?"

"Yes, Susan, and God will, one day, show Lisa the same answers that He showed you. I don't know God's timing, but I do know that He wants Lisa whole and free of all the baggage she still holds onto. So I pray."

The smell of Caroline's rolls began to draw everyone down to the kitchen table, and soon they were all chatting and having a good time. Lisa noticed the lovely new dress Hope chose to wear today, and she noticed Steve's locket was again around her neck.

Lisa asked, "Susan, what reason did you give to Mrs. Reiner when you called and asked if we could stop by today?"

"I thanked her for driving all the way down to Jefferson to be a witness at your trial. I told her you were coming to Atlanta for the holidays and wanted to stop by and bring her a small gift of gratitude; little does she know just how huge that gift of gratitude really is."

Lisa smiled at Hope and said, "Are you ready for this, Hope?"

"Yes, I have on my father's locket and lots of tissues in my purse." Then with all the innocence of someone who did not know how their words could sting, Hope said, "After today, one Grandmother down and one to go."

Gladys watched Lisa's reaction, knowing Marjorie Miller was a lightning rod for Lisa's anger. Lisa looked as if she had just been punched in the stomach. They all knew she had no intention of ever introducing her daughter to her Grandmother Miller. Hearing Hope even suggest such a thing threw Lisa into a tailspin because she had no idea Hope was even planning such a meeting. No one at the table said a word. They all understood what a bad idea this was, but today was not the day to discuss Marjorie Miller. Susan stood up and said, "It is getting late. We need to leave now if we want to get there on time. Hope, do you have your photo album? Okay, let's get going."

CHAPTER 15

———— ❧ ————

Susan could feel the tension in Lisa's body as she turned the car onto Elm Street. Glancing over at her sister, Susan noticed that Lisa was looking down at her hands, clasped together so tight that her knuckles were white. Susan thought about reaching over and taking Lisa's hand, but decided it was best to leave her alone. Only after she had slowed down the car and pulled to the curb did Lisa look up and say, "It is just as I remembered, Hope. Right under that tree is where Steve and I sat, talked, and fell in love."

Susan knew how hard this visit with its memories was for her sister, but Lisa was determined to get through it for Hope's sake. She also knew she owed this to Steve and his mother. As they walked to the door, Susan noticed that Lisa's eyes never left the Reiner's front door. The sound of music greeted them as they stepped onto the porch and knocked. Mrs. Reiner unlatched the screen door and swung it wide open and invited her guests inside. "I am so happy you took time out of your holiday schedule to come visit with me," she said as she directed them into her living room.

The chitchat was lighthearted as everyone settled in and took turns being thankful for the outcome of the trial. Mrs. Reiner made sure she made no comment regarding Hope's involvement, knowing that would be a difficult conversation—one she had no right to begin. "Hope, I understand that you live in California, right?"

"Yes I do, Mrs. Reiner," Hope responded.

"Lisa, your daughter looks just like you as a young girl," Mrs. Reiner observed. "I remember when you and my Stevie would sit on the lawn and talk. Steve was always telling me how smart you were. I think he had a crush on you."

Hope clutched the locket, trying not to be obvious as her eyes drifted from one photo to another of her father as a young boy. "I'm sorry I didn't get to meet you at the trial, Mrs. Reiner. I was struggling just to get through it and didn't feel like talking with anyone."

"Oh, don't you worry your pretty little head about me, child," Mrs. Reiner replied. "I'm not important. I was only there to tell the jury what a terrible childhood your mother and Susan had to endure."

Lisa sat forward in her chair and said, "Well, that is not exactly true, Mrs. Reiner. Actually, you are a very important person to Hope."

A puzzled look came across Mrs. Reiner's face. She obviously did not know what Lisa meant by this statement. Lisa got up and sat next to Mrs. Reiner on the sofa, took her hand, and told her the same story she had told Hope four months earlier. Within minutes Mrs. Reiner caught on to where this story was going, but she would not let herself dream that what she was thinking could be true. All of a sudden, all the pieces of the puzzle came together, and she knew Lisa's story was true.

"Why didn't I see it? Stevie tried to tell me how much you meant to him, but he was only a boy—at least my mother's heart kept saying that. Stevie was so upset when you took off; he was inconsolable, but now I know why you ran, Lisa. You and I both know what your father would have done to my boy, don't we?" Then she began to cry.

Lisa held her in her arms as old, old sorrow washed over this mother. "Yes, Mrs. Reiner, we do know, and we know that no one could have protected Steve back then. I am so sorry I was the cause of his sorrow, but I could not tell him about Hope. He would never have let me go."

"So you left him to protect him, and you gave our baby up to protect her from that monster." As these words came out of her mouth, Mrs. Reiner realized she was talking about Hope and ran to her. "You are our baby girl, Hope. You belong to my Stevie. You are his little girl," as she kissed Hope and clung to her. "I haven't lost him altogether. You are my Stevie's little girl."

Susan smiled at Hope as Mrs. Reiner repeated this several more times, trying to drive this knowledge deep into her heart. Hope didn't struggle to get out of Mrs. Reiner's embrace, although she was obviously beginning to feel a little uncomfortable.

Once Mrs. Reiner had gathered her composure, she said, "Would you like to see some pictures of your dad, Hope?"

"I would love to see all the pictures you have of my dad," Hope responded with a slight hesitation and then added, "Grandma Reiner."

That was it. Mrs. Reiner suddenly dissolved into tears at hearing Hope call her "Grandma." Lisa, Susan, and Hope began to laugh out of sheer emotion, and Hope said, "I guess I should have waited a little longer before using that name, right?"

"No, no, no, my dear," pleaded Mrs. Reiner. "I just never thought I would ever hear those words spoken to me."

"Then Grandma Reiner it is," responded Hope. "Now tell me all about my father, will you?"

Over a light lunch, Hope and Mrs. Reiner, her grandma, looked through every box of photos in the house. She told story after story, wanting to share all her memories with Stevie's little girl. They walked into his bedroom and looked at all the trophies he had earned, took out his baseball uniform that still hung in the closet, and by the end of the day, they both felt like Steve was right there with them.

Susan and Lisa sat quietly to the side, watching and listening as these two women became family. Hope took out her album and went through every photo, filling in her grandmother on her young life. Mrs. Reiner would rub her finger across each photo, trying to imagine being there when the photo was taken, wishing Steve could have been there watching his girl in that photo.

Susan leaned over to her sister and said, "Lisa, remember all the times we spied on Steve and his mother, wishing we could be part of this family?"

Lisa smiled a knowing smile, then with huge happy tears in her eyes, she turned to her sister and said, "Susan, Hope got our dream, didn't she?"

Grabbing hold of her sister's hand, Susan choked, "She sure did, Lisa, and that is perfect."

Mrs. Reiner had not planned for her company to stay much past lunch, so she had not prepared anything else, but pleaded, "You don't have to leave just yet, do you? Please tell me you can stay for dinner."

Susan was the first to answer, "We do need to get back, Mrs. Reiner. I left all three of my kids with my mother-in-law, and I am certain she needs a break by now." At seeing her look of disappointment, Susan offered, "Would you like to come over for dinner at our house, Mrs. Reiner? Scott can pick up some readymade food while I get my kids to bed, and then we can just continue with our visit. Would you like to join us?"

With pleading eyes, Mrs. Reiner confessed, "I don't want to be selfish. I know you all have tons of plans. I simply don't want to say goodbye just yet."

"Then come back with us, and we will bring you back later tonight," Hope chimed in. "I'm not ready to let you go either."

"Well, let me change my dress and close up the house; it will only take a minute." Mrs. Reiner practically sang as she rushed around getting ready. Gathering up her purse and jacket, she joyfully announced, 'I'm all set, girls, let's go."

Susan and Lisa were out the door first while Hope held the screen door for her grandmother. They were at the curb when Mrs. Reiner cried, "Oh, I forgot my camera. I just want to grab my camera so I can get some pictures of Hope, Lisa, and me for my family album. It will only take a second."

Waiting at the curb, Lisa finally glanced over at 415 Elm Street. Her eyes traveled up the driveway, imagining Steve's standing where he always stood—right at the end of the fence that separated their house from his. Her eyes then traveled back along the side wall of the house and rested on the window that had been her escape all those long years ago.

Susan leaned toward her sister and whispered, "Lisa, you and I survived. You never ever have to go back into that house again, but you do have to let it go in order to really leave it."

Not understanding what Susan meant, Lisa said, "It's just a house, Susan. That is all in the past now."

Susan knew better than to believe Lisa truly believed that was true, but she knew now was not the time nor the place. She opened the car door as Mrs. Reiner reached it and said, "Shall we go?"

As Hope and her grandmother sat chatting in the back seat, Lisa reviewed everything that had been discussed at Mrs. Reiner's home. Hope never mentioned Michael. She thought about all of the photos Hope had selected for her album, and not one photo of her and her fiancé had been included. Her choices said volumes, but she still worried. Hope has been here for three days, and no mention had been made of him. "Why? If they had broken off their engagement, surely she would have told us. What does no phone calls for three days mean? Not even her parents called her on Christmas Day. Is Hope perhaps just trying to keep her two worlds separate? Maybe we are the ones causing her discomfort. Have I been more vocal than I should have been? Have I said more than I have a right to? Yes, I am her mother, but I gave up all my rights a long time ago. Maybe Hope wants me to keep out of her other life? Hope is not a child, she is a grown woman who might resent my butting into her other life."

Lisa's attention was suddenly drawn back to the conversation in the back seat when she heard Hope say, "Grandma, this is the locket my dad gave to Lisa." Holding it up with all the tenderness, it represented to her, Hope unclasped the chain so her grandmother could open it, while she offered, "Lisa never took this off until she gave it to me four months ago." Helping her grandmother open the locket, Hope said, "See," as the locket finally fell open in her hands, "that is my mom, my dad, and a lock of my baby hair."

As Mrs. Reiner stared down at the locket, proof that her Stevie loved Lisa, Hope confessed, "Grandma, I feel like I should offer this locket to you, but I simply can't—not yet anyway. It means so much to me, knowing my birth parents loved each other, and I know my father would have loved me if he had known about me."

Pushing the locket back into Hope's hands, Mrs. Reiner pleaded, "Don't you even think of giving this locket to me, Hope. This is your birthright. Your mother sacrificed everything to protect you. She also gave up everything to protect your dad. The fact that she held onto this locket all these years so she could give it to you one day shows me how much she loved my boy, and that is enough for me."

As Hope lifted the locket and refastened the chain around her neck, she said, "Grandma, I almost didn't come looking for my birth mother. I had spent most of my college years petitioning every adoption agency in California, trying to get information about my birth parents. But back then everything was sealed tight. I had almost given up when dad came to visit me at college and handed me all of my original birth records. He knew I had been looking; he also knew my mom was not offering any help. She was afraid of who I might find. She didn't want me to get hurt if my birth mother rejected me again."

Reaching over and holding her granddaughter's hand, Mrs. Reiner responded, "I can understand your mother's fear, Hope. No mother wants to see her child rejected."

"I know why she resisted my search," agreed Hope. "But I knew I needed to have closure. I needed to know where I came from. Then when I was given Lisa's name, I had a terrible time finding her, but I did." Hope reached up to pat Lisa's shoulder as she said, "As terrible as that night was, I am so thankful I was there. If I had not been there, we all know he would have killed her, and I would never have known my mother."

Tearing up again, Mrs. Reiner added, "And I would never have known my granddaughter. I am so thankful your dad gave you those papers."

"Truthfully, Grandma, it wasn't the lack of those papers that almost made me not come," Hope corrected. "Once I found Lisa, at least the woman I believed was my Lisa, I started to make plans to fly back here to meet her. At the time, things were crazy busy at home. We were within six months of getting married, and my fiancé and his mother did not want me leaving in search of some missing relative." The acid tone in her words spoke volumes to the three women in the car.

"So you have a fiancé, Hope?" Mrs. Reiner asked with great surprise.

"Yes, I do. His name is Michael, and we are getting married next March. We were supposed to get married this Christmas, but because of the trial, we all thought it better to postpone our wedding until March," Hope explained without much feeling in her voice.

"You don't sound very enthusiastic about it, Hope," Mrs. Reiner probed, while Lisa and Susan sat up front, daring not to breathe hard, for fear of causing Hope to end the conversation. Mrs. Reiner innocently asked the questions Lisa was dying to ask. "Hope, every bride loves to share every little detail about her wedding, but I've been with you for five hours, and I'm just now hearing about Michael and your wedding." Lisa adjusted the mirror on the visor in front of her so she could see these two women without turning around and ending these questions. "Hope, do you love this man?"

Lisa's heart flew into her throat as she heard the exact question she wanted to ask innocently voiced.

"Of course I do," replied Hope.

"Hope, your mouth is saying 'Of course I do,' " Mrs. Reiner responded lovingly, "but your eyes are saying something else. Hope, don't marry this man when you have all these doubts. Marriage is hard enough when both parties go into it with no reservations. Don't think things will get better by marrying him because they won't. You are young, and you have time; take it. You make sure he is the right one for you before you marry him."

Susan had just turned onto her street as Mrs. Reiner was giving this wonderfully wise advice, so Lisa signaled her to keep going. Susan drove right past the house and turned at the next corner, hoping to hear more from the back seat.

Hope fumbled with the chain for a moment, obviously stalling before responding to this very direct advice. "I do love him, Grandma. It is just that this has been a really hard year for both of us. He is under a lot of pressure because he is running for public office and has so many important engagements to juggle. He expects me to support him in all of his endeavors, and then I went against his wishes. You see, neither Michael nor his mother were in favor of my coming back here to look up my birth mother. I came anyway and ended up taking a man's life."

"He does understand that you had no choice, right?" Mrs. Reiner probed gently.

"Oh, he understands that," Hope quickly admitted, "it is just that he feels that if I had done what he wanted in the first place, none of this would have happened. We would be married already."

"That is true, Hope, but look what would have happened if you had done what he wanted," Mrs. Reiner gently reminded her.

"I know, Grandma, we all would have lost. I will never be sorry for complicating Michael's plans because I know what I have gained. And I hope that someday he will come to understand that and embrace it as much as I do. But the problem is that it is not over, and that fact is driving him crazy. Because the authorities are now going after Prosecutor Gordon, my dad and I will be called to testify at his hearing. I have no choice in the matter. Michael can't depend on me to be there for all of his important events because we don't even know the actual date of Gordon's hearing. All of this business really irritates him to no end. Everything is so up in the air."

Mrs. Reiner was not going to be dissuaded in her pursuit of information. "Doesn't he understand the pressure all of this has caused you, Hope? I hear how it is affecting him, but does he understand that you also need support from him?"

Lisa smiled, repeating silently to herself, *thank you, thank you, thank you, Mrs. Reiner.*

It was quiet in the back seat for several seconds. Mrs. Reiner waited for Hope to answer her question, and Susan and Lisa remained silent in the front seat. Looking in the rearview mirror, Susan could see that Hope was thinking about what her grandmother had asked. All three women wanted Hope to really think about this question, and they were all willing to wait for her answer.

Finally, it came. "To be really honest, Grandma, I'm not sure he is capable of caring about what others feel. He is the only child of very powerful people. He has been reared to believe that the world should bow to his authority and that he should always bow to his mother's authority. If I marry him, and I am saying IF, I know Mrs. Gundersol will control our every move. I really don't believe he is capable of standing up to her."

"Honey, then he is not ready to get married," Mrs. Reiner affirmed.

"I know, Grandma, but if I don't marry him and try to help him get out from under her grasp, what will happen to him?" There it was—the real reason Hope was still in this deadly relationship.

Trying to bring this admission home, Mrs. Reiner asked, "Do you love him that much, Hope? Are you willing to risk losing such an important battle for this Michael's future? What if you lose? What if his mother should win yet again? Are you willing to live the rest of your life in that kind of situation? Are you willing to bring your children into a home like that?"

"No, I am not, Grandma." Hope's emphatic response surprised them all. "I have been trying to get him to stand up to his mother for three years now, but I doubt that he ever will. I care for him, and I feel sorry for him—although he would be furious with me if he ever heard me say such a thing. He is so entrenched in his family history and so proud of being a Gundersol, he has no idea exactly how pathetic his life really is. He is thirty years old and his mother still rules his life, but she is not going to rule mine—not any longer."

Mrs. Reiner smiled and asked, "So what are you going to do now, Hope?"

"I'm not sure," Hope confessed. "I have to handle this very carefully. He can get furious with me very quickly. He has never hurt me, but he can get very verbal. In the past I always made excuses for him, thinking it was because no one has a voice around Mrs. Gundersol. Because of this, I thought that around me he exerts his only place to show his power. I thought I was loving him by letting him act like a man with me, but I was wrong. I am not going to continue to allow it." Then pondering for a moment, Hope shared, "Watching the men in this family treat their women with such respect, I realized how much I was giving up for him. I want someone who can care as much for me as I do for them. I want someone like Ben, Scott, or Harry who will love me and cherish me, like I see them do with my mom, Susan, and Carol Anne. I know that will never be the case with Michael, so I am going to end it when I get home."

Everyone remained quiet, wanting to allow this declaration of Hope's to settle into a strong resolve, an unwavering commitment to action. Hope was the only one who could make this decision and the only one to carry it out. But they all knew they would be affected by that decision—or the lack of it—if she were to crumble under Michael's pressure. Only time would tell.

CHAPTER 16

BEFORE GOING TO sleep that night, Lisa bubbled over with excitement as she told Gladys what had happened with Mrs. Reiner. "Gladys, I couldn't believe what I was hearing. She asked Hope such direct questions—questions you and I had wanted to ask. Mrs. Reiner didn't mince any words, but she was still very gracious. It was amazing that she caught on to the same things you and I had picked up on; she just had the courage to drive her questions home."

Turning off the light, Gladys said, "Both you and Mrs. Reiner received some great gifts today. We just need to keep praying for Hope. Good night, Lisa."

By 8:00 the next morning, everyone knew there was going to be a wedding in the house on Saturday. Susan headed over to the Thomas' very early, while Scott called his sister, Carol Anne. "Mom and Dad are going to need my help today, Sis. You know our mom. I suspect she has already gotten Dad down in the basement and up on a ladder to go through boxes of decorations. I need to keep Dad off of ladders and be the one carrying all the decorations up and down the stairs for him."

"Sure," Carol Anne responded, "bring the kids as soon as you get them loaded in the car. Harry will be running one or two errands—one of which is picking up a wedding gift, but then he will be home most of the day and can help me with the kids."

"I should be able to pick up the kids before suppertime, Sis. Thanks for letting us dump them on you with such short notice."

Just as he had thought, Scott found his dad high up on a ladder, reaching for a box on the very top shelf of the storage room. Not wanting to startle him, Scott waited until his dad was safely descending the ladder to begin his scolding. "Mom, I told you I would get the boxes down. Dad, you know the doctor told you not to get up on any ladders anymore. Give me that box and get down from there!"

"We just wanted to get a head start going through all these boxes," Bill protested. "Your mother couldn't remember which box had those beautiful white candleholders. We haven't used them in years, but they will be perfect for a winter wedding."

"Nevertheless, Dad," Scott continued to scold, "none of us want you getting hurt. What kind of wedding will it be if we have to haul you down to the emergency room?"

"Caroline," pleaded Bill, "tell your son I'm not too old to take care of my own home."

"I'm staying out of this," Caroline chuckled. "Scott, you know there is no stopping him when there is work to be done. Bill, let Scott get the rest of the boxes down while you and I dig through these boxes. Those candleholders have to be in one of them."

As they continued to pull out the decorations, laying out the ones Caroline thought she might use, she asked, "Son, have you talked with Pastor Mark yet?"

"Yes, I called him even before Ben suggested this wedding to Lisa," Scott said as he brought down yet another box. "Ben didn't want to get her hopes up and then find out we couldn't pull this off. He is set to go."

As Caroline went through another box, she noted, "Since the house is already decorated for Christmas, I can't very well redecorate from scratch.

Besides, Lisa doesn't want us to go to too much trouble. She doesn't even want to buy a new dress for the ceremony, but Susan is going to make her. I think they are going out after breakfast. I want to hurry up and get these things arranged so I can start on the wedding cake. I need to bake the cake today so it is fully cooled and ready to decorate tomorrow morning."

"You love all of this, don't you, Mom?" Scott teased.

"You know she does, son," Bill answered for his wife. "She is in heaven, and it is extra-special because it is for Lisa."

Susan popped into the basement to let them know they were leaving, "Scott, Lisa and Hope are ready, so we are heading out. We won't be more than two hours, I expect. Lisa has that beautiful linen suit Gladys made for her last year. She actually said she was considering driving all the way back home to get it, but I talked her out of it."

"If we had thought about it a few days ago," Scott said, "we could have had Mrs. Bascom go into Gladys's house and overnight the suit to her."

Susan sat down on the stairs, completely aghast, "No one has thought about Ruth Bascom," she declared. "How could we all have overlooked her? She would be devastated if she missed Lisa's wedding. Mom, I'm going upstairs to call her right now and invite her to Lisa's wedding. She can bring Lisa's suit with her."

A few minutes later, Susan was back. "We are all set. Mrs. Bascom is going over to Gladys' in a few minutes to gather up Lisa's suit, blouse and shoes. I told her she can spend the night after the wedding since Hope will be heading back to California, and Lisa will be on her honeymoon. I knew you wouldn't mind, Mom."

"This is why weddings take more than three days to put together," Caroline protested. "You simply cannot remember every important detail, and that detail was huge. Thank you, Scott, for saving the day."

Scott shrugged, knowing he had not really remembered Mrs. Bascom, "So Susan, you don't need to go shopping now, do you?"

"Yes, Scott, Lisa still needs a few cute outfits to wear to dinner. She did not pack with her honeymoon in mind, remember?" Then realizing that Lisa had also forgotten Mrs. Bascom, Susan turned and headed upstairs to let Lisa know she would be getting married in her favorite linen suit after all and that Ruth Bascom would be in attendance.

By the time the girls returned from shopping, the cake was cooling on the baker's rack. Caroline had drawn out the design she intended to use on the cake. Bill and Scott had made several runs to different stores, gathering up special candles, food coloring, as well as mints and nuts. Bill was now at the kitchen sink, washing out the large crystal punch bowl and the cups that went with it. Scott was busy in the basement, ironing his mother's favorite linen tablecloth.

Once these tasks were completed, Bill and Scott disappeared for a few hours. They joked that they wanted to leave before Caroline thought of another job for them, but Caroline knew they had an important errand to run, so she simply smiled and sent them off.

Around 1:00 Ben and Benny arrived, having completed their own morning of shopping. "I don't know about you, Lisa," Ben teased, "but I am all ready for our honeymoon. If you don't like one or two of the shirts, you can blame Benny. He insisted that I buy something not quite so generational." Turning to Benny, he asked, "That was the term, correct?"

Benny only shook his head in fake disgust, "Getting my dad to buy new clothes is a real pain. Getting him to buy something different was almost impossible."

Wanting everyone out of her kitchen, Caroline suggested, "Since everyone grabbed lunch while out shopping, how does a fresh pot of coffee and a plate of Christmas cookies sound? I mean, I want all of you out in the living room and out of my kitchen."

Feeling as though everything was well in hand, everyone settled in for a relaxing afternoon of visiting. The conversation drifted to anything other than the wedding. Once she was certain everyone was settled in for a while, Caroline slipped out and returned to her preparations, free from prying eyes. As the visiting weaved from topic to topic, Benny remembered the story Gladys had promised to tell and asked, "Gladys, now would be a good time to tell us about your brother, Charlie, wouldn't it?"

Gladys thought about his request for a moment and then suggested, "Benny, although it isn't all sad, it really is quite a sad tale. I'd hate to introduce such a story when we should all be focused on the happy event that will happen tomorrow."

"But when will we all be together again?" Benny asked. "Hope is leaving right after the wedding, and I know she wants to hear about Charlie, don't you, Hope?"

"Actually, I do, Gladys. If Ben and Lisa wouldn't mind, I'd like to hear the story."

Looking over at the wedding couple, sitting snuggled up close together on the sofa, Gladys asked, "So do you mind a little trip down memory lane this afternoon?"

Lisa, having heard most of this story before, deferred to Ben, "Ben, would you mind hearing a story that taught me not to judge another person's life experience? You will understand once Gladys tells it."

"Sounds intriguing," Ben responded, "Gladys, we are all ears."

Gladys began at the beginning. "I had just started my senior year of high school, and life was pretty good. I had a loving home, wonderful parents, two great brothers, and I felt in control of my life. I guess you'd say I was quite proud of myself. We were not religious people, but we were good people.

"Charlie was considered the golden boy by all of us. You'd think that would have given him a swelled head and made Bill and me jealous, but we weren't. Charlie was the most loving big brother a girl could ever want. He was my protector, my counselor, my event planner, my rock. Charlie never resented my tagging along on his many errands around town. Everyone seemed to know him and like him. I remember feeling so proud when someone would ask me, 'Aren't you Charlie's little sister?' He was just one of those kinds of people that everyone wanted to have as their friend. His friends would come to our house just to hang out, but Charlie always made sure his friends treated Bill and me with respect.

"That October, Charlie was going to school full-time, expecting to graduate almost a year earlier than expected because he had taken extra classes every summer. He had just gotten a new part-time job downtown, and he was happier than I had ever seen him. One evening shortly after supper, the doorbell rang, and our lives went into a tailspin. I remember Mother's falling against our dad as the policeman at the door told us that Charlie was dead. At first, the message would not register with me. "Charlie can't be dead—not my Charlie," I remember thinking. I also remember running up to my room because I refused to listen to any more of these lies. It had to be someone else—someone else's Charlie—not ours. My father came up to my room, and I will never forget the look on his face as he told me that he needed to go down to the hospital and identify Charlie's body. He told me that I needed to come downstairs and sit with my mother.

"I didn't know how I was going to get through that night; little did I know there would be so much more to get through. Several hours later, our father returned home, now a broken man. At first he just fell into our mother's arms and wept uncontrollably. Bill and I just sat there, watching our family dissolve right in front of us. This could not be happening to our family, not ours, but it was.

"Finally, my father gathered up enough courage to tell us what he needed to tell us. My father knew his news would destroy our mother, but because it was going to be in the morning paper, he had no choice. You see, our brother Charlie was not just dead or killed; he had been tortured for hours before his death. I just kept repeating, 'Who would do such a thing to our Charlie?'

"I remember vividly the pain on my father's face as he told us about Charlie's last hours. You see, my dad knew he would not be able to keep this horror away from us, so he wanted us to hear it from him first.

"I didn't want to hear it. I didn't want to think about it. I just wanted to run, but I sat frozen, unable to process what my father was saying. I wanted him to shut up! I kept interrupting my father with, 'Are you sure that was our Charlie?' or 'You made a mistake, Dad! You must have identified the wrong person. I refuse to believe that this could happen to Charlie.'

"Amidst all of her own pain, my mother pleaded with me to stop. 'Gladys, please don't make this harder on your father than it already is. We have to accept the fact that *he* is gone.' That night, my mother could not even say his name and finally ordered, 'Please stop interrupting and let your father talk.' "

"So I did. I sat and listened to my father tell us what some horrible person had done to our Charlie and how he must have suffered; I knew I would never be the same again. I learned that Charlie had been bound and gagged and had three fingers cut off. I learned that while he was still alive, someone cut off his left ear and jabbed a stick into his right eye. He had been burned all along his arms and legs, which the police suspect was done by a welding torch of some kind, and then finally, mercifully, they stabbed him in the heart, and he was gone.

"The police told our father that they had no idea who had done this terrible thing to our Charlie. For weeks the police followed up every lead, but they all went nowhere. For months we waited for some explanation or some rational reason—something that would make sense out of all of this pain. Charlie was dead and buried, but life was not going on; everything simply stopped meaning anything to me. I hardly remember my senior year of high school. I tried to just stay numb. I was long since cried out and had no more tears in me. I didn't care about anything anymore. The truth is, I was afraid to care.

"Then almost eight months later, the police got a break. Someone came forward and told the police that a guy in their neighborhood had been bragging about 'killing that white kid.' The police finally had a name, but they could not find him. They learned that he had skipped town about a month after the killing, and no one knew where he was.

"I remember staring at the suspect's photo in the newspaper; after all, they were not sure he really was the one who had done this terrible crime; he was just a suspect. I studied that picture, trying to see something in those eyes that would explain how those eyes could have looked at my brother and done those things to him. By the time they found him hiding out in Chicago, I already knew he was the one we had been looking for.

"I remember sitting in the courthouse when they brought him in for arraignment. He was shackled hands and feet, with a crazed look in his eyes. My numbness was gone in a flash. All I wanted to do was make this guy hurt the way he had hurt my brother. I had never known this kind of anger. While he stood there with that contemptuous smug face, I wanted to kill him. I wanted to torture him like he had tortured my brother. I began to fill my heart with thoughts of what I would do to him, dwelling for hours on vivid details of exacting my revenge.

"It took many, many months before he went to trial. During that whole time, my rage was focused on him and him alone; I thought of nothing else. I read every newspaper article written about him and hated everyone who was trying to help him.

"By the time he went to trial, I was almost twenty-one. I had already lost three years of my life, reliving every moment of Charlie's last hours. I sat in that courtroom, listening to the medical examiner tell the gruesome details of our brother's last hours, and my rage became white-hot. This guy had brutally tortured my brother, and my rage grew. My rage became so huge it could not be contained to this one person. This guy was no longer just the one who had killed my brother; he was no longer the guy who happened to be black. He had now become the *black* guy who had killed my brother. Suddenly, I now hated every black guy, and then it became every black person. After all, I had enough hate to go around.

"Now before you think my hatred of blacks was simply the result of my growing up in Georgia, I need to tell you that if Charlie's murderer had been an Irish person, I would have hated everyone Irish. If it had been a Jewish person, I would have hated every Jewish person. I had so much hate inside of me, I needed people to hate just so I would not explode from the pressure of holding onto my hatred. The sad thing was, however, very few people challenged my newfound hatred of blacks. They probably assumed that I was just one of so many others who thought like I did.

"By the end of the trial, we knew he was going to be found guilty, but his being found guilty wasn't nearly enough for me. Nothing would have been enough for me. Because of his age, he was given life in prison, and I remember thinking, 'What about my brother's age?' I had an unquenchable need to see someone suffer like I was suffering."

Every listener had been quiet, allowing to Gladys tell her story without interruption. However, Benny could no longer hold back his emotions at hearing this terrible story. "Gladys, I would want to kill him too. Someone like that does not deserve to live. You had every right to feel that way."

"Benny, Benny, Benny," Gladys pleaded. "That man had almost destroyed my family. I was letting him destroy me as well. You have no idea what that kind of rage can do to you. At first, you believe it is your friend—the one companion you can count on to endure this pain you are carrying, but soon it turns on you and devours you completely. All you are left with is your rage," Gladys explained.

Benny stared at Gladys, studying this sweet old lady he had come to admire, before stating, "I understand what you are saying, Gladys. It's just that I can't picture you being that angry person."

Gladys smiled at Benny, "I was that person, Benny, and more. I thought I could contain my rage, only spewing it out at those I blamed for all my pain, but I was wrong. That kind of anger is a poison that seeps into all of your thinking. The trial was over, he was in prison, and I was now twenty-two and thought I was handling it pretty well and going on with my life—until I met Karl Carter, my future husband.

"We had gone on several dates before the topic of our families came up. I tried to avoid it, but he was persistent. At first, I tried to give a glossy overview, simply stating facts and moving on. Karl could see the rage in my eyes and wanted to know everything, but I refused to talk about it so he stopped coming to see me for several weeks. At first, I didn't care. How dare he try to invade my private world—the one I guarded so closely, but I found I really missed his company. I wanted to see him again.

"One afternoon when I saw him walking up my street, I went out and sat on the front step so he could not miss me. As he reached the front of my house, he stopped and gave me one of his beautiful smiles and said, "Gladys, are you ready to be honest with me yet? What are you so afraid of, Gladys? If I am going to get seriously in love with you, I have to know who you really are."

"Wow!" exclaimed Benny. "He didn't mess around, did he, Gladys?"

Gladys laughed. "No, Benny, he was serious. He really liked me, but he was not going to date me anymore for fear of falling in love with me—unless I came clean with him."

"What did he mean by 'come clean with him,' Gladys?" Hope probed. "Were you trying to keep the fact that your brother had been killed a secret?"

"No, Hope, everyone in our town knew about Charlie," Gladys explained. "He was talking about how I was handling my brother's death. You see, Karl could see that I had a hair-trigger temper, ready to go off whenever someone I considered an enemy crossed my path. I didn't even realize exactly how obvious my rage was to him. I had thought I was doing a better job of hiding it than I really was.

"Karl sat on my porch and told me how it made him feel when I had acted so rudely to his best friend, Tobias. He said I had no right to judge every black man, treating them all as if they had personally tortured my brother. He told me Tobias was the godliest man he knew and that he would give anyone the shirt off his back.

"I remember snickering at his description of this black man. I was so profoundly poisoned by my rage, I could not even imagine a black man's being trustworthy, but here was Karl, attesting to his friend's character. I had a real problem with that assessment—a problem that Karl knew was a deal breaker between us."

Engrossed in this tale, Benny suddenly sat up and asked, "So what did you do, Gladys?"

"I promised him I would try. I didn't really think it was possible, but I promised I would try, and he accepted my promise. Karl began by having me come to the loading dock once a week so we could have lunch with Tobias. We were both very uncomfortable. Tobias was well aware of how I felt about him, but he was always very gracious toward me. He understood the pain I was suffering from my loss. We never discussed this until years later, but Tobias was willing to tolerate my unspoken resentment because he and Karl understood that I was unaware of what was really wrong with me."

"What was so wrong with you, Gladys?" Benny asked in the most incredulous voice.

Laughing at this young man who could not imagine this sweet old lady having anything wrong with her, Gladys admitted, "I had a lot of things very wrong with me, Benny, and I will be eternally grateful to both Tobias and Karl for their willingness to be patient with me. You see, I knew I was being unfair to Tobias, just because he was a black man, but I could not let go of my anger. After a few lunches, I asked Karl if we could sit together alone, without Tobias. I even teased him that we could sneak in a few kisses if Tobias was not around."

"And he didn't go for that?" Benny asked with great surprise.

"No, he didn't, Benny. I guess I wasn't as tempting a dish to him as I thought I was," Gladys teased. "But seriously, Karl knew that he could have no future with me as long as I remained so full of anger and lost."

"Lost?" Hope questioned.

"Oh, my, yes, Hope," confessed Gladys willingly. "I was truly lost, but it was Tobias and Karl who kept lighting the way for me—even when I resented having that light shone. You see, I was actually quite happy in my misery, or at least I thought I was. So instead of getting rid of Tobias, Karl increased our lunches with him to three times a week. For months I would just sit and listen to these two friends talk, but slowly I found myself asking questions, joining in, and looking forward to our lunches together.

"You see, Tobias really was an interesting guy. He had been through a lot of terrible things in his life too, and he understood my pain. I would listen as he told stories from the Bible—stories that actually made sense to me. He was able to make that Book come alive because he really and truly believed it held the answers to all of man's questions. After a while, I actually forgot he was black and began looking forward to our lunchtime Bible studies.

"Then one day, Tobias brought his lovely young wife to our lunchtime Bible study, and everything changed in an instant. I remember turning the corner, excited to get to our regular seats at the wooden table under the sycamore tree, when I saw them. In that instant, Tobias, again, was just a black man, daring to have his arm around a black woman. Suddenly, I was filled with my old companion, rage. I remember thinking, 'How stupid could you have been, Gladys? He almost fooled you.' I no longer looked at him as the wise and kind Bible teacher I had come to admire; after all, he was just another black man, so I turned and started to run.

"Karl caught up with me a block or so down the street. He had seen the look on my face and knew I was in trouble. He begged me to come back with him, but my rage was making me blind and deaf to his pleadings. Three years of rage at every black person on the face of this earth suddenly rested on Tobias's shoulders, and I didn't care. I didn't even care if I lost Karl because of this; I just didn't care."

Benny blurted out, with some relief, "Well, Gladys, you must have cared a little because you ended up marrying him, right?"

Gladys winked at Benny and answered, "Yes, I did, Benny, but not while I was so damaged and broken. He pleaded with me to return to the table. He said, 'Gladys, it is time for us to start talking about your rage against black people, and who better to be honest with than someone who is paying the highest cost for that rage right now?' "

Gladys smiled at everyone in the living room before saying, "I thought he was talking about Tobias' paying that cost. What he really meant was that I was the one paying the highest cost for my rage, and he and Tobias wanted to help me see it.

"I finally agreed to walk back to that table one more time—that table where God's Word had been shared with me—the place I was told about how much God loves us, and the place where, just two days earlier, I had almost surrendered my heart to God. My pain was causing me to be blind with anger, deaf with rage, and comfortable with my misery. But something deep inside of me yearned to hear more about this God of love Tobias talked about, so I agreed to return to the table and try again.

"As we walked up to the table Tobias jumped up and said, 'Gladys, I would love to introduce you to my bride, Ruth. Ruth, this is Gladys, the young woman I've been telling you about.'"

Hope jumped up and shouted, "Ruth? Ruth Bascom? Tobias was her husband?"

Beaming with love and pride, Gladys said, "Yes, Hope, the very same. You see, if I had refused to return to that table that day, I doubt that I would ever have surrendered my heart to God. If I had not returned, I also know that Karl would never have married me, and I might never have known the blessing of having Ruth Bascom as my most cherished and best friend for the past fifty years.

"Hope, my returning to that table, although difficult at the time, was such a small act on my part. Simply being willing to turn around and walk back to that table with Karl changed my whole life. But Hope, God uses those simple little steps of faith and surrender to make huge changes in our lives. I shudder to think where my life would have gone had I listened to my anger that day."

Then looking over at Lisa before continuing, Gladys again tried to say something Lisa had refused to hear for the past eleven years. "You see, Hope, if I had refused and had gone on with my rage, I believe I would have turned out much like Lisa's mother, your grandmother, Marjorie Miller. My rage and pain was such a part of who I was; it would have destroyed me. And so when I see someone like Marjorie Miller, even though her behavior is indefensible, I see someone I was well on the way to becoming if Karl and Tobias had not reached out to me, and if I had not chosen to respond. Without God and His people, I could easily have become a Marjorie Miller."

"But you didn't, Gladys, and that's the point," replied Lisa with more gentleness than she had ever responded to this topic. "You accepted God's gift of Jesus, and my mother has not."

"The point is, Lisa, the only difference between your mother and me is that I accepted the help when it was offered, and she has not. Karl and Tobias were willing to keep reaching out to me, even though I was rude and skeptical. Ruth and Tobias Bascom had led Karl to faith, and the three of them brought me to Jesus. They taught me that walking with God means living a forgiven life. They taught me what it cost God to offer that forgiveness, and that I could never earn it; it is a precious gift offered to all who are willing to accept it."

Hope sat quietly studying this woman to whom she owed so much. She thought about Lisa's hearing about this same free gift of forgiveness when she was so broken and damaged by a life of drugs and prostitution. How the idea of being forgiven must have thrilled Lisa's heart! Hope pondered all that Gladys was saying about how God wants to forgive, not condemn; how He wants to restore, not reject; how He wants a relationship, not religion. "I've never heard any of this before," Hope confessed to Gladys, "I thought God was someone you had to fear, but you are telling me He wants to love me. I think I am going to need some time to digest all of this, but I promise you, Gladys, I will think about it."

CHAPTER 17

❧

Everyone was up and moving early Saturday morning. Caroline had warned them all that breakfast was going to be over right at 9:00 because she needed her kitchen to herself for at least two solid hours if she was going to get the wedding cake finished on time. Bill and Scott had their instructions, and everyone else was on his own. Once Caroline's kitchen was designated off-limits, it was out of bounds.

Scott set up the ladder in the living room while Bill separated the decorations Caroline wanted them to hang in the exact places she had already determined. After forty-five years of watching her decorate this house, Bill knew not to question, but to simply do as she had instructed.

Lisa watched them spin their decorating magic for a few minutes before deciding to run upstairs and get her shower. Susan was due in about an hour to help with her hair, and then all that would be left for her to do was double-check her suitcase and then enjoy the celebration.

Gladys was locked in Caroline's room, handling some secret gift wrappings. Having nothing else to do, Hope wandered downstairs and sat on the staircase to watch Scott and Bill. A few minutes later the doorbell rang and Bill, having his hands full, asked, "Hope, could you get that for me?"

"Sure, Mr. Thomas," Hope called out as she ran for the front door. She swung it open and standing right in front of her was Ruth Bascom, with her arms full of Lisa's wedding suit, blouse, and shoes. At first, Hope simply stood there staring into Ruth's face, not offering to take anything out of her hands, nor inviting her in. Ruth could have reacted in a hundred different ways at this obviously rude behavior from Hope, but as always, Ruth simply smiled and said, "Why hello there, Hope, how are you this morning?"

Hearing Ruth's voice startled Hope out of her thoughts, and she quickly responded, "I'm so sorry, Mrs. Bascom. Let me take some of these things, and please come in." Hope laid the garment bag over the banister and placed Lisa's shoes on the second step. She immediately turned back to Mrs. Bascom and said with teary eyes, "I am so happy you made it, Ruth. Your being here means the world to all of us."

Ruth immediately recognized the difference in Hope's demeanor this morning, compared to how cool she had been during their last meeting and thought to herself, "Something has changed in this young woman."

Hope took hold of Ruth's hand and led her into the study, saying, "Ruth, Gladys is locked away upstairs wrapping gifts, Lisa is in the shower, the kitchen is off-limits to everyone until the wedding cake is decorated, and the living room is a danger zone with ladders and garland all over the place. Besides, I wanted to have a few minutes alone with you—if I could?"

Ruth studied this girl, wondering what had made the drastic change in her attitude toward her. Then she responded, "Certainly, Hope. What can I do for you?"

"Actually, Ruth...you don't mind me calling you Ruth, do you?"

"Of course not, Hope," Ruth replied.

"Well," hesitated Hope for an instant, trying to decide how to start, "first, I want to apologize for how I acted the last time we met. I know I was rather cool toward you, but I don't want you to get the wrong impression." Hope sort of giggled, "Actually, I did give the wrong impression.

You see, you might have gotten the idea that I was rather distant because of your being black, but honestly, Ruth, that was not the reason. You see, I am not a religious person at all, and I feel really uncomfortable around religious people. Lisa and Gladys pray all the time, telling me how important God is to them. But then, they started telling me about this Ruth Bascom, the godliest person they knew, and I was a wreck. I felt trapped and ill-prepared for whatever religious stuff you were going to show in front of me. Honestly, I was so nervous about *who* you were, I didn't even notice *what* you were. Does that make sense to you?"

Ruth laughed. "Yes, it does, Hope. The last thing any of us wanted was to make you feel uncomfortable."

"Oh, I'm not uncomfortable anymore, Ruth. Yesterday Gladys told us all about you and Tobias. She told us how you two taught Karl that God loved him, and then the three of you taught Gladys the same thing. You three loved Gladys through her struggle with anger, and because you did that, Gladys was able to do the same thing for my mother. I will love you until the day I die for what you and Gladys did for my mother." Starting to cry with gratitude, Hope broke down. Ruth gathered Hope in her arms as she said, "Ruth, seeing how your religion has changed their lives makes it something I want to have in my life too. I know it took something more than human willpower to turn around my mother's life; it took something as big as God. But Ruth, even though this seems like such a natural thing to do when I'm back here with all of you, I don't think it will work for me back home in California—not with my family and friends. I'm not saying I am not going to become a religious person, but I think it is something I do need to investigate."

Upstairs, Lisa had finished her shower, wrapped a towel around her wet head, put on some casual clothes and had slipped down the stairs and stood quietly outside the study. A moment later, Gladys joined her as they listened to Ruth gently explaining the difference between being religious and being forgiven. As Ruth and Hope continued to talk in the study, Lisa and Gladys stood praying that Hope would understand what Ruth was saying.

Ruth knew she was going to shock her listener with her next comment. "None of us want you to become a religious person, Hope. A person who becomes religious is someone who has created some manmade rules he thinks will impress God. Then they use those rules to pass judgment on other people. Sweetie, religion is man's way of climbing up to God, but being forgiven is accepting what God did to reach down to us. God sent His only Son, Jesus, here to us to take our place and pay the debt we all owe. The gift of salvation is free to all who will accept it. People who live a forgiven life can never behave haughty or arrogant, using themselves as some kind of spiritual measuring stick because to live a forgiven life is to always know that God's forgiveness has been offered to all. It cannot be earned because it is free to all who will accept it. Hope, all we have to do is confess to God that we are not perfect. Now that isn't so very hard, is it? We all know that none of us have lived a perfect life, right?"

Hope quickly agreed, "Perfect? Not even close, Ruth."

"That is what sin is, Hope. It is not being perfect, so Jesus came to be perfect for us, and all we have to do is accept His perfect and free gift so we can begin to live a forgiven life as God's child.

"Hope, I always carry this booklet that my Tobias wrote many years ago. I'd love to give it to you, if you don't mind. You can read it at your leisure, and then, only if you want to, you and I can talk about what it says."

Hope protested, "Ruth, I can't take your booklet," and in the hallway, Lisa's heart and emotions felt crushed until she heard Hope explain, "That would be like my giving someone my locket. That booklet is your connection to Tobias."

"Sweetie, this is not my one and only copy. I have hundreds of these booklets at home," Ruth explained.

Taking the booklet, Hope read the title, *Pray for the Peace of the City*, by Tobias Bascom. "Ruth, I'm hoping this booklet allows me to get to know your Tobias better. Gladys really loved him after all, didn't she?"

"Yes she did, Hope. Tobias was a very godly man who walked a forgiven life and taught others what it means to be truly forgiven and then to walk in that forgiveness. After you read it, you and I can talk, but only if you want to, Hope. Would you like that?"

Hope smiled, "I'd like that very much, Ruth. I will read it on the plane tonight, but right now let's go find my mom and Gladys and get this wedding party started."

CHAPTER 18

B<small>Y</small> 10:00 A.M., Caroline had the wedding cake finished and displayed on the dining room table. Only then did she invite Gladys and Ruth to join her in the kitchen to help with the final preparations of the wedding dinner that was to be served after the ceremony.

Susan finished fixing Lisa's hair, makeup and nails by 10:30, after which Susan and Hope left to pick up Mrs. Reiner, who had been invited to join in this family celebration. Lisa walked into the kitchen and asked, "Can I help with anything?"

"Absolutely not," all three women responded in unison and started to chuckle. Gladys then said, "Lisa, you look especially beautiful today. Susan did such a great job with your hair, and she would be very upset if you chipped those beautifully manicured nails before your wedding."

"But Gladys, I am getting so nervous sitting around doing nothing," Lisa pleaded.

Caroline checked the clock and said, "Lisa, it is 10:45. The boys will be here in thirty minutes, and you still have to get your wedding suit on before the photographer arrives to take pictures. Susan and Hope will be back with Mrs. Reiner any time now, and we should be finished with all this preparation by then. Why don't you go upstairs and get dressed so you are ready to greet Ben when he walks in the house?"

"Is Ben going to see his bride before the ceremony?" questioned Mrs. Bascom.

"Yes," Lisa affirmed as she continued to explain. "Ruth, since we are not young kids, and this is a simple family wedding, we decided it would be more fun if we all enjoyed the day together. Besides, Ben has already seen me in my favorite suit. Ben told me that he bought Benny his first real suit yesterday because he is going to stand up with Ben as his best man. I can't wait to see my two men all dressed up today."

Checking her watch, Ruth admonished Lisa by stating, "Well, they are going to be here in a few minutes, and you are still going to be in those jeans. If you don't march upstairs and get dressed now, you will end up getting married in jeans."

Lisa checked herself in the full-length mirror as Susan knocked on the bedroom door and entered. "I love that suit on you, Lisa. Gladys really did a great job on it."

Lisa smiled into the mirror as she said, "I remember the look on Ben's face when I stepped out of the dressing room at the jail. I suspect I will see that same look when he sees me in it today. Susan, who would ever have imagined my life turning out this way? I never knew I could ever be this happy."

"Don't you dare start crying, Lisa," Susan warned. "I put lots of mascara on you this morning, and even though it is not supposed to smudge, let's not risk it today of all days." Hearing excited voices downstairs, Susan said, "We need to head downstairs and start greeting your guests, Lisa."

Lisa and Susan quietly slipped down the stairs, trying not to be seen. Lisa stood in the hallway, trying to control her emotions. Hearing the excited voices of all these people who had come to mean so much to her was causing waves of gratitude to wash over her. "Susan," she whispered, "I'm not sure I can do this. I should not have allowed you to put all this makeup on me. I am going to blubber like a baby once I see Ben. I know I will."

Susan laughed at her older sister. "Lisa, you and I never learned how to manage happiness. It is almost a scary feeling to us, isn't it? Don't you worry about messing up your makeup. You just stay in the moment today and enjoy every single swell of happiness that comes to you. If you cry, you cry. Today is all about you and Ben, so simply enjoy it and don't worry about anything else." With this last admonition, Susan gave her sister a loving nudge toward the opening as they joined those waiting in the family room.

Talking with Harry, Ben had his back to the doorway and did not see Lisa enter the room. Benny, standing right behind his dad, saw Lisa before anyone else and began tapping his dad on the back and suggested, "Dad, you might want to turn around right now."

Ben turned around to see his bride-to-be waiting. Lisa had not worn this beautiful royal-blue suit since the day in court when her mother testified. Ben excused himself and quickly made his way to Lisa and said, "You look beautiful, Lisa. Everyone is here, so we should get this show on the road."

Family and friends quickly took their seats while Ben, Lisa, Benny, and Susan took their places in front of Pastor Mark. Ben and Lisa had made it clear that they wanted this to be a casual ceremony without pomp and circumstance—only family and close friends witnessing their eternal pledge to love and honor each other. They had written their own vows and wanted this ceremony to be a witness of God's grace in their lives. Beaming with happiness, Lisa slipped her arm under Ben's arm and started forward when Lisa Anne suddenly and loudly called "Wait!"

Lisa turned and watched as her niece, Lisa Anne, ran toward the kitchen, returning almost immediately with a beautiful bouquet of lilies and white hydrangeas, wrapped in a beautiful baby-blue silk ribbon with cascading baby's breath. Beaming with pride, Lisa Anne walked up to Lisa and offered the bouquet and said, "Auntie Lisa, I made this for you to hold during your wedding."

Smiling down at her beloved niece, Lisa accepted the bouquet and said, "Lisa Anne, this is perfect. Look how it goes with my suit. You did a wonderful job!"

Lisa Anne quickly returned to her seat next to her grandmother and said, "Now you can begin, Pastor Mark."

Smiling his acknowledgment to Lisa Anne, Pastor Mark turned his attention to the bride and the groom and began, "Ben and Lisa, neither one of you wanted a traditional wedding ceremony today. Everyone in this room knows you two love each other, so before I launch into what that kind of love means for the two of you, I have asked several of these witnesses to share with everyone what this union means to them. You knows who you are, so as your turn comes, simply stand where you are and share your thoughts."

The first one to stand was Gladys. "For eleven years I have prayed that God would send someone into Lisa's life who would love her without judgment. Ben, I know you love my Lisa with all your heart, and I know that Lisa loves you. Witnessing Lisa's fight back from the very pit of hell, learning to first trust that God loved her and had forgiven her, then learning how to love herself and accept love from others, has been an amazing thing to witness. Today, Ben, God is giving you a precious responsibility—one I know you take very seriously. Lisa is placing her trust in you, and so am I. Knowing her history, I would trust very few men with her care, but Ben, before all of these witnesses and with all my heart, I place my girl's future in your care because I know what kind of man you are."

As soon as Gladys finished, Ruth Bascom stood. "Lisa, you know that Tobias and I were never able to have children. You also know that I love you as much as any mother could possibly love her child. You know that I know your strengths, and I know your weaknesses. Today, as you two stand before God and pledge to love and honor each other, I challenge you both to make this pledge: to always remember how much you both have been forgiven, and therefore live a forgiving life; never holding onto wrongs, never repaying evil for evil. I pray a blessing on your life together, one that is filled with the same kind of love Gladys and I knew with our beloved husbands. I pray that fifty years from now you can look back and know that God used each of you to bless the other in ways that no other person on the face of this earth was allowed to do for this person to whom you are pledging your love today.

As Ruth took her seat, Benny cleared his shaky voice, turned around, and spoke from his heart. "What I want to share sounds a little selfish after hearing Ms. Gladys and Ms. Bascom, but it does come from my heart. When my mother died, Dad and I only had each other, and even though my dad is a great dad, I used to lie in bed at night and worry about what would happen to me if something happened to him also. Today, standing here next to my dad, seeing him so happy makes me happy too. Not only for him, but for me as well. I know I truly have a complete family now. In front of all of you, I want to say to Lisa, I love you and am so glad you are marrying my dad. I know you love him, and I know you also love me. As I look around this room, I feel so happy because every one of you is now family to me." With a huge smile, Benny turned his attention to Hope and said, "Now I even have a big sister."

Finally, it was Susan's turn. Taking her sister's hand, Susan said, "For so many years I felt the burden and responsibility of being the only one in the world who loved and cared what happened to you, Lisa. Way back then, I didn't know that God loved you more than I ever could have, so I carried a burden that was much too heavy for me. One day God sent Aunt Gladys into my life and yours, and I didn't feel so alone where you were concerned. Knowing someone else was sharing in the caring made the burden easier to bear. Today, you stand here loved by many wonderful people, Lisa, not the least of whom is Ben." Then turning and addressing Ben, Susan laughed. "Ben, do you remember the first time we met? Boy, did I dislike you that night. I remember wishing you would choke on that pastry you were eating. I had no idea that the day would come when I would willingly hand over my sister into your capable care. I'm glad that God does not listen to our foolishness and hold our words against us. When I think of how God used all of this to bring Lisa to God, then to bring the truth of Hope to all of us, and even bring Mrs. Reiner a little bit of her Steve back to her, I want to cry with thanksgiving. Ben and Lisa, may God grant you both many years of happiness and may you both always remember that all of this has truly come from the hand and heart of God Himself."

Pastor Mark stepped forward to complete the ceremony. "Well," he smiled, "I had intended to give a long speech about what love is, and where it comes from, but after what we have just heard from Gladys and Ruth, my words would seem redundant.. I was going to challenge you both to keep the pledge you make today, but that too would seem redundant. I was going to remind you that all good things come from God, but again, I was beaten to the punch. And finally, I was going to admonish you that your union affects everyone around you, but Benny showed us all a real-life example of that truth. So what is left for me to say?

"Ben and Lisa, it is such a privilege to stand in front of the two of you to-day, hearing how you both understand that this person standing beside you is God's gift to you. As you listened to these people speak, you both know that a marriage is between two people, a pledge to love, honor, respect, and cherish that other person as they need to be loved, honored, respected, and cherished. But the truth is, although this marriage is between the two of you, its impact will affect everyone you love. By the way you treat each oth-er, you will either bless or harm all those who love you. Forgive each other quickly and completely. Look for ways to uplift each other, not to tear down. Be the first person to come to the other's aid and the only one you run to for intimate comfort. Always be loyal to each other in your conversations with others. There is physical betrayal, emotional betrayal, and verbal betrayal; always remain loyal to this person to whom you are pledging your future, and God will bless your union with His grace.

"I know that you both have written your own vows, so Ben, I will ask you to go first, and then you will follow him, Lisa."

Ben's chest heaved with emotion as he turned toward Lisa, took her hands in his, and struggled to control the nervous giggle that threatened to overtake him. "Lisa, I have always used humor to mask my feelings of deep emotion. I do not want to do that today. Today, as I stand here in front of you, I want to express my complete emotional honesty. When Benny and I lost Beverly, a huge part of me died with her. I buried myself in my job, both of taking care of Benny and providing for the two of us. I was afraid to look at what I had lost for fear of being crushed by the loss. Lisa, I cherish the hours of serious conversation we enjoyed as we got to know each other. I knew you were trusting me with something so very precious—an intimate view into your private world, how you think, and what you believe. Watching your courage gave me courage. I found myself opening up to you with such honesty that I felt with you I could once again become a whole person. I trusted you with my most secret thoughts and fears; you not only supported me and understood me, but you challenged me to become a better, more loving father and friend. Lisa, I love who I have become because of our relationship. I vow to keep our relationship honest, and I commit to you my present and my future."

"Benjamin," Lisa said with a clear, determined voice, "I stand here before you, a woman who knows the gift I have in you. Everyone in this room knows where I've been and what I have done, and I do not take for granted the forgiveness of God or of these people present. In my whole life, I have only loved one other man besides you, and that was Hope's father. I will always remember the night that I told you all about Steven. I told you that I will always love him because he is Hope's father, but even more so because Steven loved me with his whole heart—at a time when I so desperately needed to feel loved. I needed to know if you were a strong enough man to accept this truth without feeling jealous or making me feel guilty for my past. Ben, the compassion and understanding you showed to me told me everything I needed to know about you. Ben, Steven holds my past, but you hold my tomorrows. I vow to love and honor you as the head of our home and the guardian of my heart. Trust has always been difficult for me, but today, in front of God and all of these witnesses, I pledge to you my whole heart, unmasked, to love you and trust you without reservation."

After blessing the exchange of rings, Pastor Mark prayed a prayer of blessing on the couple and loudly announced, "I now pronounce you husband and wife. Benjamin, you may now kiss your bride."

Within a few minutes Caroline had dinner on the table, and all of the guests were seated. The wedding meal was wonderful, and as food was being passed around, many commented on the lovely ceremony they had been privileged to witness. After the meal, they watched as Lisa and Ben cut the first piece of cake before turning the rest of the cutting back to Caroline. After enjoying the cake, the guests made their way back into the family room to watch the newlyweds open their wedding gifts. When all of the gifts had been opened, everyone followed the couple outside as they left for the Plantation for their three-day honeymoon.

As Mrs. Reiner followed Hope back into the house, she mentioned, "Hope, Scott and Susan invited me to come along with you to the airport. They know I'm going to have a hard time saying goodbye to you, and perhaps my helping you gather your things will give us a little more time together. May I?"

Sliding her arm around her grandmother, Hope responded, "Grandma, I'd love your help. This has been an amazing few days for me. I found you, and I've come to know so much about my father, I feel as if I actually know him. I hate the idea of leaving you and going back to California so soon. I want more time with you, but I promise we will keep in contact."

After Hope had secured her luggage and Christmas gifts, she stepped out into the hallway, opened the large linen closet door and gathered up a set of fresh linens for the bed. Stepping back into the bedroom, Hope asked, "Grandma, can you help me strip this bedding for Mrs. Thomas? Ruth will be staying in this room tonight, and I would like to put clean sheets on the bed before I leave."

The two laughed as they made the bed, remembering how Ben and Harry carried on during the wedding dinner. "Those guys are a riot, Grandma. I love how this family just loves to be together and how graciously they have accepted me. Don't get me wrong. I love my family, but it is going to be hard going back to California, knowing what I need to do."

"So Hope, have you made a decision? Mrs. Reiner cautiously probed, "Are you going to call off your wedding?"

"Yes, I think so," Hope replied with less determination than Mrs. Reiner was hoping for. "I just don't know what will happen to him if I walk out of his life. Maybe I'm the one who is supposed to help him get free of his controlling mother, but if I fail, then my life will be ruined. I just don't know what I am supposed to do. Can I really be that selfish and only think of me and not care what happens to him? Gladys and Ruth keep talking about forgiveness; shouldn't I forgive Michael? Everyone has forgiven Lisa for her past, and look how that turned out."

Mrs. Reiner studied the face of this granddaughter she hardly knew. *Could she possibly be this naive about life? Would pointing this out be of any help right now?* "Hope, I've only known you for three days, and I do not want to tread into areas where I am not welcome."

Looking up with a puzzled smile, Hope responded, "Tread away, Grandma. If you have something to say, I want to hear it."

"Okay, but first, I want to say I don't know Gladys Carter or Ruth Bascom at all. I don't know what they said to you about forgiveness, but I do know both of these women are wise and experienced. I cannot imagine that either of them would counsel you to marry someone you are not sure you love or whose love for you is in question. I would suggest that you talk with them again because I fear you must have misunderstood their meaning. Hope, please take your time and make sure you are doing the right thing for the right reason before you marry this man."

Hearing Scott calling that it was time to leave for the airport, Hope walked over and hugged her newly found grandmother and said, "I promise, Grandma. I'm glad I have three very wise, seasoned women in my life. I know you are only a phone call away, and I promise I will think about what you have said."

Mrs. Reiner quickly changed the subject, gathered up the bundle of Christmas gifts for Hope, but determined to talk with Susan as soon as they dropped Hope off at the airport.

As soon as Hope was safely aboard her flight and Scott, Susan, and Mrs. Reiner were back in the car, Mrs. Reiner asked, "Susan, I don't know your Aunt Gladys, or her friend, Mrs. Bascom, at all, but I had quite a disturbing conversation with Hope regarding something she thinks they said to her."

Curious as to what this could possibly be, Susan turned around and looked directly at Mrs. Reiner and asked, "What did Hope say?"

"I'm not trying to meddle in Hope's affairs, but remember my conversation with her in your car on Thursday, when we talked about this Michael of hers?" The acid tone in Mrs. Reiner's voice when saying his name was not missed by either Scott or Susan.

"Yes, I remember that conversation quite well, Mrs. Reiner. Lisa and I both were thrilled at how direct and to the point you were. We were also glad that Hope listened to your concerns about Michael."

"Well," paused Mrs. Reiner, "Hope's resolve didn't last very long. It seems that sometime between Thursday and today, both Mrs. Carter and Mrs. Bascom made Hope think it was her responsibility to forgive him for not being the man he should be. I cannot believe that either one of these women would have counseled her this way, but Hope drew this conclusion from their comments. Now she is determined to go home, forgive this man, and proceed with her wedding plans. This foolish girl believes it is her responsibility to save this man—as Gladys did Lisa." Almost pleading, Mrs. Reiner asked, "They could not actually believe that is best for Hope, can they?"

"Absolutely not, Mrs. Reiner," Susan replied in disgust. "I don't know where Hope could get such an idea. None of us want Hope to marry this guy. We don't understand why she feels so responsible to make him happy when he obviously doesn't care about her happiness. I will talk with both Gladys and Ruth, and we will try to straighten this out with Hope. I'm just glad that Lisa didn't know about this turn of events before taking off on her honeymoon; it would have ruined it for her."

CHAPTER 19

＊

As Hope walked through the gangway door, she spotted her dad standing alone. Forcing an empty smile, she knew that this meant her mother was still angry with her and that Michael was also making a statement by his absence. She could always count on her dad to be there for her, and she did not want to make this harder on him than her mother already had. So, as usual, Hope disregarded her disappointment, smiled, quickly hugged her dad and pretended everything was just fine.

Feeling like she had a foot in each world, Hope found herself unwilling to share all of the wonderful experiences she had enjoyed in Atlanta— at least not just yet. Wanting to protect her dad from feeling hurt, she decided not to mention getting to know her birth father or his mother. The chitchat on the ride home was restricted to the weather, always a safe topic, and the difference between the traffic in Los Angeles and Atlanta. For guys, sports are always a safe subject, but since neither she nor her father cared much for sports, that was never a conversation path for them.

Westbound red-eye flights are always hard on the body, so Hope went straight to bed when she got home. Determined to sleep well into the early afternoon, she could avoid her mother for at least one more day. She hated feeling this way about her mother, but as long as her mother continued to be Mrs. Gundersol's lackey, the less she shared with her, the better.

Hope set her alarm for 3:00, climbed into bed, and wondered if Michael would even show up tonight. She had returned early so she could accompany him to some big fundraiser, but that concession would not matter to him. Teaching her not to disappoint him was always much more important to him these days. Shortly before drifting off to sleep, Hope remembered the pamphlet from Mrs. Bascom, but sleep quickly overtook her. "That pamphlet will just have to wait for another day," she sighed.

By 5:00 Hope was up, showered, dressed, and waiting for Michael. If he was coming, he would be here any minute. Walking into the living room, Hope sat in the wingback chair beside the front window so she could see his car turn into the driveway. She could hear her mother in the kitchen and knew she should go in and break the long silence that was building between them. She thought, "Tonight will be hard enough. Forgiving Michael for how he treats me is more than I can handle; having to give in to my mother for never defending me against Mrs. Gundersol is too much to ask of me right now."

The loud clicking of the mantle clock had begun to wear on Hope's nerves. Suddenly she spotted Michael's red convertible turn into the driveway. She watched him slip out of the car, check his hair in the side mirror, slam the driver's door, and swagger toward the front porch. Studying this man with whom she had agreed to spend the rest of her life, she wondered what she had ever seen in him. Sure, he was handsome and dressed well. He certainly knew how to enjoy spending money he had never earned himself. He could take her places and introduce her to well-connected people she would never meet otherwise, but what he could do for her mattered little to her. *"What, if anything, had drawn me to him?"* she wondered. *"Can I think of one thing to love about this man who is now standing at my door, waiting for me to answer his demanding knock?"*

Forcing a friendly smile on her face, Hope took a deep breath, opened the front door and invited Michael into the house. "Good evening, won't you come in?"

Michael planted an uneventful peck on her cheek as he quickly slid past her. *"That kiss was nothing a man in love would plant on his soon-to-be bride,"* she couldn't help but think. Obviously he was still angry that she had traveled east for Christmas. Hope knew this evening was going to be another one of their difficult nights—one of many they have had these days. "May I offer you something to drink or do we need to get going?"

"We have time, Hope," barked Michael with that demeaning manner she always associated with his scoldings. "I will take a Scotch and water, easy on the water. Tonight's fundraiser is going to be long and tedious for me."

As Hope went over to her father's liquor cabinet, she thought to herself, *"Tedious for you? What about for me?"* Pouring his drink, she wondered, *"How long will it take you to make any personal comment to me about me? Many nights I have gone all evening without one single comment directed to me—apart from corrections or instructions from you."* Checking her reflection in the mirror above the liquor cabinet, Hope made sure her thoughts were not obvious on her face, then she turned with a smile, handed Michael his drink, and asked, "So did you have fun skiing up at Mammoth? I saw in the paper that you had almost seven inches of new snow. That must have made your trip fun."

"I had a great time there. I didn't realize how tired I was with all these boring public events my parents keep scheduling for me. I was able to avoid the press and had ten whole days to myself. It actually felt good to be just a person on vacation."

Hope waited for just one question about how her holiday had gone, but regrettably knew there would be no such questions. Whenever he was displeased with her, he gave her the silent treatment. She had observed his mother use this technique on him enough times to recognize it in him. Hope struggled for something safe to say. "So how many people do you think will be attending tonight?" As she waited for his answer, Hope longed to be sitting at the Thomas' table, laughing with Ben and Harry, or sitting in the family room talking about something interesting with Scott and Susan, or even sitting on the floor beside Benny, watching the little kids. Actually, Hope wished to be almost anywhere but here with him when she heard him answer, "Tonight is my mother's invention. She has invited about three dozen big-time contributors to a sit-down dinner at the Marriott downtown. I hate these things. I would rather have a casual, open bar and appetizers kind of gathering—one I can slide in, make an appearance, and duck out. They are much easier on me than a sit-down, but my mother never listens to my opinions."

Hearing him describe this gathering, Hope realized that her mother and father would not be invited to this kind of event. They were not big-time contributors and would not fit in well. Mrs. Gundersol was nothing, if not acutely savvy. Political connections were her stock and trade, and she knew how to use them to her advantage. With knowing this about her future mother-in-law, Hope was always puzzled that Mrs. Gundersol was so keen on pushing this wedding forward. Staring over at this man she really hardly knew, yet knew much too well to really love, she mused to herself, *"I have nothing to offer you politically. I have no great family connections; actually, just the opposite, according to your mother. So why is she so dead set on our marriage? Why isn't she working on you to dump me? I don't get it. If it were up to her, we would have the wedding next week, pomp and circumstance aside. She has said repeatedly she just wants the wedding over with. Why?"*

Standing up and handing Hope his empty glass, Michael said, "I guess we better get going. With traffic, we have at least an hour drive in front of us."

Hope took the glass but did not move right away. There never was a good time to question Michael, especially shortly before he was expected to do something he did not want to do. Since there never was a good time, Hope decided to ask, "Michael, why do you want to marry me?"

"Hope, don't be stupid. Get your coat or we will be late," he retorted.

Standing her ground, Hope demanded, "Michael, do you even love me?"

Angered at being questioned like this, he stormed over to the door, opened it, and said with his "I-am-serious" voice, "Hope, I'm here, aren't I? I'm taking you to an event as my significant other—an event with the most important people I know. What does that tell you?"

"Actually, Michael, it does not tell me very much. The fact that you did not say you want to marry me because you love me is rather a big deal to me," countered Hope. "As I come to think of it, I cannot even remember one time when you have actually said you loved me."

"Now you really are being stupid, Hope. We have been engaged for over a year, and we are getting married in the spring. I am making you Mrs. Michael Gundersol, a position most women would die for, and what do I get instead? You walk out on me during the holidays with no way to reach you, and I am not supposed to question your loyalty. But you can question mine?

My mother, father, and I have accepted you as my future wife, even though you continue to disrespect my mother's advice and have taken off three times now to visit people who can do you nothing but harm. My father has had to call in some pretty big favors in order to keep your birth mother's legal problems out of the local press. Don't you understand that we cannot afford to be connected to such people, and yet you refuse to co-operate in any way? Do you really want to continue this discussion about who it is that is really being the disloyal one in this relationship?" Seeing that familiar look of wilting come over Hope, he knew she was again beginning to surrender her will to his and closed with, "Hope, I know you have always felt less than whole because you were adopted. I understand that you don't feel worthy of someone like me loving you, and so you always need extra reassurances. Hope, you need to understand that your lack of self-confidence can be tedious and makes you a little too needy sometimes. You do need to work on that issue, but right now we need to get going. Go get your coat and meet me at the car."

Hope stood there trying to figure out what just happened. Again, he had taken a challenge directed at him and turned it into an indictment of her; a reflection on her self-doubt because of her adoption. Adjusting her coat collar as she looked in the mirror, Hope asked, "Am I really that broken? Am I truly so needy that I demand constant reassurances from him and that this neediness is what is making him withdraw from me?" One quick beep of his horn signaled she was taking too long, so Hope grabbed her purse, checked for her house key, closed the door behind her and determined, "I need to be less needy tonight; I'm just not so sure how to go about it."

The hour-long drive to the Los Angeles Marriott was quiet. Michael reviewed his canned speech several times before turning on the radio, trying to avoid a repeat of their earlier conversation. As they pulled into the underground parking garage, he slid a placard with his name on it into the corner of his windshield so the parking attendant would see that he was entitled to VIP parking. Directed to the second-level parking garage, he pulled his car into the empty space right next to his parents' Mercedes. Seeing a photographer standing by the elevator, Michael hurried around the car, opened Hope's door, and helped her out. He then whispered quietly in her ear, "I'm sorry about our conversation earlier, Hope. You know I love you, don't you?" Michael knew the photographer was sliding around the support post to get a better shot. Knowing this photo would make it into the morning column; he waited until the guy was in place to plant his kiss.

Unaware of this ruse, Hope took his action as sincere and enjoyed this infrequent show of affection from him and allowed him to guide her toward the elevator. Tonight she was not going to question his motives. She was not going to drive them both crazy with questions and demand reassurances. She knew she needed to grow up and stop all of this second guessing.

The evening went as smoothly as could be expected, considering Mrs. Gundersol would never air her dirty laundry in public. Although honey was dripping from her lips, ice would not have melted on her tongue. Hope had become accustomed to this type of behavior from her, but her duplicity always stung. Her job tonight was merely to sit quietly, sharing no opinions and drawing as little attention as possible. She was simply

Michael's significant other tonight—although she never felt very significant at these affairs. Other than when photos were being taken, he was scarcely around. She tried walking the room with him but found it mind-numbing. After Michael had answered the same question ten times, she found herself mimicking his pat answers in her head. Then Hope considered how she would have answered that same question with a real sense of purpose—something she always found missing in his answers. Eventually, Hope found herself sitting back at the table playing with her coffee cup, hoping her watch was just broken. Michael seldom stayed long at these events, but tonight felt endless; she wanted only to go home.

Tired of waiting, Hope grabbed her purse and headed for the ladies' room to freshen up her lipstick, anything to fill the time. She had finished washing her hands when something rather strange happened. A woman who had followed her into the ladies' room had taken a seat by the window and had openly stared at Hope as she had applied her lipstick. By her attire, Hope reasoned the woman had not come from the event, and she obviously did not work at the Marriott either. Hope tried to ignore her and go about her business, but she could feel this woman's cold stare boring into her. Trying to get a quick glimpse of her in the mirror, Hope wondered, *"Could she be a reporter? I need to be careful. Michael is always warning me to be careful of their tricks and not to say anything that can be taken out of context."* Hope finally slipped her lipstick back into her purse and started for the door, which was right beside this woman. Trying to appear casual, Hope nodded and smiled as she said, "Good evening."

Never changing her expression, the woman muttered something under her breath. It was evident that she did not care to hide her disgust, which made Hope feel more than a bit nervous. People—even those who are just bystanders, as she obviously was—often have strange ideas about those in the public eye. Hope quickly slipped past the woman and made her way back to the ballroom where she would feel safe; albeit bored. By the time Michael was finally ready to leave, the woman's rude behavior was ancient history. Hope did not think to mention it to him on their way home.

CHAPTER 20

Hᴏᴘᴇ ᴡᴀꜱ ᴀɴxɪᴏᴜꜱ to return to work on Monday morning. The office was officially closed for the holidays, but she knew several managers would be there who simply could not stay away. She had not yet been entrusted with an office key but was certain she could gain entry this morning. She wanted to throw herself into the waiting project so she could stop thinking about Michael. Thinking about her husband-to-be should be a bride-to-be's normal dilemma, but nothing was normal about it. She had more questions than answers and since her conversation with her grandmother, she did not like any of the answers. As she pulled into the parking lot, she noticed Mr. Davenport's car was already there, as were several others. Knowing the receptionist would not be one of them, Hope sat in her car, writing out her list of thank-you note recipients and waited for someone with a key to pull into the parking lot.

Another manager came out of the side door and made his way to his car. Hope remained in her car. Two others had jumped into their cars so quickly and taken off she had no chance of reaching the door before it slammed shut behind them. She watched as he opened his trunk and removed several binders and started back toward the side door of the office. Hope quickly gathered up her purse and keys and made a dash for the same door. "Good morning. Mind if I slip in the door with you, Josh? I have some rewrites to do."

Josh held the door open and allowed Hope to enter, "Have a nice holiday, Hope?"

"Sure did," was all Hope was willing to offer before excusing herself and making a beeline to her office and closing the door behind her. She turned on her office light, removed the project copy from its folder and spread it out on her desk, but she could not stop going over Michael's cold remarks from the previous night. Noticing her boss's familiar red-inked notes in the margin meant he had been in her office recently. Hope reviewed his notes and tried to concentrate on the suggestions in the margin, but her eyes would not focus through her tears. Fearing someone might see her crying, Hope quickly dabbed away the tears and scolded herself, "Stop this right now. You always read too much into his behavior. Last night was not such a bad evening. Even Mr. and Mrs. Gundersol were nice to you. What more do you want? Michael keeps telling you to stop the fairytales and to grow up. Did you expect him to sweep you off your feet, carry you into another room and make mad, passionate love to you?" Hope turned and looked at her reflection in the mirror that hung above the credenza, "It wouldn't hurt. Is this how our marriage is going to be? Is he so focused on his political career that he doesn't need affection from me? Why am I supposed to make every effort to show him my love and support, but he doesn't have to do anything to convince me that he loves me? Why is this forgiveness thing such a one-way street?"

Squaring her shoulders and forcing a smile, Hope turned back to her desk, only to see her boss standing in the doorway. "Hope, what are you doing in the office? Didn't you go to Georgia for Christmas?" Noticing the glisten of tears in her eyes, Davenport asked, "Are you okay? You look a little upset. "

"I'm fine, Mr. Davenport, I think the jetlag is just hitting me this morning, but as soon as I get to work on this project I should be fine."

Wanting to change the subject, Hope asked, "I noticed that you added several additional points to your memorandum, and I was just starting to read through them. Is there anything else you wish to add before I begin?"

"No, Hope, I came into the office yesterday afternoon and went through all of your notes. I'd much rather be here working than being dragged around a mall. You'd think Christmas would drain my wife of the thrill of trekking through malls, but her energy is endless. I like the way your edits did not change the tone of my comments. When I saw you in your office, I wanted to stop by and tell you that you did an excellent job. Once you have gone over these last few additional comments, I think we will be ready to send this to the printer."

"Thank you, Mr. Davenport. I love working here. Once I have reviewed these last changes, I will put it on your desk so you can do a final perusal. However, the art department has not yet finished their inserts, so we will have to hold off sending this to the printer until they get that to me. Since tomorrow is New Year's Eve, the printers will not even start on this until Thursday." Davenport just smiled as he went on his way, leaving Hope to her work.

By lunchtime the biggest project she had ever attempted was on Davenport's desk, and she knew he was very satisfied with her work. Hope climbed into her car and headed for the mall, feeling better than she had when her workday had started. Needing to replenish her supply of thank-you notes, she made her way to her favorite stationery store on the second level of the mall. As she entered the store, she pulled out the thank-you note list she had made that morning and noticed something rather odd about it. At the top were the names of her mom and dad and two siblings. That was not odd. They had always been at the top of every Christmas thank-you note list she could remember. However, the next several names—Lisa and Ben, Benny, Mrs. Reiner, Gladys, Susan and Scott, Ruth and, of course, Mr. and Mrs. Thomas, her gracious holiday hosts—were quite different this year. She could not help but smile as she read through this list. "They are my family, and I can't wait to be with them again." Her eyes drifted to the bottom of her list and noticed she had just written

"The Gundersols"—not Michael's name and his parents' names. Michael should have been at the very top of her list, but she knew she did not want him there. That thought bothered her. Actually, she realized she did not want him on her list at all. These days there was very little about him or his parents for which she felt thankful.

As Hope lifted her purchase off the counter and headed for the door, she had a strange feeling of being watched. Securing her wallet deeper into her purse and tucking her purse close to her body, she lengthened her steps and made a quick right turn as she cleared the doorway. She remembered the coffee house was only two doors up the street and made her way quickly to one of the tables toward the back of the shop. Positioning herself with her back against the wall, Hope tried to look calm as she studied every person entering the shop. This was the second time in one hour she had experienced this strange feeling. No one seemed interested in her, so after a few moments Hope gathered up her purchases and made her way to the mall exit.

Feeling calmer as she reached her car, Hope unlocked her door as she reprimanded herself, "What a drama queen you are, Hope! Who cares enough about you to be following you around?" Once in her car, Hope started her engine, then adjusted the rearview mirror to check her lipstick. "You silly little girl. Michael would make such a big deal over your behavior, if you were foolish enough to tell him." Straightening up the mirror, Hope caught a glimpse of a woman standing between the two cars directly behind her. Straining to get a better look, she was certain she had seen this woman before, but where? Putting her car into reverse, Hope reached up and made sure her car door was locked before backing up much farther than necessary in order to clear the parking space. She wanted to get a better look at this woman who was standing between the two cars, without any packages or making any attempt to gain entry into either car. Just as Hope had her car in position, the woman quickly dashed in the opposite direction, making sure her face was turned away from Hope.

By the time she arrived back at her office, Hope had convinced herself this was simply a woman who was disoriented about where she had parked her vehicle and was not spying on her. After lunch on Mondays had become Hope's regular time to call Lisa's answering machine in Jefferson, Georgia. She would usually jabber on about whatever had gone on during her weekend, but not today. Lisa was still on her honeymoon and would not even get home to Jefferson until after New Year's. Tapping the receiver, Hope really wanted to call and chat with her mom. "It is funny how quickly you come to depend on another person. I wonder if she and Ben are having a good time at the Old Plantation? Ben is sure crazy about her, and she turns to mush whenever she is around him. I am so glad they found each other."

Digging through her purse, Hope was certain her pocket phonebook was in there somewhere. Then she remembered stuffing it into the upper pocket of her overnight case when she was packing to come home. "I should have unpacked yesterday and put my little phonebook back into my purse. I have Grandma Reiner's phone number in it, but now I don't have it with me."

Hope quickly jotted down a reminder note to put her phonebook back in her purse, slid the note into her pocket and headed down the hall to meet with the art team. As soon as she entered the conference room and saw Judy, the art team coordinator, Hope remembered where she had seen the woman at the mall. Seeing Judy standing there jogged her memory because the two looked so similar. She was certain that the woman at her car was the same one who had entered the ladies' lounge at the Marriot the night before. Hope wondered, "Why would a reporter care to follow me around? The next time I see her, I am going to go right up to her and tell her to stop following me." Then remembering Michael's admonition not ever to talk to anyone, Hope decided it best to simply avoid this snoopy reporter.

Around 4:00 Judy stopped by Hope's office and asked, "Are you just about finished, Hope? You and I are the last ones here, and you don't have a key."

Hope grabbed her purse and turned off her office light. "I'm sorry! Were you waiting for me to be finished? I didn't even think about how the alarm and door would be secured." Hope followed Judy to the main entrance and waited while Judy set the alarm and locked the door. In late December, it starts getting dark by 4:00, so the security lights were already on in the parking lot. As they turned the corner of the building, Hope noticed three cars were in the parking lot. Judy's car was next to the building with her car parked beside it, but the third car was parked against the back fence and backed into the space. Hope did not mention this fact to Judy. Unable to see the driver from this distance, Hope noted the car's type and color and then quickly climbed into her car, locked the door and started her engine. She wanted to make sure she was able to follow Judy out of the parking lot and onto the busy street before that car had a chance to come near her.

That evening as she and Michael drove to the Gundersol home, Hope decided to mention this strange woman. "Do you have reporters following you around?" she casually ventured.

"Sure, it is just part of the political game." He responded with a tone that warned Hope he was not interested in this line of questions.

Ignoring his tone, Hope continued, "Well, some woman reporter has been following me around, and I do not like it. She was in the ladies' lounge at the Marriot last night, she was standing near my car at the mall today, and then I know it must have been her sitting in her car in my work parking lot when I left tonight. What in the world does she think she will learn from me?"

Looking puzzled toward Hope, his tone quickly changed as he asked, "Are you sure it was the same woman? Also, what makes you think she is a reporter? Did she question you?"

"No," Hope replied. "Besides you told me not to talk to reporters, remember? Who else could be following me around? How can you stand this type of invasion of your privacy? Doesn't it get old?"

"It sure does," he chided, "but I've found ways to lose them when I really want my privacy. In this business, you need reporters. It's when they stop following you around that you had better start to worry. So if she didn't ask you any questions, what makes you think she is a reporter?"

"Who else could it be? I'm going to start watching for her car so I don't get surprised by her again. At least it should be easy to spot. It is a maroon Chrysler convertible with a white top. I'd suspect there are not many of those on the road." Hope was so busy congratulating herself on keeping down the drama queen routine and simply stating facts that she did not notice how quiet Michael had become.

As soon as they pulled into his parents' driveway, Michael excused himself saying, "I need to make a phone call, Hope. I should have confirmed our reservations for tomorrow night before I picked you up tonight. You go ahead into the house, and I will be there in a few minutes."

It was bad enough walking into the lioness' den with Michael; having to do it alone was treacherous. "I don't mind waiting here with you. Isn't there an extension right inside the garage door?"

His reaction took Hope by surprise. "No, I said for you to go on in. I don't need your babysitting me while I make a phone call."

"Michael, you know I don't like to be alone with your parents. Why can't I just wait for you?"

His tone became both ugly and threatening. "Because I told you to go inside, Hope. Why do you always have to argue with my instructions? Can't I ever count on you to do exactly what you are told?"

Hope lifted her jacket and purse out of the back seat and headed for the front door. She knew this was something more than forgetting to confirm dinner reservations, but when Michael became like this, there was no talking to him. Hope was ushered into the large solarium, Mrs. Gundersol's favorite room. The city views from the floor-to-ceiling wraparound windows were truly impressive, and since all of her Christmas decorations were still up, the room took on a winter-wonderland atmosphere. The lovely decor would have been spectacular if not for the fact that Estelle Gundersol was sitting center stage and immediately barked, "Where is Michael?"

"He needed to make a phone call but will be right in." Hope knew better than to do more than answer the questions posed to her. She wondered who would be joining them for dinner but knew better than to ask.

"Harold," Estelle barked at her husband, "take Hope's drink order and then go find him. Clint and Victoria will be here any minute, and Michael needs to be in here to greet them."

Hope quickly waved her hand, declining a before-dinner drink. "Mr. Gundersol, I believe Michael is on the house extension in the garage."

Without saying a word, Estelle walked over to the house phone setting on her beautiful mahogany desk, lifted the receiver, cupped her hand over the mouthpiece and listened in on the conversation. The look on Estelle's face as she overheard her son's private conversation scared Hope. Slamming down the receiver made it obvious that Estelle did not care that her son would know someone had been listening and barked, "Harold, go out there and tell Michael to get off the phone and get in here now."

Hope watched as Mr. Gundersol set his drink on the bar and headed out the side door toward the garage. She pondered the difference in both Mr. Gundersol and Michael whenever Estelle was present. Both men were strong, determined, take-charge kind of men, pushing their weight around and enjoying it; but around Estelle, they both changed into meek, submissive little boys, afraid of making her angry. Hope studied Estelle's face as she began rifling through some papers on the desk. *What kind of person does it take to force such strong-minded men into such passive followers?* Hope suspected that Estelle had never lost a single argument with either one of these men—or anyone else for that matter.

As soon as Michael walked into the house, Estelle ordered him to follow her to the back den. Even with the door closed, she was obviously giving him a tongue lashing. Seeing their guests pulling into the driveway, Harold quickly knocked on the den door. All three of them came walking back into the foyer as if nothing had happened. Smiles all around was the order of the day. Harold graciously led the guests into the solarium and played bartender. Estelle, still quite upset, but knowing how to play her part well, kept the conversation flowing. Well-trained at following his mother's lead, Michael made sure their guests remained the center of the conversation.

Accustomed to being ignored during these VIP gatherings and daring not to join in, Hope did her best to feign interest in the conversation. On numerous occasions a guest had turned to her and asked her opinion, but having no idea how Michael would want that question answered, Hope had learned how to deflect these questions. Michael would quickly answer on her behalf. Once or twice, she had not been able to sidestep a direct question and gave answers she had heard Michael give on occasion. She had learned later that although she had given the correct answer, she had given it to the wrong person. Michael was always playing both sides of the aisle and how was she to know which answer went with which side? Therefore, Michael warned her about answering any questions that were not related to the weather.

Hope found that when you are not engaged in the conversation, it is difficult to feign interest, causing the dinner meal to become tedious beyond measure. Tonight this was especially true, given how the evening had started. Having sat through two years of these monotonous dinners, Hope was astutely aware of all three of the Gundersol mannerisms. Casual guests would not pick up on them, but hundreds of these meals to her credit had finally made Hope rather an expert on all of their little foibles. Estelle's strained smile, accompanied by a slight twitching of her right eye, meant Estelle was boiling mad under her calm façade. The fact that she was pushing all of the discussion topics toward Harold meant she needed him to carry the majority of the conversation for fear of breaking her practiced calm façade. Usually, Estelle was always the center of every conversation at her table—but not tonight.

Harold, like Hope, had not been in the den earlier that evening. All he knew was what he saw on Estelle's face when she opened the den door, and that was enough.

Michael seemed more distracted than usual tonight. He was having trouble holding up his end of the conversation. More than once he excused himself from the table, something Estelle usually forbade, but tonight seemed to actually encourage. Each time Michael returned to the table, he seemed rattled and unfocused. Hope noticed a slight bead of sweat at his temple—even though the temperature in the house would not merit it.

As the evening came to a close and after the guests were gone, Hope knew that whatever had started with that phone call would not be discussed in front of her. The Gundersols, although brutal toward each other, never aired their dirty laundry in front of "outsiders." Tonight was one of those nights Hope was glad to be counted as an outsider and could not wait to get home. She was certain that Michael would never explain tonight's power struggle, and she was right. The drive home was quiet. Hope found herself actually feeling sorry for him when he turned into her driveway and said, "I made a few calls tonight. That woman in the maroon Chrysler works for a gossip magazine. She cannot be trusted and has been known to make up things when she cannot get an exact quote. Hope, under no circumstances are you even to acknowledge her. If you see her again, just walk away, do not talk with her, and do not even listen to her if she tries to talk with you. Do you understand me? Now get in the house, and I will call you tomorrow. I have several more phone calls to make tonight, so I need to get going."

CHAPTER 21

❧

NEW YEAR'S EVE morning began early for Hope. Her private line ringing startled her out of a much needed slumber, but forgetting the three-hour time change, Hope dove for the receiver, expecting to hear her mother's much anticipated voice on the other end. "Hi, Mom, how is the honeymoon going?"

Hope was startled to hear Michael's irritated voice on the other end of the line, "Hope, it is me. Something has come up, and I will not be able to escort you to that New Year's Eve bash after all. Some out-of-town business just came up, and I will be gone for three days."

The flat tone of his voice, coupled with this obviously practiced little speech, caused Hope more questions than answers. Without thinking, she questioned him. "Michael, what kind of out-of-town business could you possibly have over New Year's?"

The tone in his voice became angry and impatient, and Hope immediately knew she had crossed the line. "What do you know about my business? How dare you question my motives! I do not answer to you."

Uncharacteristically, Hope took the safety of this phone call to voice one of her longstanding issues. "I know, Michael. You only answer to your mother, right? And by the way, I did not say a word about your motives, but now that you mention them, should I be worried?"

"Hope, I don't know what has gotten into you lately, but I don't like it. You used to be such a cooperative partner, but now you question everything I do. I have a lot of responsibilities on me, and I cannot have you second-guessing my every move. We are getting married in three months, and then we will proceed right into the main season of my campaign run. I will not tolerate a wife of mine not giving me her absolute support. Do you hear me, Hope?"

"Then maybe we should consider postponing the wedding for now. I have no control over the trial back in Georgia, and you seem to be so focused on your business, you don't really have any time for me anyway." Hope stopped short of making this a clean break. She so wanted to simply scream "Forget it," but then who would be there for him in his time of need?

"Hope, there is no postponing this wedding. Why is that always your comeback? Eight months ago, you couldn't wait to become Mrs. Michael Gundersol. We were supposed to get married last weekend, remember? But then you decided to take off and go looking for your long-lost birth mother—a decision all of us warned you against making. But oh, no, Hope knew better. I have put up with all of your stubborn willful behavior, believing you only needed to grow up a little, but I am done with it. You better come to your senses and join the team or else."

"Or else what? Will *you* call off the wedding? I doubt that. And are we not talking about *our* wedding and marriage? So what team am I supposed to join? The Gundersol political team, perhaps? I do not believe I am cut out for your family business. I cannot face a lifetime of this." Taking a deep breath and steadying herself, Hope finally stated the obvious, "Michael, I still care about you, but I no longer wish to marry you. The cost is way too high for its seeming benefits. You need someone who likes the Gundersol lifestyle; I do not. So Michael, you are free, and so am I. The wedding is off." The absolute wash of freedom at saying these words out loud surprised and energized Hope. Nothing he could say would now dissuade her from calling off this wedding, so Hope simply placed the receiver back on the base and ended their last conversation.

Checking the time, Hope decided to jump into the shower before calling Grandma Reiner. She knew her grandmother would be pleased that she had finally called off her wedding and could not wait to share the news with her.

As Hope was drying off, she heard the house phone ringing and wondered who would be calling this time of morning. Five minutes later, that answer was obvious. Hope stepped out of the bathroom right into the face of her mother, "Hope, what is this about your calling off the wedding?"

Pushing past her and heading toward her bedroom, Hope responded, "I see Estelle wasted no time putting you to work this morning, Mother."

"Of course Estelle would call me with this kind of news," Jean's response was both defensive and angry. "What are you thinking, Hope? You are ruining your chance of a great future with Michael. That man is going places, and he wants to share that journey with you as his wife."

"No, he doesn't, Mother, and that's the point. He does not know how to share. He does not share his business, his goals, his dreams, and certainly not his emotions. I have tried to be understanding. I know his mother rules that family with an iron fist..." then turning toward her mother, Hope added, "among other people, but I am convinced that he really does not love me."

"That is absolutely preposterous, Hope. He has stood by you for two years, waiting for you to grow up enough to take you as his bride. We have all tried to be patient while you took off and looked for your birth mother. He understood how important that was to you, didn't he? We changed the wedding date to accommodate you, remember? Estelle told me that her son is devastated over this breakup. He loves you, Hope. Michael is still a young man, even though he has all of this responsibility riding on his shoulders. What is it you want from him? Don't you think you are being just a little bit selfish right now?"

"Mother, I know he is under a lot of strain now. I also know how much pressure Estelle puts on him as well. The idea of that woman controlling and dominating my life from now on is intolerable to me. I always felt my job was to make him feel loved and cared for—for himself—not just because he is a Gundersol. I've watched how his parents treat him, how they demand so much more from him than he is actually capable of doing. I know someone has to love that man and show him he has worth beyond the family checkbook. You and Michael's mother convinced me that was my job, and I tried! I really did."

Jean pleaded, "Hope, he is a wonderful man. If I were willing to have a talk with Estelle about backing off a little and giving you two some time to work things out, would you at least consider giving him another chance?"

"A chance to do what, Mother? Give him ten more chances to show me all the ways he doesn't respect me or my opinions? How about ten more ways he can show me he doesn't love me?" Deciding to put all her cards on the table, Hope added, "Mother, do you realize that he and I have seriously dated for two years, and he has never even tried to make a move on me? Do you realize that we have been engaged for a year and that I am still a virgin? About a year ago I was actually convinced that he might be gay, but one night when he had had too much to drink, he told me about an affair he had had during college; as a matter of fact, he got rather graphic about his escapade. I found myself feeling rather jealous of the girl. Either he was lying then or he is lying now. Either way, I have never been the beneficiary of his physical affection."

Not knowing how to respond to this level of honesty from her daughter, Jean scrambled for something to say. "Hope, maybe Michael is just trying to show you, his future wife, the honor and respect you deserve. Maybe the fact that he is showing such self-control is exactly the way he is showing you how much he does love you. Maybe that kind of self-control is why he gets so irritable with you sometimes. Did you ever think of it that way?"

"No, it never occurred to me that he was doing that, Mother. So if that is true, then Estelle is not the only woman in his life who is putting undue pressure on him. Maybe that is why he was so angry when we had to postpone the wedding. Could that be why he withdraws from me whenever I try to get close to him?"

"Maybe, Hope. Don't you think you owe it to him to reconsider this? I will talk to Estelle, and you talk to Michael, okay?"

As Jean closed the door behind her, Hope fell onto her bed in tears and cried, "Just fifteen minutes of freedom is all I had." Hope longed to return to the shower, if only to experience a few more moments of that wonderful feeling of self-determination. "Why is it my job to rescue him? Why must I be the bigger person here? Why does my mother seem to care more about his future over her own daughter's?"

Sitting up on her bed, Hope replayed the conversation with her mother. "She will talk with Estelle, right. When has Estelle ever listened to my mother? Even if she is successful, that won't last long—not with that woman." Looking longingly at the telephone next to her bed, Hope decided not to call her grandmother; after all, she had nothing good to report; besides, she remembered her grandmother's reaction when Hope shared this same concern with her. What a different reaction from that of her mother's. "Hope, personally I am glad you are still a virgin. With all your doubts about this Michael, I would think you would be happy that you have not taken this relationship that far. If you end up breaking it off with him, it is best you have not shared your most precious gift with someone who obviously does not care enough about you to appreciate that gift."

Hope curled up with her pillow and tried to sleep. She wished her mother would show the same care for her as she did for Michael; but in any event, she needed to make some serious decisions about her life, but she was too tired to do so right then. With a sigh, Hope rolled over and pulled the covers up over her head, "Tomorrow is soon enough."

CHAPTER 22

———— ⚜ ————

Lisa's New Year's Eve morning started quite differently than her daughter's. A gentle tap on the door signaled their morning coffee was setting outside the door of their honeymoon suite. Ben grabbed his robe, cracked open the door barely wide enough to lift the silver tray that held a carafe of freshly brewed coffee and two china cups. He poured two cups of coffee, walked around the bed, set Lisa's coffee within her reach, bent down to kiss his bride and said, "Coffee is here, Lisa. Time to rise and shine."

Not yet comfortable with letting Ben see her in all her morning glory, Lisa slid into the bathroom, brushed her teeth and hair, then slipped into her new silk robe that Gladys had given her as a honeymoon gift. Never one for wearing much makeup, Lisa was used to being seen without it so just a quick touch of lipstick was all she needed to feel quite dressed up.

Lisa picked up her coffee cup and joined her husband on the balcony. Although quite chilly this early in the morning, the view was well worth the discomfort. Ben patted the empty seat next to him on the two-seater lounge and tucked the woolen throw around his bride. "What a beautiful morning this is!"

Lisa snuggled close to Ben, sipped her coffee and said, "Ben, it scares me to think about how close we came to never meeting. Do you know how much I love you?"

"Lisa, not nearly as much as I love you. You and I were meant for each other. I don't know how, but I know God would have used something to bring us together, and that is enough for me."

"What is on the agenda for today, Ben? I know we have that huge dinner party and concert this evening, but what will we do to occupy our day?"

Ben waited a second before answering, then smiled, "Lisa, I know we said these four days were just for us, but I know you are dying to talk to Hope. I wouldn't mind checking in on Benny, so how about we take a walk down to the dining room, have a bite of breakfast and then find a private phone in the lobby and make a few phone calls?"

Beaming with delight, Lisa responded, "That's a great idea, Ben. I know Scott and Susan have Benny's New Year's Day all mapped out, but he will still be home until at least 11:00. I'm not sure what Hope's plans are, but I can at least leave her a message to let her know we are thinking of her."

During breakfast Ben decided to bring up a topic that had been bothering him ever since the first day he knew he was going to ask Lisa to marry him. "Lisa, have you thought about what we should do about Gladys? I hate the idea of her living all alone now that you will be moving in with Benny and me."

"Ben, Gladys, Ruth and I talked about this way before you actually asked me to marry you. As soon as I suspected our friendship was moving in that direction, I told Gladys I was determined to remain single if it meant that I would have to abandon her at this time of her life."

A puzzled look crossed Ben's face, then that familiar chuckle Lisa had come to love, "So obviously, you settled this issue without me, right?"

"Actually, Ruth Bascom came up with the answer." Lisa chuckled. "She isn't getting any younger either, and her neighborhood is getting a little seedy. Now that her eyes are causing her trouble, she fears she might not be able to drive much longer. Her house is too far away from the bakery to walk, so Ruth offered to sell her home and move in with Gladys. That way she will be close to the bakery, and neither she nor Gladys will be alone. They both knew it would have to be this way before I would feel free to accept your proposal."

Ben leaned back in his chair and said, "You mean I have been worrying about something you women have already taken care of?"

"Ben, there was no way Gladys was going to allow me to use her as my excuse for walking away from you. She knew my loyalty to her would have been a deal breaker for me. Ruth is putting her house on the market soon after the holidays, and she will move in after we get my things cleared out."

Ben took hold of his bride's hand and said, "I love it when a plan comes together."

Lisa smiled and quoted Jeremiah 29:11, *"For I know the plans I have for you," declares the Lord, "plans to prosper you and not to harm you, plans to give you a future and a hope."* Ben, Gladys quoted that verse to me every day during my recovery. At first I resented it. Eventually, I came to believe in it. Now I am living it. God does keep His promises—if we will simply trust Him."

After breakfast they touched base with Benny. "Dad, I'm having a great time. Scott and Harry are taking me to a professional wrestling match at the big arena this afternoon. Tonight they are getting a babysitter and Scott, Susan, Harry, Carol Anne and I are going to the midnight showing of the new *Rocky* movie. You don't mind, do you, Dad? I know you and I were going to go see it together, but I can watch it twice."

"I don't mind, Benny," Ben reassured him. "We watched all three of the other *Rocky* movies two or three times, remember? It never gets old, right?"

"Right, Dad. Are you and Lisa...*Mom*...coming back tomorrow?"

Ben practically moaned at the thought of ending this wonderful time alone with his new bride. "Yes, we are, Benny. We should be back around 1:00, so you need to be packed and ready. Gladys and Ruth went back to Jefferson yesterday, right?"

"Yes, they left yesterday morning. I'll be ready well before you get here, Dad. Have a great New Year's Eve, and I'll see you guys tomorrow."

Glad that Benny was having such a great time, Ben handed the phone to Lisa so she could call Hope. "I'm almost afraid to call her, Ben. I never know which side of the rollercoaster I will experience with her. One day she is madly in love with Michael, and the next she is ready to call off the wedding. One day I am riding high, feeling like she has made a good decision, and the next conversation I am plummeting down the other side, despairing over Hope's indecision. Is this what every parent experiences, or is this simply the consequences of not having been in her life for the first twenty-two years?"

Ben smiled and suggested, "Lisa, it might be a little bit of both. You don't feel right speaking out because you don't think you have the right. Lisa, I've heard lots of parents talk about how hard it was watching their grown kids make bad decisions. I'm talking about parents with good kids and parents with rebellious kids. Kids are kids, and they have wills of their own. Sometimes they just won't listen, and the parents have to love their kids either way. No one ever said being a parent is easy."

"I'm learning that," Lisa agreed. "I guess I used to daydream about how my little girl's life was playing out, and it was always perfect and wonderful. It was obviously much better than it would have been living with me, and for that I will be forever grateful. I know I made the right decision. I gave her life, and then I gave her a chance at happiness. She is an adult and has the right to blaze her own trail in life. I just wish she knew that God loves her and that she can turn to Him for guidance."

"Lisa, I don't believe in coincidences. Your daughter came back here just in time to save your life, right? She knows a family is here who loves her and wants the best for her. She heard the gospel several times. She heard it, and she witnessed it in your life, in Gladys' life and even in Ruth's life. There is no way that girl could miss the truth that God is in the business of making people whole again, that He loves us, forgives us and wants to bring wholeness and healing to people who will simply respond to His love. She heard that message loud and clear so we simply need to continue praying for her and be there for her."

Lisa pondered his thoughts for a moment before replying, "Ben, I'm just not sure it is a good idea for me to call her right now. I do not want to risk spoiling our last day here, and I don't think I could help it if the phone call goes badly."

"Lisa," Ben counseled gently as he handed over the phone, "do you really think not calling her will avoid that? You are worried about her so just call her, and we will handle whatever comes. Avoiding it will not make it go away."

As Lisa dialed the operator to place the long-distance call and charge it to their room, she smiled at Ben and said, "That is another reason I love you, Ben. You always encourage me to do the right thing—even when it is hard."

Lisa was surprised to hear her daughter's voice on the other end of the line, "Hello, Hope. Ben and I are just checking in. We wanted to make sure you got home safe and sound and to tell you how much it meant to both of us having you at our wedding."

Ben sat there as proud as could be listening to Lisa maneuver through the conversation, avoiding pointed questions but showing real interest in what her daughter was sharing. "Your mother means well, Sweetie. She must really believe that Michael is the right man for you."

Ben watched as Lisa's face took on a look of real concern as she said, "But Hope, you are the one who will have to live with this decision—not her. I don't know Michael at all, so I don't feel comfortable giving you advice. Except I do want to say that if you have doubts, then it is best that you call off the wedding until your doubts have been cleared up."

Lisa listened patiently as Hope went through all of the reasons she did not feel right calling off the wedding. "Sweetie, I think you must have misunderstood what Ruth was saying about forgiveness. As a matter of fact, I am quite certain she would not have meant that. Forgiveness does not mean you do not have the right to set boundaries in your life. You can forgive him for what he has done to you without allowing him to continue to mistreat you. You do not have to marry him to prove you have forgiven him. I know this for a fact because both Ruth and Gladys have been talking to me about this very subject for months now. You see, I am someone who has been forgiven so much, as you well know. For the past eleven years, God has been working in my life, first restoring me back to health and then teaching me how to love and be loved. He forgave my past and has given me a future.

"But I just could not accept the idea of ever forgiving my mother for what she did to me. For years I refused to even discuss this topic because it was too painful a thought. How could God ask this of me? So God did what He always does; He kept loving me and growing me into the person who would, one day, allow Him to take me to the very place I feared the most—to my most painful hurts. I realized these were the ones I needed to hand over to Him so my healing could become complete.

"You see, Sweetie, forgiveness is not having to accept the same old behavior from someone who is hurting you or mistreating you. Forgiveness is not having to say that what the person did wasn't really awful. Forgiveness is not saying that they are free from God's discipline for having done what they did."

"Then what is forgiveness, Mother?"

"Hope, forgiveness is telling God that He is God, and I am not. Forgiveness is finally letting go of the right to seek revenge or demand retribution for the wrongs you hold against that person. Forgiveness is actually an action you take before God, rather than before that person.

"Judging is different than assessing that someone has done something wrong. Judging does include that, but it goes much further. Judging includes demanding or petitioning God to take punitive action against this person—as if we have the right to order God to punish someone upon our request. Doing this is man's way of playing God. Thinking we have the wisdom to decide another person's punishment, desiring to withhold any chance of offering God's mercy is something only a perfect and wise God can do. Every time we stand in judgment of another, we are playing God."

"So I can forgive him but stand my ground and refuse to marry him? He thinks that if I refuse to marry him, I have not really forgiven him."

"He would like you to believe that, Hope, but that is not true. Forgiving him is simply releasing any claim you have against him. It does not require that he accept it or understand it; you just have to extend it first to God and then to him. What he does with that forgiveness is up to him, but you are then free of the burden."

Lisa hesitated for just a moment then decided to share her own struggle with this subject. "You know, Sweetie, I'm saying this as much for me as for you. I have held onto my mother's offenses my whole life, thinking I could never forgive her. I thought forgiving her would mean she would never be held accountable for what she did. I also thought forgiving her meant I was saying what she did wasn't really all that bad, and I could never do that. To be honest, for years I would not let Gladys or Ruth even get close to this topic because my hatred of my mother was so strong. I wanted to hold onto my right to demand justice for all I went through."

"Mother, I can certainly understand that. Your mother was horrid," Hope affirmed.

"Yes, she was, Hope, but as long as I hold onto my rights, I also hold onto my hurts. My not forgiving my mother does not hurt her; it hurts me. But Hope, even if I forgive her, it does not mean I have to prove it to the world by letting her back into my inner circle and continue to mistreat me, and that is the point. Forgiveness is simply letting go of your right to demand justice. It appears that we both need to do a little forgiving now that we understand what it really means."

"I guess so, Mom," Hope replied without much conviction.

"Hope, doing right will not always be easy, right? But Sweetie, for the long haul, doing right is easier than doing what's easy and living with a wrong for the rest of your life. Believe me, I have done both. I have to get going, but just know that Ben and I are praying for you as you decide what you will do."

Lisa joked as she hung up the phone, "I'm glad God has a plan here because I sure don't. I know what I want for her, but I don't get to make the decisions in Hope's life. But I do know one thing —there are no coincidences in this world. I can see God is working in my girl's life, and I can trust Him."

Ben stood up, took Lisa by the hand and suggested, "Why don't we take a few minutes to look around this beautiful old plantation. Scott and Susan have been coming here for years and love it. I think that lovely private dining room over there is where Scott told me he asked Susan to marry him. Every anniversary since, they have had their special dinner in that room, so let's go take a peek at it."

Ben slid the ten-foot-tall hand-carved mahogany pocket doors wide open and allowed Lisa to walk into the old plantation study first. Bookcases filled with period-appropriate books gathered over the years and donated to the plantation lined the walls. Sprinkled among these books were black and white photos of the painstaking labor required to restore this old plantation house back to what it once was. A plaque on the wall told about the team of investors who had purchased the house from the original owners in the early nineteen twenties. That plantation had been boarded up for over sixty years after being ransacked and left in ruins during the raid on Atlanta toward the end of the War Between the States.

As Lisa read the plaque her eyes fell on an all-too-familiar name, and she cried out, "Oh, Ben, do you know what this place is? Look!"

Ben leaned down and looked at the name Lisa was pointing to and read out loud, "This plantation was owned and operated by the Stewart Family from 1795 to 1865 when the Civil War broke the back of slavery, and the family could no longer maintain the property. Returning home from being wounded at Savannah, Mr. Charles Stewart, the second master of the plantation, simply had the windows boarded up and lived the rest of his life at the home of his only daughter, Elizabeth, some five miles away. It is said that he never returned to the old place but could not part with it. For fifteen years after his death, the investors pleaded with Miss Elizabeth to sell the place so it could be restored before it was too late. However, knowing her father's wishes, she refused to sell as well. On her deathbed, she gave her son permission to sell the property but only if it was to these investors who had promised to bring it back to all of its original glory."

"Ben, do you know what this means? This is the Stewart Plantation."

"Yeah, so?" Ben studied his wife's eyes as she kept repeating this over and over. "Obviously this means something special to you. Are you going to keep me in suspense or are you going to tell me what is making you so very excited?"

"Ben, the Bascom family were slaves on this very plantation. Ruth's husband, Tobias, wrote a book about his grandfather and his sisters who were all born on this plantation. Ruth told me that in the mid-fifties Tobias worried that, because they had no children to pass the family history on to, all of his family history was going to die with him. She said that Tobias had promised his great aunts that he would write a book about his great-grandmother, Hannah, and her three children. Ben, I've read Tobias' book. I simply never connected this Bed and Breakfast with Tobias.

"Tobias was born up in Harlem, New York, but because Harlem was a dangerous place for young black boys, the seven-year-old was sent back to Atlanta to be reared by The Sisters, as they were affectionately called. Ms. Pearl and Ms. Ruby always called him 'Toby-Boy,' out of respect for their older brother. Toby-Boy grew up hearing stories about life as a slave on this plantation. These stories were so much a part of his young life, he had a really good picture of life on this plantation. A few years back Ruth allowed me to read the story, and it is a wonderful read. Tobias called it *–Treasure in a Tin Box.*"

"Lisa, do you think Ruth would allow me to read Tobias's story? Maybe you and I can help her get it published someday. After hearing Gladys tell her life story the other day, knowing how important Tobias is to our lives, I think we owe it to him to get his family story out there so others can read it. After all, if Tobias had not loved Gladys through her anger, she might have lived her whole life in that stew of anger. If that had happened, there would have been no wonderful Aunt Gladys and Ruth Bascom to come alongside of you when you needed the help. I don't even want to imagine my life without you. So you see, we both owe Tobias a huge debt of gratitude."

Perusing the shelves of the library, Lisa's eyes lit on a leather-bound ledger high on one of the shelves. "Ben, can you reach that ledger on the top shelf?"

Ben spotted a folded library ladder leaning against the side panel of the bookcase, pulled it out and climbed up to the top shelf and lifted down the dusty leather-bound ledger. Afraid she would not be allowed to open it if she asked permission, Lisa quickly undid the leather ties that held it closed and laid it open on the closest available tabletop. As she suspected, this ledger was Master Stewart's slave log showing purchases, trades, births and deaths of all his property. Lisa scanned the names, hoping to find what she was looking for.

Turning the brittle yellow pages with care, both Ben and Lisa searched for the name Tobias, Pearl or Ruby. Halfway down the sixth page was the entry for which she was searching: Boy Tobias, born to Esther, the house cook, June 25, 1847—healthy.

Five pages later was another entry: Twin girls, Pearl and Ruby, born to Esther, the house cook, October 10, 1852—both healthy.

"Ben, we found them! That first entry was Tobias's grandfather, and this entry is 'The Sisters.' Do you think the management would allow us to copy these pages? I would love to take them back to Ruth as a gift."

Ben lifted the ledger in his huge gentle hands, smiled at Lisa and said, "Let's give it a try, Lisa. If they won't, then we can get your camera and try to take a photo. Actually, I think you should run back to our room and get your camera before we talk to anyone in management. I will wait here and protect the ledger. Here is our room key, but hurry. One way or the other, we are not leaving here without proof that we found the Bascom family history."

CHAPTER 23

$\maltese$

ON CREST VIEW Drive, New Year's Day was heating up. Harold Gundersol walked into the solarium and abruptly ordered Estelle's assistant to leave the room, something quite out of character for him. The unmistakable tone in his voice caused her to leave without even looking in her boss' direction.

Taken aback by this sudden show of assertiveness by Harold, Estelle decided it best to remain quiet, curious about what was behind her husband's strange behavior. She watched as Harold closed the French doors behind the assistant, then waited until he returned and took the seat next to her before asking in a very acid tone, "So what has you all fired up?"

Harold, not yet ready to answer this challenge, stood up, walked to the wine closet, poured himself a stiff drink, downed it, returned to his seat and then asked, "Just how long have you known about this Marla person?"

The shocked look on Estelle's face confirmed the answers to several of Harold's questions. He did not even wait for a response before adding, "So you do know who I am talking about? Don't bother denying it; once I found out, I had my accountant go through all of your bank records."

Feeling violated at having her personal records invaded, Estelle flew into a rage, "How dare you, Harold! Those accounts are my family money. How did you gain access to them?"

"That isn't really the point here, Estelle," Harold bellowed right back. "Don't you remember? About ten years ago you added my signature on those accounts. So I had every right to do what I did, but you did not. Estelle, if I could find out what you did, don't you think any inquisitive reporter could find it out?"

Not accustomed to being anyone's target, Estelle stood up and thundered around the solarium, "Harold, I don't know what you are implying here, but I do not like it."

"You don't like it? YOU don't like it? Estelle, we have spent the past twenty-eight years prepping Michael for office. We sent him to the best schools, groomed him for public office, given him the Gundersol dynasty, and it is all ruined. If you had told me about this Marla six years ago, maybe we could have done something, but no, Estelle thinks she knows everything. Does he know that you have been paying off this woman for the past six years?"

"No, Michael does not, but he does know that I know about her. I found out about her by accident six years ago. Apparently, he had met her during his junior year at Berkley. She was already married and had two kids. Her husband wasn't wealthy, but he was well-connected; she loved his connections but not him. At first, our son was just a boy-toy for her, but she really had her hooks into him and had no intention of letting go of him."

"Did you actually talk to her?"

"Of course I did. Do you think I was going to sit back and allow this woman to ruin our future?"

"You mean our son's future, don't you, Estelle?"

"Don't be ridiculous, Harold. But let's be honest with one another. You and I both know how much we want that future. So she and I met twice; neither meeting went well. She wasn't interested in divorcing her husband, but neither was she willing to give up Michael."

Then Estelle decided that if Harold wanted to know it all, then he deserved to hear it all. "Brace yourself, Harold. Michael is the father of her third child. The kid is now five years old and her husband was convinced it was his, but Michael knows the truth."

Harold sank down into his chair as if just being punched in the gut, "So where does Hope fall into all of this? If Michael is so madly in love with this other woman, why the charade with Hope?"

Harold could see a look of pride come over Estelle's face as she began to explain, "Harold, this Marla was married and had no intention of divorcing. Michael knew his political future would be ruined if Marla was ever discovered, but he also refused to let her go. So we decided he would ask Hope to marry him—just for show. He does not love her, but you and I both know how important it is for him to have a beautiful wife on his arm for political clout."

"And Hope is okay with this?"

"Harold, don't be so naive. Why do you think I started cultivating a friendship with Jean Winslow five years ago? It certainly was not because she is such an interesting person. Get real! Jean loved all the events to which I took her, and she was so easy to manipulate. All I had to do was make a casual suggestion, and Jean would run with it. I started out hinting at all the benefits Hope would have being married to my son, and Jean's eyes glazed over like a deer in my crosshairs. I worked on her for almost a year before I told Michael what I was doing."

"How did you talk him into this little scheme of yours, and how did this Marla take it?"

"Well," Estelle responded, "that was a little harder. At first neither one of them would go for it. Our son wasn't willing to give up Marla nor was he willing to walk away from his political future, so he came around faster than she did. That was when I agreed to start paying her for her silence. Harold, you know that money talks, and it was talking her language—for five years.

"Michael agreed to start dating Hope during her senior year of college as long as I agreed to cover for him when he went to meet with Marla.

It seemed like a good plan. Hope was as naïve as her mother and didn't ask many questions. He didn't love her, and that was all this Marla cared about. Everyone was happy—until last spring."

Harold was now very confused. "You mean when Hope took off for Atlanta?"

Frustrated, Estelle retorted, "Same time, different reason, Harold. You see, if everything had stayed status quo, we would have been home free. Michael found it easy to keep Hope in line. If she balked at something, all I had to do was take Jean out to lunch and drop a little hint; she would automatically run home and work on Hope. I had done such a good job of convincing Jean this was the best life path for her daughter, she never had a clue she was being manipulated."

Harold turned to Estelle and asked, "So what changed the status quo?"

"Marla did," Estelle declared with all the bitterness of a woman unaccustomed to not getting her own way. "Last May, Marla's husband and oldest daughter were killed in a car accident. Remember when Michael decided to go on the unscheduled ski trip last May? He was really up in San Francisco with Marla. That is why he didn't make a fuss when Hope decided to take off for Atlanta. He was glad to have her out of his hair for a few days, but then she returned sooner than he expected, and Marla wanted to change the plans."

"Change it how?" Harold quipped. "Does this Marla think he is going to marry her? How old is this woman anyway?"

"Harold, there is no way he can marry this woman. She is eight years older than him. She was married before, and the daughter who died in that accident was from a messy affair. There is not enough money in the world to clean her up enough to pass muster with the press. That is just not going to happen, but Michael is absolutely under her control and will not listen to me."

"Estelle, this is entirely your fault. For Michael's whole life, you have dominated him. You actually suck the oxygen out of every room you enter. He was never allowed a dream or a goal that was not orchestrated by you. You taught him to accept your will as his own. You trained him to knuckle under to your will. So why are you so surprised that he would find another you—his normal? The only difference between the two of you is that she could offer him affection and sex, and he likes his new normal."

Estelle was finally out of answers. "So Harold, what do we do now?"

"I don't think there is anything we can do now. Marla is in the driver's seat, and our son is her passenger." Harold thought for a moment and added, "Estelle, we have spent hundreds of thousands of dollars on his campaign, and it is all going up in flames. Do you think this Marla has a number in mind? Everyone can be bought. It is just a matter of finding the price."

"But Harold, even if we could pay off this woman, I don't think either Michael or Hope will go through with this loveless marriage. Lots of people join together for the perks that come with marriage. You and I certainly did."

Harold quickly agreed, "Yes, we did. You wanted my name and connections."

"And you wanted my family money," quipped Estelle right back at him. "But the difference is, you and I both knew what we wanted and were willing to negotiate a marriage deal that satisfied what we both wanted. Hope has no interest in politics, and she doesn't seem to care about the financial benefits of becoming a Gundersol. She actually wants Michael to love her. He, on the other hand, still wants his political future but does not want to pay the price for it. Our stupid boy seems to think he can have both worlds."

Harold paced the floor trying to figure out his next move. "So where is he right now?"

Frustrated by her lack of control in this new situation, Estelle barked, "He is out trying to track down Marla. Apparently she has been in town for the past three days and has been stalking Hope. Last night on the drive over here, Hope told him about this reporter who keeps following her around, but when she described the car, he knew exactly who it was. That was who he was talking to on the phone last night."

"So Marla is here in L.A.? How did Michael know where to reach her?" questioned Harold.

"Because she always stays at the same motel when she comes here to be with him," Estelle snapped with all the venom she could muster. "From the little bit I overheard of their conversation, she is on a rampage of destruction; Michael is in a panic. Only now does he realize that she is actually willing to destroy his future if she does not get her way. He is convinced that she intends to expose all of this to Hope in order to blow up the wedding plans. He thinks she would even go so far as to go directly to the papers and spill everything if he won't call it off."

Pondering this new twist, Harold warned, "I can't believe this mess. For years I worried that my son was gay. Not knowing about Marla and watching how coldly he treated Hope, I suspected he was trying to keep his secret under wraps. Others have also questioned this, and I have spent tons of money keeping a lid on those suspicions. Estelle, calling off the wedding might quiet down Marla a little longer, but it will most assuredly revive the suspicions about his being gay. I don't see any way out for him. He has made a real mess of his future."

"Harold, I think we can still salvage his career. Marla can be bought off; I know it. Once she settles down, Michael will be able to think straight again; he will come around. He wants his future as much as we do, and he knows about the rumors. As soon as we get Marla packed off, I will invite Jean and Dan over for a nice dinner. I need Jean working on Hope while I work on Michael."

Harold stood up in disgust and started for the door, then turned and ended this conversation. "Well, our son might be stupid enough to think he can have both worlds, but that illegitimate kid of his will never be a Gundersol. That woman is never to step foot in this house. Estelle, you had better let go of some of that family money that got you here, and send that woman packing—and quick." With this declaration, Harold turned back toward the door.

Only half-joking, Estelle voiced her sinister thought out loud, "Too bad that wasn't Marla in that car accident last spring. Come to think of it, it would cost us a whole lot less to arrange a fatal accident with a certain maroon Chrysler than to try to pay her off."

Before slamming the door behind him, Harold thundered, "Just take care of it, Estelle, and I don't care how."

CHAPTER 24

✦

THE SECOND DAY of January began with a bang—literally. Ben and Lisa both sat up out of a sound sleep at the pounding at their bedroom door. "Dad, are you awake?"

Ben fired back, "I am now, Benny. What is so all fired important it couldn't wait until breakfast?"

"Dad, get dressed and come out into the living room," Benny pleaded.

Ben grabbed his robe and headed out to find out what was bothering his son. Before he had a chance to ask, Benny shoved the newspaper at him and said, "Dad, read the front page."

Ben only got through the first paragraph before taking off down the hallway to his bedroom. Lisa was almost dressed when he entered their room with a look on his face that made her want to run. "What is it, Ben?"

Ben handed Lisa the paper and then put his arm around her for moral support as she read the headline:

THE GEORGIA OBSERVER

Serving the citizens of Jefferson, Georgia, for over 100 Years

TWO LOCAL LADIES MUGGED AT GUNPOINT

Late yesterday, Ruth Bascom and another elderly lady who does not wish to be identified, were found beaten and robbed at the home of Ruth Bascom, 741 Chestnut St, Jefferson, Georgia. A neighbor said he heard loud voices coming from Mrs. Bascom's home and saw two young men running from the property around 8:00 last night. As he entered her open back door, he could see both women lying on the kitchen floor, badly beaten. Police were immediately called to the scene, and both women were taken to Jefferson Memorial where they were treated and released. Ruth Bascom is the owner of Bascom's Bakery, and it is suspected that these young men thought there might be cash hidden at the house. The police have a good description of both suspects and their get-away car.

Practically hysterical, Lisa cried, "Ben, why didn't someone call us?"

"I'm so sorry, Lisa, apparently they did. We didn't get here until almost 11:00 p.m. last night, and I didn't even think about checking my answering machine. Right after Benny went out front to pick up the morning paper, he checked the answering machine. There were two messages from Gladys saying they were both okay and are back at her house. You finish getting dressed so we can get right over there."

"They were probably over at Ruth's house packing for the move. We need to get Ruth moved out of that house today. We can close up the bakery for a few more days, and all of us can get her packed and cleared out in a day or two."

"Lisa, first things first. We need to get over there and make sure they are both okay. Grab your shoes and put them on in the car. After we have made sure they are okay, we will worry about some kind of breakfast and put together a moving plan."

Lisa, Ben and Benny walked into Gladys' kitchen right at 7:00 a.m. and were not really prepared for what greeted them. Sweet, kind, gracious Gladys Carter was standing at her sink with a huge shiner on her right eye and her left arm was in a sling. She still greeted them with a warm smile. "It looks worse than it is, Lisa. It could have been so much worse." Signaling them to lower their voices, Gladys explained, "Ruth is still asleep. The doctor said that thug separated her left shoulder when he twisted her arm, demanding she tell him where she had hidden her bakery money."

Ben pulled out a kitchen chair and demanded that Gladys take a seat. "Gladys, let me make the coffee. You sit down and tell us all about it. How did you get hurt?"

Gladys started to chuckle as she admitted, "Actually, this is my fault. The thug never touched me. When Ruth fainted from the pain of having her shoulder pulled out of the joint, both those boys took off quick. I simply lost my head. I was so frightened all I could think about was getting to the phone and calling the police." With a little smirk, Gladys lifted her sling and confessed, "I tripped over Ruth's leg running for the phone, hit my cheekbone on the corner of her kitchen counter and knocked myself silly. I guess when I fell, I tried to use my arm to brace myself and jammed my elbow. It is nothing that won't heal. Ruth was the one who was really hurt."

While sitting in Gladys's kitchen chatting, Benny produced the front page article. "Ms. Gladys, why didn't you want your name in the paper? It just says 'another elderly woman who wishes to remain anonymous.' "

Knowing what she was about to say would send Lisa into panic mode, Gladys carefully chose her words. "You see, Benny, when those thugs left they took my purse."

"You mean they took all your money?" Benny missed the real danger in her reply, but Ben and Lisa did not.

Getting up quickly and heading for the phone, Ben announced, "I'm calling a locksmith and having all the locks changed this morning.

Then Benny and I are going down to Hodges Hardware Store and get security locks for all of the windows. I am installing a floodlight as well."

Lisa quickly agreed saying, "Gladys, it was foolish of you and Ruth to come here last night, knowing those criminals have your I.D. That means they know where you live, and they have your house keys. How could you sleep here last night knowing this?"

"Because, Lisa, there was a police car out front all night." Turning back to Ben who was busy looking up a locksmith, Gladys asked, "Ben, you know Maxwell Grover, don't you?"

"Sure I do, Gladys, but the captain would never spend payroll funds assigning Max to sit sentry on your house."

"That's exactly what Max said when he was ordered to drive us home from the hospital last night. When Max was a young boy, Ruth and Tobias had served as his youth leaders. He didn't even ask permission. His shift was up, so he just parked out front to make his presence very obvious. He left a few minutes before you got here."

Then remembering her car, Gladys asked, "Ben, on your way back from Hodges, could you take my spare car key off Lisa's key ring and let Benny drive my car back here? I don't want to leave it over in Ruth's neighborhood any longer than I have to."

"Sure will, Gladys, I'd be happy to."

Lisa knew Ruth would have to approve the closing of the bakery for two more days before talking about putting together a moving party, so Lisa did not mention their plans to Gladys. Sipping her coffee, Lisa decided to reread the article that had started her day with such a panic. After reading it, her eyes glanced down the page where another familiar name jumped off the page at her.

District Attorney Stanley Riggs Vows to Bring Former Prosecutor Gordon to Trial.

Months of vigorous negotiations on Gordon's part have proven fruitless. Riggs continues to promise the citizens of Jefferson justice. To quote the district attorney, "My office will offer no plea-bargain to Gordon. We have a tentative trial date set for early April."

Lisa made a mental note to call Hope later that day to see if she was aware of the trial date, but right now she needed to focus on Gladys. Benny was given the task of making toast, while Ben scrambled some eggs. Lisa set the kitchen table, and Gladys was ordered to stay put.

As soon as the table was set, Lisa slipped out of the room and made a phone call to Atlanta. Bill Thomas needed to hear this news from family. As expected, Bill and Caroline promised to clear their calendar and drive down that afternoon. The second phone call was to Scott and Susan. Susan offered to help Lisa pack her things and move them over to Ben's, while Caroline was assigned the task of keeping Gladys and Ruth comfortable and out of the way. Scott and Bill were to help Ben and Benny pack up Ruth's house. With all these helping hands, it would not take long to pack up all of Ruth's personal belongings and get her settled in. Selling her furniture and putting the house up for sale could wait; Ruth's safety was the primary concern for now.

An hour later Benny carefully pulled Gladys's car into her garage, locked it up tight, brought the keys into the kitchen and laid them on the table. "Hi, Mrs. Bascom, sorry to hear about what happened to you last night."

Ruth, still quite groggy from the painkillers the doctor had prescribed, replied, "Thank you, Benny. I am just grateful to be alive. To tell you the truth, I think those boys were actually more frightened than I was."

Angry at any words of sympathy, Benny retorted, "Good, I hope they are frightened at the prospect of jail time too. I just don't understand how God could let this happen to you two of all people."

Ruth reached over and patted Benny's hand as she said, "God isn't responsible for what happened yesterday. God isn't Santa Claus, keeping a list of who is naughty or nice. God never promised us that we would be free of all the bad stuff. Benny, we live in a broken world. Broken people do terrible things to people."

"But Mrs. Bascom," pleaded Benny, "if God can't protect His own children, what are we supposed to do?"

"Benny, God can and does protect His children most of the time, but sometimes, for reasons we do not understand, He allows trials in our life. God wants us to trust Him and respond with all the grace that He alone can pour into our life. This sick world needs some beacons of light that will shine His grace and mercy. Who better to shine that light than those of us who live in that light every day, Benny? We are to trust Him. Trust that He will give us the strength to be His light to all these broken and damaged people. Do you think those boys could steal my most valuable possessions, Benny?"

"They sure tried and look how they hurt you," Benny responded.

"Yes, they sure did hurt me, that is for sure. But Benny, I am safe and sound in the perfect will of my heavenly Father—my most prized possession—while they are lost, blind, frightened, and wasting their lives. I am not saying they should not be tracked down and face the consequences for their actions. They need to be stopped before they take the life of someone not yet ready to face his Creator or before someone else ends their life before they are ready to do the same.

"Benny, bitterness is a root that grows quickly and takes over our life. Accusing God of failing us because we cannot see His bigger picture is telling God He cannot be trusted. I, for one, refuse to allow some young delinquent to limit, or define, my ability to trust in a God who has proven Himself over and over in my life. Benny, that would be giving those punks way too much power in my life."

Benny pondered Ruth's answer for several moments before replying. "Mrs. Bascom, when someone hurts those you love, it is hard to remember that the Bible says, *"For God so loved the world..."* and that *world* includes them as well. It is easy when I am sitting in church, but here, seeing the suffering they caused, it is a lot harder."

"Benny, do you think God has favorites? Can God be holy if He plays favorites? When you hear about someone else suffering through some tragedy, do you ever think, 'Why wasn't that me?' or do you just ask that question when it is you who is facing a tragedy? If "**God so loved the world…**" is only true for His favorites, then God is not holy. If it isn't true now, when we are the targets of a tragedy, then it isn't true when we sit in the safety of our church pew. God loves all of us all of the time. The worse these broken people behave, the more their behavior shows how much they need to be told that they need a Savior, right?"

"Right!" Benny smiled in agreement.

By 6:00 that evening, Lisa and Susan had all of Lisa's things packed and moved to Ben's place. Lisa brought in the last box from the car and suggested, "Let's not waste time unpacking right now. The guys should be finishing up over at Ruth's house, and I want to be at the house when they get there."

Susan picked up her purse and suggested, "The guys will be starving, and I know Caroline was busy keeping Gladys and Ruth out of the kitchen, so can we stop by Mario's and pick up some pizzas?"

"Great idea, Susan. I think Ben has a coupon for Mario's on his fridge. I'll get it and call in an order so it will be ready when we get there. How about one cheese, one sausage and one with just veggies?"

"Sounds like a plan, Lisa, but Ruth is on some heavy painkillers. Pizza might be a little much for her. Have Mario add a cup of his wonderful minestrone soup, just in case."

The guys pulled into the driveway just as the girls showed up with dinner. Ben quickly washed up, then set up a TV tray for Ruth and brought in her soup, drink and 7:00 painkiller. "Caroline, how have your patients been today? Did they follow instructions and stay off their feet?"

"Ruth did not even try to protest," Caroline replied. "Her shoulder constantly reminded her that she needed to let others do for her." Then turning toward Gladys, Caroline added, "Gladys, on the other hand, was fit to be tied. She could not read because her glasses pressed on her black eye, and the sling made it impossible to knit, so I kept her busy instructing me where every clean dish was stored."

As soon as everyone had settled down to eat, Caroline announced, "Around 3:00 today the police stopped by to say they have the boys in custody. They brought by a photo lineup, and both Gladys and Ruth were able to pick out the boys. Do you know they are only sixteen years old, and this was their third home invasion? Last year these boys shoved an old man down a flight of stairs, breaking his leg. For that they only got six months in minimum security at the youth camp. They've only been out for five days."

Ruth gave Benny a knowing smile before saying, "It is hard to feel too sorry for such hardhearted boys. Makes you wonder what kind of life they must have had to be able to toss an old man down a flight of stairs and manhandle a couple of old ladies. I sure hope the courts do more than slap their wrists this time—not because it was me this time. These boys are headed for real trouble, and they need to be taken off the streets."

Scott excused himself and headed out to his truck. A few moments later he came walking back into the living room with Gladys's purse. "Aunt Gladys, those boys did not take your purse. When we got over to Ruth's place and started packing, I found this in a box you must have been packing when those boys broke in. Everything seems to be there."

Embarrassed at forgetting she had put her purse in the box, Gladys said, "Ben, I'm sorry I put you to all that trouble having the locks changed."

"Not a problem, Gladys, better safe than sorry. Besides, all of your locks were so old any ten-year-old could break into this house."

While the family enjoyed a quiet respite from a hard day's work, none of them were aware of the danger surrounding Hope out in California.

CHAPTER 25

HOPE ARRIVED AT work early that Thursday morning. Everyone gathered in the staff kitchen to catch up on the holiday news, discuss all of the New Year's Day ball games and chatter about the two new automobiles parked in the lot that morning. Glad for these distractions, Hope was certain no one would ask how she had spent her New Year's holiday, and she was correct, no one did. Sam Silverstone was busy collecting on the office football pool while others moaned about some call by the refs that should have gone the other way. Feeling safe from any prying questions, Hope happily set off for her office, content to spend her day buried in work, always a happy distraction for her.

Around 11:00 Mr. Davenport stopped by Hope's office with a request. "Hope, I signed up a new client over New Year's. He has been struggling with another agency for months, but they just cannot deliver the quality product he demands. I told him I would put my best people on his project and make sure we serviced his needs with speed and quality."

Wondering why Mr. Davenport was telling her this, Hope asked, "How can I help you with this project, Mr. Davenport?"

Giving a sheepish smile, Davenport asked, "I was wondering if you could do me a tremendous favor this morning, Hope. I know this is asking for something out of the ordinary, but I want our client to see that we will go the extra mile to service him. If I loaned you my company car and paid for the gas, would you be willing to drive up to Pacific Palisades and pick up seven boxes of time-sensitive materials from our new client? Ordinarily, I would simply order a courier service, but this client needs to feel like we are hands on with this project. You are the only one who worked over the holiday and isn't under a work deadline."

"I'd be happy to do that for you, Mr. Davenport," Hope replied. "But would you mind if I take my car? I don't mind putting the extra miles on it, and I would feel much more comfortable driving my own car."

"Not a problem, Hope. Stop by the front desk, and Nancy will issue you a gasoline credit card and give you written directions to the client's home. In good traffic this is over a two-hour drive, so I will tell him to expect you around 2:00. You should be back on the road by 2:30 and back here, barring heavy traffic, by 5:00." As he turned to leave, Mr. Davenport stopped and said, "Hope, I really do appreciate this."

Twenty minutes later, Hope jumped into her car, anxious to get on the road for this important mission. She was thankful Mr. Davenport trusted her with such an important client's needs that she did not even think to look around the parking lot for that maroon Chrysler LeBaron. Hope studied the map issued to her and was on the freeway within a few minutes.

Hope made good time and was already in the Palisades ninety minutes later, oblivious to the car that had made every turn she had since pulling out of the company parking lot. As it turned out, Hope was not the only driver being followed that day. The driver of the maroon Chrysler stayed two car lengths behind Hope's little Mazda sedan while the driver of the gray Buick Park Avenue kept only one car between him and his prey, Marla Brown.

Hope slowed down around the winding curves of the Palisades, but not to enjoy the spectacular vistas. She needed to be able to read every street sign, not wanting to miss her next turn. Spotting the street sign she was watching for, Hope slid around the corner and stepped on the gas in order to coax her gutless little car up the steep grade that was taking her up to the third street on the left. The large estates perched atop this plateau, with their magnificent vistas, made Hope embarrassed to pull into the impressive driveway that led to her destination. Hope was so distracted by its beauty, she did not notice the maroon Chrysler slide on past the driveway and slow down. More experienced at trailing their prey, the gray Park Avenue ducked into a driveway farther up the street.

Hope nervously rang the doorbell, practicing her opening speech for the person who answered the door. Having been on the lookout for this guest, the housekeeper quickly opened the door and invited Hope into the marble-covered vestibule. "Hello, I'm here on behalf of my employer, Mr. Davenport. I am to pick up some important boxes from your employer."

"Yes," the housekeeper replied with a gracious smile. "They are all right here. Let me call Matthew. Some of them are quite heavy, so Matthew will load everything into your car. I do need to see some identification, please."

Embarrassed at not being ready with her identification, Hope opened in her purse and quickly produced her driver's license, saying, "One can never assume anything when turning over important documents to total strangers."

The housekeeper, with years of experience in handling important people's valuable possessions, inspected Hope's license, making sure she was who she said she was and then excused herself in order to find Matthew. Hope counted the boxes, knowing she was to pick up a total of seven. There was no way she was going to sign for less than seven since that was her charge by Mr. Davenport.

Ten minutes later Hope pulled out of the driveway, made her way down the steep, winding street that delivered her to the two-lane road that would lead her back down to Palisades Drive. Anxious not to be late arriving, Hope knew she had enough gas to get to her destination. But she also knew she should fill up before heading down the Palisades and then onto the busy Los Angeles freeways. She remembered a quaint little shopping center shortly before her last turn and remembered seeing a gas station in that center. Pulling in, Hope jumped out and began pumping gas. It had been years since any gas stations in California provided personal service at the pump. Hope listened as the clicking of the gas meter signaled gallon after gallon filling her tank. Her eyes perused the beautiful ocean view and she was so mesmerized by her view that she did not hear someone walking up behind her.

Startled by the feel of hard metal being shoved into her side, Hope turned and saw the woman from the Marriot and the mall, standing right next to her, ordering her to step away from the gas pump. Flashing the gun so Hope would understand she meant business, the woman ordered Hope to walk toward the side parking lot beyond the gas station's building. Hope did not have time to think about what would happen to her valuable cargo; all she could think about was the look on this woman's face and the gun in her hand.

Marla pushed Hope forward, ordering, "Slide in from the driver's door and be quick about it."

Hope did as she was told, never taking her eyes off the gun in her captor's hand. As soon as they were back out on the road, Marla explained, "I do not intend to hurt you, Hope. I just needed you to obey me and give me time to explain a few things without interruptions. My name is Marla Brown; you and I both love the same man."

As Marla drove, Hope quickly realized the woman was hysterical. With every curve her speed increased, and she began talking very quickly, determined to fill in Hope on her six-year romantic history with Michael. The squeal of the tires began to send Hope into a panic, but Marla was so intent on telling her well-rehearsed story she was not paying any attention to her rapid acceleration and speed. The excessive speed, coupled with the gun in Marla's hand, made it difficult for Hope to focus on her words. Marla was more focused on the reaction of her captive than the car's excessive speed, let alone the fact that the same gray Buick Park Avenue that had followed her for the past two-and-a-half hours was again behind her.

For these two women, the whole world was now limited to the two of them and what they had in common.

Fearing they could easily go off the highway at the next curve, Hope reached for her seatbelt and quickly fastened it while Marla continued to rattle off her well-rehearsed facts like a machine gun...ratta-tat-tat... Hope did her best to absorb what was being said, but feared this woman was too upset to be trusted with a gun that was pointed in her direction. Finally, Michael's name sunk in, and Hope asked, "Michael? Are you talking about Michael Gundersol?"

"Of course I am. Haven't you been listening?" The unsettledness of her response frightened Hope who tried to calm her down. "I don't know anything about any relationship you might or might not have with Michael, but you need to know that I called off our wedding and our relationship two days ago. Personally, I don't care what happens to him from now on."

It was obvious to Hope that Marla did not believe a word she was saying. "You are only saying that because you are afraid of me. I told you I do not intend to hurt you. I want you to know that you are being used."

"Used by whom?" Hope studied this woman's face. She was clearly much older than Michael but obviously involved with him in some way.

"By Michael and his mother, of course," Marla explained. "You see, he and I have been together for six years. I met him when he was still at Berkley. Even though I was married, he and I loved each other. That was enough for us. Six years ago Michael got me pregnant, but I decided to tell my husband it was his kid. I had already been divorced once, and I liked the lifestyle my husband provided. He was so busy making a living and doing his thing, I was free to come and go as I pleased. Michael knew his mother would never accept me, so we kept our affair a secret for a while. Then he got careless, and Estelle found some letters from me in his bedroom; everything hit the fan."

Stunned by this news, Hope clarified, "So you are telling me that Estelle has known about you and the baby for five years now?"

"Yes, does that surprise you? Estelle came up to Berkley the winter our boy was born, and the three of us had a powwow—at least that is what she called it. I called it a *business meeting.* She brought her checkbook, I brought our boy, and Michael brought nothing. Michael is never any good at taking a stand, but I suspect you know that about him by now. Whenever Estelle is around, he doesn't dare breathe without her permission. I've always been rather surprised that he even dared to make love to me without her permission, but then he is still a man after all."

Throughout grad school, we were allowed to play house as long as we kept it all a secret and as long as my monthly checks kept coming in. Then when the Gundersols began ramping up the political machine and grooming Michael for his destiny, Estelle wanted to change the game. She made several trips up to Berkley in order to convince us that Michael needed to be married in order to have a solid backstory for this political life. We all knew I was never going to be that person. She told us she had someone in mind—someone who would give a good impression and would be easy to control." Grinning snidely toward Hope, she asked, "You do realize she was talking about you, don't you?"

Hope returned the snide grin and responded, "I'm beginning to realize it."

Marla began to relax and calm down, even placing the gun down between her legs, confident she had now gained Hope's full attention. "Michael and I went round and round about this matter at first. He did not want to get involved with you, but he is nothing if not practical. He wants what he wants. I know he wants me, but he also wants his political life. I cannot be part of that. Once he convinced me that yours would be a loveless marriage—totally for show, I agreed to go along with it as long as he kept his hands off of you. He was certain you were such a compliant little thing—always so easy to distract and willing to go along to get along. He had me convinced we could do it.

Hope now had all the answers she needed. Michael was simply using her, and she had let him. He was every bit as bad as his mother—nothing but a selfish, conniving, cheat whose personal goals would always trump anyone else's needs. "So why are you telling me this truth now?"

"So you do know I am telling you the truth then?" Satisfied of this huge victory, Marla explained, "Because everything changed last spring."

"Last spring? We were planning our wedding last spring. We were supposed to get married on the first of December. Everything was planned, and then I flew to Atlanta." Hope stopped short of offering an explanation for this trip. This woman did not deserve to know why she did anything.

"I know, Hope. You see, just as you were trying to decide whether or not you were going to go look up your birth mother, my life was tossed upside down. My husband was taking my daughter over to a friend's house to spend the weekend when a truck ran a red light, broadsided them, and both my husband and my daughter were killed."

Hope was shocked at the lack of emotion in this woman's voice as she related this account.

"Hope, your little trip was a godsend to us," Marla offered.

Hope flinched at this statement and thought, *Godsend? What do you know about God sending things? You talk about your husband and daughter dying in a terrible car crash like it is just a chess move in some casual game you are playing.*

Continuing with her story, Marla said, "Michael wanted to be by my side and was glad you took off. That way he didn't have to come up with some elaborate story about going on some ski trip or something, but then you came back too early. For six months we have been trying to figure out how we can have it all, get you out of our lives, have each other, and still have Michael's political career. After all, now I am a respectable widow and who would dare go digging up the history of my dead child? Estelle doesn't believe we can pull it off, but Michael and I think we can—as long as you go along with things. You need to keep your mouth shut and tell the press you are calling off the wedding because of your birth mother's problems. That excuse will not reflect badly upon Michael. The press will write something about how he tried to stand by you as you found out all this terrible history and how you even killed your own grandfather—but to no avail. Then we can wait a year and quietly get married after he is already in office. People will forgive anything if their politicians just promise to make sure they are passing bills that make life easier for them."

Turning to look straight at Hope, Marla asked, "So what do you think?"

Before Hope could even put a thought together, the car that had been following behind them, pulled into the oncoming lane and began to pass them on the left. Hope saw him first and shouted, "Look out, that idiot is trying to pass us with a curve right ahead. Marla, hit the brakes and give him room to slide back into the lane right in front of us, or we will all go over the cliff."

Marla hit the brakes, but the brake pedal went right to the floor. Shouting that she had no brakes, Marla began pumping the pedal, hoping something would begin to grab; however, the road was steep, and the curve was fast approaching. Both women began screaming as they realized the gray car had pulled alongside them and was deliberately maneuvering his car closer and closer to force theirs over the embankment. Marla instinctively turned her car away from his, but the cliff was immediately adjacent to them. They both felt the right front tire's leaving the pavement and skidding on the loose gravel of the shoulder.

Hope screamed, "Turn the wheel back," as she reached for the steering wheel and helped Marla force the car back onto the pavement and back toward the gray car. Just as the Chrysler bounced into the Park Avenue, the driver instinctively corrected his steering, which put him right into oncoming traffic. Hope looked up to see a car turning the bend, heading right at the gray car. Hope reached over Marla's arm and laid on the horn as she frantically pointed toward the oncoming car. Only then did the driver of the gray Buick hit his brakes and pull in behind Marla's LeBaron. Hope spun around to quickly look at his license plate number, committing it and his description to memory. She commented, "If we get through this, at least we will be able to tell the police who was trying to kill us."

Marla leaned her whole weight against the steering wheel, forcing the tires to squeal as she tried to keep her car from going off the cliff as they made the next turn. Looking ahead, Hope recognized where they were and said, "Marla, the next curve is Pelican Point. It is a sharp curve with an unobstructed cliff. If we don't stop this car, that man will have lots of room to force us off the cliff. See that stone pillar way to the left of the road—right before the curve begins? Head for that pillar. It is the only thing that will stop this car."

Marla forced the wheel of her car as far left as she could manage, crying, "Help me, Hope! Grab hold of the wheel and help me turn it." Both women used all of their strength to force the LeBaron into the oncoming lane and as they felt the left tire leave the pavement, both women turned toward each other, covered their faces and braced for the impact.

Confused and in lots of pain, Hope struggled to free her seatbelt, but her body had slammed forward on impact, jamming the belt buckle. Hope looked at Marla, who was still unconscious and obviously badly injured. She tried shaking her awake, but then saw her head had hit the steering wheel. She was bleeding from a huge gash on her face. Looking beyond Marla in the dimming light of a winter sunset, panic quickly set in as Hope saw the gleam of a flashlight coming toward them. Hope struggled to see beyond the glare of the light, hoping not to see that same sinister face that had glared back at her just moments before. Working more determinedly to release the seatbelt, Hope panicked as she saw that someone coming closer to the car. Her mind screamed, *What if it is that guy again?* Unable to move her leg without excruciating pain, Hope wondered, *What did we do to make this guy so angry? Why does he want to kill us?*

Overwhelmed with pain and fear, Hope cried out, "God, I know You love me, and I did pray that prayer that Ruth said You would always hear and accept. Dear God, my soul is in Your hands, and I do trust Your promises. If this is the end for me…God, in Jesus' name, I come to You."

Someone was screaming something at her, but she could not understand what he was saying because the sirens were so loud. *Sirens?* That means help is here. Hope strained to hear what the voice behind the light was saying to her. She forced herself to concentrate until she finally understood his words. "Cover your face! We need to remove this shattered windshield so we can put a safety blanket over you. We need to use the Jaws of Life to break the bracing on this convertible so we can lift you two up and out. Protect your face."

That conversation was the last thing Hope remembered before letting the blackness of unconsciousness take over.

CHAPTER 26

Hᴏᴘᴇ ᴡᴀs ᴡʜᴇᴇʟᴇᴅ back into her hospital room after having her leg set and cast. The impact of the accident had driven her knees into the dashboard, snapping her right thigh bone. Heavily medicated, Hope struggled to answer the questions the officer was asking. "Hope, can you identify the other car?"

Hope closed her eyes and envisioned herself turning around in Marla's car, "It was a two-toned, gray on gray Buick Park Avenue with black leather seats. A parking sticker in the lower right corner of the windshield had a seagull or a pelican standing on a rock. The license plate number was XXL-555."

"That is wonderful, Hope," the officer responded. "How good of a look did you get of the driver?"

"I got a very good look at him; so did Marla."

Hope did not notice that the officer ignored her reference to Marla, instead suggesting, "I think we need to get a police sketch artist over here right away while it is still clear in your head. In the meantime, I'm going to put out a BOLO for this car. I'm almost certain we will find it was stolen, and that it has been dumped somewhere. Maybe we can get prints or other evidence off of it."

As soon as the officer left her room, another man entered and introduced himself, "Hello, Hope, I am your attorney, Samuel Parker. I have been retained to represent you, so I do not want you talking to anyone from now on without my being present."

Hope started to respond when the officer walked back into the room and asked, "And who are you, and how did you get past the desk?"

Parker gave his most practiced "I-have-every-right-to-be-here" kind of look, but before the officer could even respond, Hope asked, "So Mr. Parker, who retained you and who is paying you?"

Smiling a smile that only a greasy, conceited player can produce, Parker patted Hope's hand and said, "Hope, now don't you worry about a thing. It is all taken care of."

"Well, since I am not guilty of anything except being naïve and gullible, I doubt that I will have any need of your services, Mr. Parker. I suspect Estelle Gundersol is picking up your tab, so you can go back to her and tell her to stay out of my business. I do not need you filtering my words for me."

Parker picked up his briefcase and quickly excused himself.

Hope turned toward the officer and said, "I guess I hit that nail on the head. Officer, a minute ago, you said you suspected the car was stolen. Why?"

"Almost two hours before your accident, Hope, the LAPD received a tip that Marla's car was going to be involved in a fatal accident."

"A tip? You mean that man really did intend to kill me?" Hope could not quite believe all of that was coming to light.

"Not you, Hope—Marla. We had a BOLO out for her car but could not find it."

Puzzled by this news, Hope asked, "But who would want to have Marla killed?" Even as the words came out of her mouth, Hope already knew the answer.

"Michael Gundersol called in the tip himself. He was in a panic, having spent the past three days searching the greater LA area for Marla

Brown. I don't know all of the details; however, I do know that he over-heard his own mother telling his father that the plan was set. Their guy had found Marla, and the plan would proceed that night. I guess Michael stormed into their room, confronted them and demanded to know what the 'plan' was. Once he realized his mother had hired a hit on Marla, Michael immediately called the police and told them everything. Once the accident was reported, Mr. and Mrs. Gundersol were taken into custody for questioning. We need to find the driver and get him to flip on Mrs. Gundersol. With all their money, we will need a rock-solid case before we go after her."

Amazed at what she was hearing, Hope said, "So Michael called the police on his mother? I can hardly believe he had the nerve. Maybe there is hope for him after all. That also explains why Estelle sent over her lawyer. Obviously, she wanted to keep me quiet. The person she really better be fearful of is Marla." Then with honest concern, Hope asked, "Officer, how is Marla? She is going to be okay, right?"

"I'm not sure, Hope. She is still in surgery. Her injuries were much more extensive than yours because her side of the car took the full and direct impact."

Twenty minutes later, a broken and bewildered Michael came into Hope's room. "Hope, I am so sorry about everything. You were not sup-posed to be in that car with Marla."

"Well then, that makes everything okay doesn't it, Michael? The of-ficer just told me that you did try to stop it, and that does count for some-thing. I know all about Marla. She told me everything before that man tried to run us off the cliff."

Collapsing into the chair beside her bed, Michael buried his face in his hands and said, "I'm glad it is over. I never wanted to hurt you, Hope. I just didn't know how to get out of it."

"Is Marla hurt badly? You do realize that no matter how sick and twist-ed your relationship is with her, she does love you."

Michael sighed. "They just rolled her out of surgery, but they won't tell me anything. They won't even let me see her." He lifted his head and admitted, "I've really made a mess of things. I was willing to ruin your life so I could get what I wanted. I had no idea my mother would go this far. I really didn't."

"Michael, you are still young. You can still build a life for yourself—and Marla—if you want to. You've never needed your parents' help; you just didn't want to work for the life you really wanted."

He stared off into space for a moment and then admitted, "My mother will never forgive me for betraying her. All my life I did everything she wanted—except giving up Marla. I just couldn't do that. But she will never forgive my betraying her by calling the police." Turning back to Hope, he concluded, "Hope, I can never have the life I want now. I need my mother's money and my father's name and support. I've lost both today. I've lost everything."

Without another word, Michael walked out of Hope's room and her life for good. As she watched him walk down the hallway, Hope realized that although he seemed truly sorry for what had happened, he was still more concerned with what all this meant to him and his future. Hope thought about everything Michael had said and done today and concluded that, as much as Michael could love anyone, he did love Marla. *"At least he did do the right thing by calling the police. But now, as the full weight of his heroic decision comes to light, Michael is beginning to waffle—something he is very accomplished at doing."*

Hope leaned back against her pillow, realizing exactly how lucky she was to finally be rid of all three of the Gundersols. Looking up at the ceiling, Hope said, "God, I am so thankful. I am lying here in a hospital bed with a broken leg, having narrowly escaped a near-death experience. My fiancé just walked out of my life for good, and I can truly say I am thankful."

With a realization that made her shudder, Hope added, "I could have been married to that man. I could have had children with him. Estelle could have been my mother-in-law and without knowing it, I could have been forced to share my husband with Marla. But God, none of that is true now, and I know it is not because I was too smart for them. It is because

I promised Lisa I would pray Jeremiah 29:11 as a prayer to You—until I understood what it meant. God, I do understand it. People make plans. Sometimes their plans walk all over people, abuse and misuse them for their own purposes. God, I want to know and to start following Your plans for my life. I want to follow Your plans for the rest of my life, and I want to stop being gullible and foolish."

A few minutes later a very sheepish Jean Winslow entered her daughter's room. "Hope, your dad and brother are fishing in San Diego. I just talked to Dad on the phone, and he wanted me to tell you they are driving back tonight. He will be here at the hospital first thing tomorrow morning."

"That's good, Mother, I'm glad. For a few minutes there today I was afraid I'd never see my family ever again," Hope confessed.

Mortified at learning everything that had happened, Jean began to cry as she confessed, "I wasn't sure you would want to see me after all of this. I had no idea Estelle could go this far to get her way. I was so full of pride and blinded by Estelle's wealth and connections, I let her maneuver me into pressuring you to stay in that relationship. I knew you were miserable, but I kept telling myself it would get better once you two were married. Somewhere deep inside, I knew I was lying to myself and to you, but I let the promise of such a vast fortune coming to you cloud my judgment. Estelle had me hook, line and sinker, and I let her. That woman gets whatever she wants."

"Well, Mother, that might not be true any longer. Estelle's dream of another generation of political power, privilege and prestige has been shattered. Michael, her tool to achieve all of these lofty dreams, has finally turned on her and betrayed her. The cherished name of Gundersol, the name that would always open every door for her, is now tarnished beyond repair. And finally, Mother, all of Estelle's treasured family money will probably not keep her out of prison. That is quite a fall for someone who always believed she was untouchable."

Jean sat quietly thinking about everything her daughter had told her. Almost too afraid to ask, but knowing she needed to know the answer,

Jean finally asked, "So you have not yet said what is going to happen to us. Are we too broken? Did I betray you to the point that you cannot forgive me?"

Hope smiled at her mother for a moment before saying, "I have a long recovery ahead of me. I will be here in the hospital for at least three more days, then the doctor wants me off my feet for at least a month before he will release me to return to work. You and I have a lot to talk about. I have a wonderful family in Atlanta and Jefferson, but I realize it is not a competition. I do not have to choose one over the other. I am blessed to have both. I want you to know this part of my family the way I have come to know them, and I want them to get to know you. Mother, this family is all about forgiveness. I want you to meet all of them and maybe, someday, you and I can talk about how I became a follower of Jesus. He is the One who teaches us that to live a full life, you must start with asking for forgiveness—first from Him. Then He wants us to walk a forgiving life. I know you don't understand what I am talking about right now, but you will because I can truly say that I do forgive you, Mother, with all my heart."

As an act of true repentance, Jean suggested, "Hope, we need to call your mother and tell her what has happened to you. Do you have her phone number?"

"Mom, it is in my purse, and that was left back in my car at the gas station when Marla kidnapped me. Besides, I think Lisa has already moved into Ben's house, and I don't have that number yet."

Jean considered her options. "Hope, I could call your Aunt Gladys. She should know how to get hold of Lisa. I would think Gladys' home number would be easy to find."

Smiling at hearing her mother refer to Gladys as "your Aunt Gladys" thrilled her heart. Seeing her mother so anxious to include her "other" family, Hope quickly agreed, "Mom, you can call information and ask for Gladys Carter's phone number. She lives on Hayter Street in Jefferson, Georgia." Then remembering the nurse telling her that no long-distance phone calls could be made from the hospital room, Hope suggested, "I guess you will have to go down to the lobby and use one of the public phones."

Saddened at the idea of not being the one to tell them she was all right, Hope decided to focus on the fact that her mother was now willing to make this call for her. Jean grabbed her purse and headed for the door when Hope cautioned, "Mother, please make sure they know that I am all right—especially Gladys. I don't want her sitting at that house all alone worrying about me."

Several minutes later Jean returned to Hope's room full of smiles and excited. "I was able to get through to Gladys Carter for you, Hope. What a sweet lady!"

Frustrated at such little information, Hope prodded, "So what did you tell her? You didn't get her upset, did you? You did ask for Lisa's phone number, right? Did you call my mom and tell her what happened to me?"

Jean pulled the chair closer to Hope's bedside and lifted the hospital phone onto the bed, saying, "Hope, you won't believe it. When I called Gladys' house, Lisa answered the phone. It just so happens that your whole family is at Gladys' house tonight. Why is a long story for another day, but they are calling here in just a few minutes because they all want to talk to you."

Beaming with excitement, Hope grabbed the receiver on its first ring and said, "Hi, Mom! First off, I am fine. I don't want you to worry about me."

Jean's eyes welled up with tears as she watched her daughter's face light up. As she listened to this one-sided conversation, she thought about how foolish she had been. How could she have been jealous of Hope's new family ties and so blinded by Estelle's pride-centered friendship. Much of this heartbreak had been her own fault. Jean looked at Hope and thought, *"I doubt that I would have been so generous to forgive someone who had betrayed me."*

Hope interrupted the questions being fired at her. "Mother, I really am okay. So everyone is at Gladys' house tonight? Can you put me on speaker phone so I can tell you all what's happened to me? No, Mother, not about the accident—something even more important. I'll wait until you get the phone on speaker so everyone can hear it together."

Jean smiled at her daughter, assuming the important news was going to be that Hope had finally broken off the marriage, but she was soon to realize that Hope's news was much more important.

Two clicks and several background voices could be heard suggesting putting the telephone in the center of the room, then Hope could hear Scott in the background saying, "Wait, we need to go wake up Ruth. She would want to be here for this. Tell Hope to wait just a moment while I bring Ruth into the living room."

Lots of excited chatter could be heard while everyone got seated and then she heard, "Go ahead, Hope. We are all ears," announced Lisa.

Hope took hold of her mother's hand, leaned over and gave her a kiss on the cheek, then started, "Hi, everyone! I need to tell you I am all right. I have a broken leg and am pretty banged up, but I will be fine in a couple of months."

Several people tried to shout comments, but Hope quickly took control of the conversation saying, "Everyone, I know you all want to know all the details about the accident, but can we please set all that aside for right now? I promise I will tell you every horrid detail in a day or two, but right now I want to tell you all something so much more important. It's something I know you all want to hear.

"First of all, I need you to know that my Mother Jean is sitting here beside me, and she has not heard what I am about to tell all of you. Since you are all my family, I want to tell you all at the same time, so here goes. Ruth, are you there?"

"Yes, I'm here, Hope," Ruth called out.

"Ruth, remember last Saturday morning when you and I talked in the den?"

"Yes, Hope, I remember our conversation," Ruth called out.

"Well, everyone, Ruth explained to me the difference between just being a religious person and being a person of faith. She told me exactly what that means, and then she gave me one of Tobias' booklets to read.

"During your wedding, Mother, I was struggling with lots of things. I was trying to decide if I was going to go through with my own wedding plans, knowing I could never really be happy with Michael. I was also struggling over my decision to become a person of faith. I knew I needed to pray the prayer that Ruth and the pastor said God would always listen to, so during your wedding ceremony, Mother, I did pray that prayer. God did hear it; I absolutely know He did."

The people sitting in Gladys' living room lit up with excitement at hearing this wonderful news, but everyone was careful to remain quiet so Hope could continue. "Then on Monday evening, when Michael took me back home, I told him the wedding was off for good. I told him I could not marry someone I did not really love, and I told him I did not think he really loved me."

Lisa gave Susan a quick high five at hearing this news as Hope continued, "I've found out a lot of ugly information today. I also have had lots of my questions answered, but I don't want to waste this long-distance call talking about the Gundersol family. I want to talk to you about what I've learned.

"I started out believing my life was just one big mistake—given away as an infant, that disaster at the bakery and then the trial—were all just part of some cosmic joke with me as the naïve and gullible main character. But tonight, having just gone through a second attempt on my life within a year, my fiancé finally gone forever, and most likely at least two more trials in the near future for me, I know my life has not been nor will it be a big mistake. I now know the Creator of the universe has a plan for me, and I am excited to find out what that plan is.

"I've learned that although my life seems to be spinning out of control, the One who controls everything has my life in His hands.

"I've learned that I do not have to choose between my two families. It is not a competition where for one to win, the other must lose. I actually have one big wonderful family.

"I've learned that I need to never be afraid to face the truth—even though painful—it is always better than living a lie.

"I've learned that powerful people do not have power over me, and that I should never surrender my right to stand up for truth—no matter what they threaten to do to me. I must never ignore my inner truth and allow others to heap guilt on me or shame me into going along simply to keep the peace. I have learned that peace at any cost will never produce real peace.

"Today, as we were flying around the curves of the highway, with a steep cliff right outside my window and a man trying to force us off the road, I realized that life is much like that curvy road. At times, we have a beautiful vista with blue water spread out as far as we can see, then we hit a curve and everything can change in a flash. What was beautiful only a few moments earlier is now treacherous and life-threatening. After the crash, when I thought that hit man was coming to the car to finish us off, I discovered a rescue squad was there to help me. I realized that life is too full of curves in the road to try to maneuver through it by myself. I want to live a life of faith—the same life Tobias talked about in his booklet, the same life Gladys and Ruth taught you to live, Mother, and I want my mom and dad to come along on this journey of faith."

The hospital P.A. system announced that visiting hours were now over so Hope quickly brought the phone call to an end. "I don't really want to end this phone call. I want to tell you guys so much more, but we will have the rest of our lives together. Just know that I love all of you and will come back there as soon as I am allowed to travel. This time I would like to bring my mom and dad with me. I want them to get to know all of you and love you all as much as I do. Good night, everyone! I love you all."

A huge celebration of thanksgiving erupted at Gladys' home that evening. Repeating every word of Hope's confession of faith, Lisa's joy was overwhelming. Gladys hugged Lisa as she said, "Lisa, you know the curves in the road Hope was talking about reminds me of Dickens' 'It was the best of times; it was the worst of times,' right? This is certainly one of those best-of-times moments."

"It sure is, Gladys," Lisa agreed, her eyes filled with happy tears as she was finally able to add the one missing part, "and because my girl has experienced her own *Epoch of belief*, I know that my *Spring of Hope* has come to me as well."

As everyone began to settle into quiet conversation, Lisa took hold of Susan's hand and silently walked out back for a few moments alone with her sister. For several minutes, they simply sat together in the stillness of the night, allowing Hope's confession of faith to fully sink in. Susan could hear her sister's breathing change from a contented sigh to a more rapid rhythm as she suspected Lisa was reliving the image of her little girl flying around those dangerous curves. Susan remained quiet, not wanting to force the conversation. The sky was clear, and all the stars were out—as if God Himself was putting on a celebration display tonight. After all, one more of His precious little lambs had been rescued tonight and was now safe and sound.

Almost reverently, Lisa slid her arm around her sister's waist and whispered, "You know, Susan, all those childhood prayers really were answered, weren't they? God has given us so much more than either one of us could have imagined. I've been sitting here thanking God for all the ways He has shown us He loves us—us—you and me—the Miller girls.

"Susan, in my worst of times, I still loved you, but I also resented you. You were moving forward in life, happy, safe, and loved by so many while I was stuck in a lifestyle no one could justify. I was so full of rage and excuses back then. You kept coming back—no matter how I treated you."

"Because I loved you, Lisa," Susan cried through thankful tears.

"I knew you did, Susan, but I couldn't hear what you were saying to me at the time. You wanted to wipe away my excuses and make me face who I was, and my rage would not allow that. So God sent Gladys to me. At first, I played the same game with her. I presumed she had no inkling what it felt like to live with crippling rage. I assumed she had always been this perfect, sweet old lady I was observing—someone who could never know my kind of rage."

Starting to chuckle out of embarrassment, Lisa turned and faced Susan directly as she confessed, "Susan, do you know the night I realized how much God loved me?"

Susan was too emotional to answer her sister. She simply smiled and shook her head no.

"I had been living with Gladys for about three months. She and Ruth would sit with me every evening, telling me all about how much God loves us all. I would usually sit quietly trying to ignore what they were saying. I had run through all of my excuses, and they had fallen on deaf ears. No matter what I said, these two women had a Bible verse ready and waiting for me.

"Well, one night Gladys decided it was time for me to hear her story— the same story she told Hope and Benny right before my wedding. But with me, Gladys went into much more detail about exactly how ugly she had become while in her rage. She emotionally undressed herself to me so I could see that she really did understand what I was battling inside. She showed me all her scars that night, using words I could fully relate to. I remember sitting and looking at this lady I had come to admire, telling me that she had been where I was. She was honest and transparent, and I loved her for that. Only then did I realize this Jesus she was talking about was the One who had changed her from that rage-filled person that I identified with into this sweet and kind person I so wanted to become. I realized that this same Jesus had put this wonderful woman in my life because I needed a flesh-and-blood example of what Jesus could do for me if I would just trust Him.

"That night I surrendered my heart, my rage, my excuses, and my past to God. It wasn't easy, but it was so worth it. Seeing how God had changed Gladys gave me hope that He could and would change me also. I cannot imagine that night in the bakery when I faced my daughter, if I had not had those years of restoration and healing before meeting her. Because Jesus forgave me of my past and changed who I was, I could be as honest with Hope as Gladys had been with me. When you stand before people as a forgiven person, you are able to be open and transparent because you know that the change was all God's doing.

"Then God sent Hope back into my life. I wasn't expecting it. I wasn't even asking God for that. I only wanted Him to keep her safe. He had done so much for me, how could I ask Him to bring my girl back to me? But God knew that Hope needed to see all the love in this family. She also needed to see our faith in action. Seeing what He had done for Gladys and me showed her He is real, and He can change our lives if we will trust Him."

"Don't you forget Ben," Susan teased. "Ben is a really huge gift."

"I know. I do not deserve any of this, but God did it anyway."

Then turning back toward her sister, Lisa said, "Susan, tonight, hearing my daughter say she had accepted God's forgiveness makes me realize that I need to do something I have struggled against ever since I was forgiven. Gladys and Ruth have been challenging me to take a real step of faith and to finally forgive Mother for my childhood. For a long time I have refused, believing she does not deserve to be forgiven. But Susan, I have been forgiven so much, how can I refuse to forgive her—regardless of how she responds? I need to go see our mother; but would you come with me? I do not expect her to behave any differently than she always has, but her reaction is not what must guide my actions. I need to tell her that God is in the business of forgiving everyone—you, me and her. I need to be free of the burden of carrying this weight around with me. I intend to make sure Marjorie Miller has heard the truth, and then I will finally be free."

Susan smiled at her sister. "I would be honored to go with you, Lisa. Hope is a wonderful thing, isn't it? As children, hope was never part of our lives, nor was it ever a part of our mother's life. We know that God is not that big ogre up in the sky who enjoys beating us down, but our mother still believes that. We know He has a plan for our lives and that He can be trusted to direct our paths through all the twists and turns of life—if we will simply accept His love and trust His heart. It is the only way to flood our lives with His hope. Our mother needs to know this hope is available to her as well, and she can only know it if she knows the kind of God who offers this hope."

Lisa slipped her arm around Susan, and the two started back toward the house. "You know, little sister, God's hope really has returned, hasn't it? Just imagine, we two Miller girls have become so safe and secure in

God's love to the point that we are willing to go face the lioness in order to share this wonderful truth with her. I am so filled with gratitude that I cannot think of a better way of showing it than to share it with our mother. What she does with it is up to her, but I need to try. After all, Susan, this is not the end; it is only the beginning.

Dorey Whittaker

Dorey lives in central Virginia with her husband, Bruce, and they have been married for forty-seven years. They reared two daughters, enjoy their four grandchildren, and have partnered together in lay ministries for over forty years.

Accidently poisoned by arsenic at age three, Dorey was left practically deaf until age twelve and illiterate until age sixteen. She knows the struggle to forgive those who have caused so much damage to her life; and the pure joy and blessing that comes when you finally surrender your rights to hold onto feeling of justifiable revenge. She learned that forgiveness is a gift you give to yourself.

She knows how it feels to face tremendous obstacles, shame, and ridicule for being one of the many "left behind" children. She was told, "Just get over it and move on." Dorey knew how broken she was. She also knew that God was her only hope. What once was her greatest shame, has now become one of her greatest victories.

We all must decide our life path. Either accept the label of victim, with all its excuses readily at hand, or choose to follow God on His path to real self-worth. Dorey shines a light on God's path to living a victorious life.

Visit Dorey's website to read her personal life experience:
Doreywhittakerbooks.com

Made in the USA
Columbia, SC
03 June 2017